Extra
Innings

Lynn Stevens

Play Hard!

Lynn Stevens

Published by Lynn Stevens
www.lstevensbooks.com
Cover design by Najla Qamber Designs
ISBN: 978-1-69-885844-9

FOR BEAN AND DAVE

TOP OF THE 1ST

Acid waved in my stomach, reaching for the peak of my throat.

Stop it. You can do this. Just go at it like you own the place. Stride up to the coach like Mom does when she's on the donation hunt.

The fields sat at the southern end of Jackson Memorial Park: one for softball, one for baseball. I had parked on the baseball side by a beat-up orange truck. The boys were already there, tossing balls and joking loud enough that I heard them through the closed windows of my car. Thankfully, the softball field was empty. Taking a deep breath, I climbed out of the car, pulling my equipment from the backseat.

Maybe it was my BMW, or maybe it was me, but the only sound I heard as I stalked toward the field were birds chirping to one another. No doubt the guys recognized a girl when they saw one. Mother Nature blessed me a bit too much in the boob department for anybody to mistake me as a boy.

I strode onto the soft dirt of the field and straight toward the older man with the clipboard. Coach Bernie Strauss stared back at me. He was easily six-eight with tree trunk legs and arms that UFC fighters would die for. He looked more like a Marine Corps drill instructor than a summer league baseball coach. I totally wanted to test him by shouting "Semper Fi."

I stopped in front of him, waiting for what I knew was coming.

"Softball practice ended about twenty minutes ago." He sounded like he ate gravel for breakfast.

"I'm not here to play softball, Coach." I straightened my back and channeled my mother's unbending confidence. "I'm here to help you win the city championship this year."

No one laughed like I expected. So I exhaled, relaxed. Big mistake.

"Get off my field. I ain't got time for this," he shouted loud enough that birds scattered from a nearby tree. Coach Strauss turned his back to me and continued to bark at the team. "If you don't get back to practice, you'll be running laps in three … two …" His slight Texan accent made the "you's" sound like "ya's".

The boys started throwing and stretching again, but they didn't stop watching us.

"Coach –" I began.

"I ain't your coach."

I lost my cool, just like my father. "This is bullcrap. Look at your registration sheet." He didn't, so I snatched the clipboard from him and pointed. "See the name Vic Hudson? Well, that's me. I paid to play. And I fully intend to. It isn't against the rules."

Coach ripped the clipboard from my fingers and flipped to another page. I waited. He read. I tapped my foot. That's not nearly as dramatic on a dirt infield. The boys stopped warming up again.

He looked me up and down. "Fine. I'll give you a shot, Hudson. You suck and you're gone."

"I can deal with that."

"Get out there." He pointed at a tall, super skinny boy. "Delvin, warm her up."

I tossed my bag into the dugout and jogged onto the field. It didn't take me long to figure out why Coach Strauss told Delvin to warm up with me. He kicked his leg like a pitcher and tossed a pretty nasty fastball. If I had to guess, he could hit ninety from the mound on a good day. It would've been stupid if I said anything, even though every ball he threw at me stung my fingers like tiny pricks of a hundred safety pins. I didn't even try to throw my hardest. I warmed up like it was any other day.

Then he began stepping back. One step here, then another.
Idiot.

I threw hard and high to make my point. Delvin had to reach to get it. He may throw harder, but I can throw farther.

"Alrigh', get in here," Coach yelled. He raised his eyes at Delvin, who shrugged. "I know most of you from last year. We only got two potential newbies. One's a girl. Anyone got a problem with that?"

If they did, they sure as hell weren't going to tell Coach Strauss.

"Good. I expect you to treat her like you'd treat anybody else." He looked at me and softened his tone. "What position do you play, honey?"

"Third." I glared at him. He smirked then turned back to the team. Before he could open his mouth, I said, "And I'm not your honey."

His head snapped back like he'd taken a right hook to the cheek. "Excuse me?"

I pointed at Delvin. "Do you call him 'honey'?"

Delvin's cheeks glowed light pink with either rage or embarrassment. I didn't know which and really didn't care.

Coach didn't answer me though. His chin grew beet red, which crept up his cheeks all the way to his pale yellow crew cut. Steam came out of every clogged pore on his face as he yelled, "Everybody at third. Jayden, get your ass to first." He sneered at me and I expected to get kicked off the field. "We're going to field some grounders and see who handles them best. I'll hit you three then rotate. Hudson, ladies first."

Crap. Me and my big mouth. He's going to either hit me a line drive at a hundred miles an hour or make me go so far out of range that I make an ass of myself.

I jogged to third and dug my cleats into the stubborn dirt. The rest of the guys lined up along the fence, amused grins matching Strauss's own jack-o-lantern expression. Coach tossed the ball into the air.

Crack.

I jumped spread eagle and dropped my glove between my legs, catching the line drive. I came down ready to throw to first, but Jayden wasn't on the bag. He stood three steps off with his mouth open. Smiling, I rolled the ball back to home plate.

Coach didn't give me time to get back into position when he hit a grounder to my left. In a game, the shortstop would've played it, but this was a different type of game. I dove and knocked it down. My throw to first was in the dirt, but I was on my butt when I whipped it across the infield. That shouldn't be held against me. It was an almost impossible play.

The last ball went up the line. I hustled and would've had it clean until it hit the bag. It took a nasty bounce that was nearly out of reach. I jumped and brought it down barehanded, throwing to first off balance as I fell into foul territory.

I stood up without looking to see if Jayden caught it and walked to the fence to wait for my next turn. The guys gawked at me as I leaned against the fence, ignoring them. I'd made my point. I could field. My next time up, Coach hit some routine grounders.

After rotating through every infield position, it was time for batting practice.

"You're up," Coach announced as he pointed his chunky finger my way. "Delvin, pitch to her."

While Delvin threw some warm up tosses, I pulled my large batting gloves on, stretching them over my long fingers. The shin guard came loose as I walked to the plate, but I didn't dare adjust it. Not yet anyway. I'm a switch hitter in softball but more natural from the right side. So that's where I started when I stepped into the box. I wasn't entirely certain I could hit a fastball from the left anyway.

Delvin dug at the rubber. I did the same at the plate. Kicked some rocks out from under my right foot. Buried my left foot in the front of the box. Right arm cocked at a ninety degree angle, my bat perched above my shoulder, I waited. A trickle of sweat ran down my cheek. This felt more like a playoff game than a practice.

My swing was graceful as I rocked the fastball over Jayden. He stretched, revealing his dark walnut skin. His long braids smacked his back as he dropped to the ground. Jayden could jump for a big guy.

"Nice," Coach said.

The Asian boy behind the plate whistled low and said, "Sweet."

Delvin tossed a few more pitches before Coach snapped at me to get to third. I didn't hesitate, grabbing my glove and hustling onto the field.

"Get in the dugout," Coach commanded after everyone had hit.

I stood at the end of the bench, waiting for the axe to drop. I'd played well enough to warrant sticking around, but I was still lacking the mandatory testosterone. If Coach told me to go, I would. It was his team and I wasn't about to make things worse by throwing an epic hissy.

"We got a tough schedule this year. Last year, the Rebels kicked our ass to take the district. Well, half those boys can't play no more.

4

Hell, we're missing three of our own. It's time we take our game to the next level. The Rebels need to rebuild more than we do. We can take 'em. Now get outta here. I'll see you tomorrow." He glanced my way. "All of you."

I grabbed my gear and practically bounced out of the dugout when Coach called me and Shane Anders back.

Shane was short, plump, and had a face pot-marked by zits and craters. Something told me that his dad made him play to get him out of the basement. Coach Strauss towered over him. Shane tremored a little.

"Alright. Vic, what's your real name?"

"Vic."

He sighed, sending a poof of peppermint my way that didn't conceal his bad breath. It smelled like he didn't bother to brush his teeth in the morning. Ever. "Don't bullshit me, girl."

"I'm not, Coach. Vic's short for Victoria."

He stared at me and shook his head. "Fine. Here's the drill. We practice every day at the same time, at the same place until the first game. Ain't hard to remember. No excuses for tardiness or missin' a game. Miss a practice, you don't play the next game. Bring your own equipment. Forget your glove or your cleats, you don't play.

"Games start next week. Your jersey will be clean. If it ain't, you ain't playin'. We play on Tuesdays, Thursdays, and Saturdays for six weeks. Team that wins their district plays in the city championship tourney. I don't know nothin' about either one of you, but there are a couple of boys here that could move on to college ball. Scouts look at summer programs, too, especially if they're already interested in a player. Neither one of you is goin' to play baseball at the next level. I just ask that you don't screw it up for everyone else.

"Now get out of here. Today's practice was a short one. Tomorrow's not gonna be this easy."

Shane took off in a hurry. It was obvious he was scared of Coach. We watched him run to a small pickup truck and scamper in.

"Can I ask you something, Vic?" Coach crossed his arms and glared at me.

"Yeah, sure."

"Why're you here?" He nodded toward the empty softball field. "You could be playin' ball over there. Tell me the truth."

I knew the question was coming, but I didn't expect any sincerity behind it. "Softball isn't baseball, Coach. It may seem similar, but it isn't the same. I wanted to play ball one more time. That's all."

He nodded, then turned away from me and started gathering his bats.

"Am I really on the team?" I asked. I needed absolute confirmation.

"Yeah, got no choice." He straightened up and smiled at me. "Looked at the regs. Doesn't say this team is for boys sixteen to seventeen. Just says players. But you already knew that, didn't you?"

I smiled. Of course I did. "See you tomorrow, Coach Strauss."

He grunted and I took off to my car, trying not to skip like a ten-year-old.

I'm in. I'm going to play ball again.

BOTTOM OF THE 1ST

Mom's Lincoln sat in the driveway when I got home to Grandma Hudson's new house in St. Louis. My father wasn't happy when she decided to move, but I was thrilled. The first thing I did was look up the district for summer ball.

The hood was still warm on Mom's car. At least she hadn't been here too long. This didn't bode well. I pictured the scene I'd walk into. Grandma would be in the wingback chair Grandpa had loved and she refused to get rid of. Mom would be sitting on the couch, still as an icicle with a cup of hot tea in her hand. Neither would say a word.

They never got along before Grandpa died. Now it was worse. Grandma had never wanted my father to marry Mom. She thought Mom was "too stiff" and "too flaky." When I first brought up the idea to move in with Grandma for the summer, Mom freaked out until I explained the reason why. She didn't approve, but she agreed so I could play ball.

I opened the front door with the intention of shouting "I'm home" when I heard … laughter? From the kitchen? Cautious that I was stepping into another dimension, I tip-toed toward the unusual sound. I'd heard Mom laugh, of course. And Grandma too, just not at the same time and in the same room.

Mom sat at the table with the traditional mug of tea in front of her. Grandma stood at the sink drying the kettle.

"And then I told him that he broke an old lady's heart," Grandma

7

said, putting her hand on the sink to steady herself. She was laughing so hard she snorted like a hog.

This only raised my suspicions that something was wrong in the universe.

"Mary, I can't believe you used the 'old lady' card on that poor man." Mom put her hand to her chest to stifle the hilarity.

"Well, it worked." Grandma set the kettle in the sink then noticed me. "Oh, Victoria. You have impeccable timing." She pulled a bowl of strawberries from the counter. "Here, have a strawberry."

Tension exploded in the room when the laughing stopped as if on cue.

"What's going on?" I took the bowl from Grandma and sat across from Mom at the table. The strawberries burst with flavor. I hadn't realized how hungry I was as I scarfed half the bowl.

Mom looked at Grandma, who raised her eyebrows, and began the slow talk like I was either deaf or five-years-old, "Vicky, there's a function this Saturday –"

"Can't make it. I have practice." *God, these strawberries are sweet.* I sprinkled some sugar over them anyway. Maybe if I kept eating, Mom would give up.

"It's in the evening, Victoria." Mom sighed.

"I don't want –"

"Your father will be expecting you –"

"To make an appearance," I finished, wiping juice from my chin. "Wait, he's coming home?"

"He'll be in Saturday afternoon and will leave Sunday."

"Well, I don't want to go. Can't you get me out of it for a change?" I totally sounded like a spoiled brat, but I was so sick of the events or functions or whatever I kept getting forced into.

"You know I can't."

"You've never even tried!" I slammed the bowl with a thud, spilling precious strawberries across the table.

"Now, you know that's not true," Mom said as she put her hand on my forearm. "Your father –"

I yanked my arm away. "Mom, I don't want to go."

"You don't even know what it's for."

"Probably some campaign financing thing like it always is. Show off the trophy wife and the trophy daughter."

I hit her where it hurt the most. Mom hated being called a trophy wife. She was more than that. If it wasn't for all her work in the early days, the Senator wouldn't have made it out of the city council.

"That's enough, child," Grandma said in a soft voice. I was in trouble. She wasn't a fan of my father's politics, but he was still her son. "You will go. It's for charity."

I felt my stomach fall to my feet and looked back to Mom. "Is that true?"

She nodded.

"What charity?" I was fighting a losing battle.

"American Lung Association. Your grandmother organized it."

I gave Grandma my best why-didn't-you-just-tell-me glare. She stared back at me with an equally defiant expression. Grandpa died of lung cancer, even though he quit smoking his pipe right after my father was born.

"Is it formal?" I asked, sighing loudly and sounding too much like my mother.

"Of course. We'll get you a new dress –" Mom began as she grinned in triumph.

"Can't I wear one that I already have?" I hated dress shopping with Mom. She made me try on everything and I never wanted any of them.

"Fine, you can wear the one your father loves." She tilted her head in thought. "That pink chiffon –"

"Oh no. I'm so not wearing that ever again. I'll wear that black dress I wore to the Inaugural Ball."

Mom threw her hands up. "Fine. And your father said you can bring Theo if you wish."

I sat up straighter. She didn't really say I could bring my boyfriend. "Are you serious?"

"Go call him so he can get a tux," Grandma said. She picked the bowl of strawberries from the table and popped one in her mouth.

I kissed each one on the cheek and ran down the short hall to my room. Theo and I weren't exactly seeing eye to eye lately. Maybe this would turn things back into a positive swing. I closed my door and listened to some crappy country song playing as Theo's ringback tone.

"Hey, what're you doing Saturday night?" I asked when his deep, soft voice answered. He could have a career as a late night D.J., but Theo's goals were much higher than that.

"Packing. Why?"

I fell back on my small bed. "There's this thing I have to go to and I can bring a guest."

"I get to go to one of the Senator's fundraisers?"

I rolled my eyes. "No, it's a charity thing."

He paused. "Yeah, I'm free. What time?" When I didn't answer right away, he jumped on it. "Did you forget to ask, Victoria?"

He never called me "Vic" or "Vicky", claiming he preferred my complete name. Funny, I never called him Theodore.

"Yeah, Theo, I did. I was in shock, I guess. Anyway, it's black tie."

"I've got a tux."

"Great. I'll text you the details."

"Okay," he said with a huff. Something crashed in the background. "Crap."

"What're you doing anyway?" I asked.

"Getting the luggage out of the basement." He groaned and something else fell. "I'm starting to pack for our trip. Still wish you were going."

A small pang of guilt sat on my gut. Some of the incoming seniors at Xavier Academy went to Europe for a few weeks every summer. I opted out to stay home and play baseball. "You'll have fun without me. Besides, I've been there and done that."

"But not with me."

The pang grew into a beach ball size rock in my stomach. Then I realized he hadn't even asked about practice. "Aren't you going to ask how today was?"

"Today?" Another small crash in the background. "Oh, right. Your first practice. Slipped my mind."

"Gee, thanks."

"Well, I'm assuming that since you aren't crying, you didn't get kicked off the team."

"Because I'm such a cry-baby, right?" I stood up and started pacing. *What the hell is he thinking?*

"That's not what I meant and you know it."

I didn't feel like fighting with him so soon after making up from the last one. "Coach had no reason to kick me off."

"Except that you lied on your application."

"No, I didn't," I said, probably with too much force, but I was tired of being called a liar.

"Okay, fine. You did mislead the league."

That I couldn't deny. "Better."

"And that you *are* of the opposite sex." He grunted again and I heard the distinct sound of something silver falling on the wooden floor. "I doubt the guys on your team didn't fail to miss that."

"Point?"

He sighed. "Victoria, I just hope it's worth it. You know that if your father finds –"

"Don't go there, Theo. He won't find out." I fell back onto my bed just as Mom knocked on the door and opened it at the same time. "Look, I gotta go. Mom's here."

Theo hung up without saying anything. I tossed the phone on my pillow.

"Hey, honey. I'm sorry to interrupt." She sat down beside me and took in every inch of my room. "This must seem so cramped to you."

"Nah, not really." I hadn't thought about it much, but it could probably fit in my room at home twice, maybe three times. I had a simple single bed with a mismatched patchwork quilt. There was an oak nightstand and a matching four drawer dresser. Grandma didn't decorate it with my tastes in mind, but it felt more like me than the princess room back at Chez Hudson.

"Oh." She glanced around the room again. Mom never left the house in anything less than the perfect outfit and perfect helmet hair. "I need to get to the Tea Room for a meeting. Are you sure you're going to be okay here?"

I sat up and tried to read the expression on her face. "Yeah, I'll be fine."

She patted my knee and walked out of my tiny bedroom, leaving me with that feeling that something was wrong and it was somehow my fault. The Lincoln started in the driveway as I headed down the hall to the kitchen. Grandma stood over the sink of fresh strawberries, humming to herself. She amazed me. Grandma was in her late sixties, yet acted twenty-five. She rarely stayed home for long. If there was a charity event, she was there. If there was a protest, she'd be right up front, much to my father's dismay. Her appearances increased more and more after Grandpa's death.

After forty-five years of marriage, Grandma didn't have anyone to keep her in-check anymore. She went into full hippie mode. Her silver hair grew to her waist and she started wearing clothes that hadn't seen the light of day in decades and probably should've remained hidden.

She also became a lot more fun to hang around.

"Why didn't you tell me sooner?" I asked

She dropped the strawberries back into the colander and stared at the ceiling.

"Come on, Grandma. You planned it. You could've told me instead of letting Mom lead the ambush." I leaned against the archway and crossed my arms, waiting for an answer.

"Because I wasn't going to demand that you go. And I know you don't like these functions." She turned toward me, drying her hands on a pale yellow towel. "And I didn't expect your father would fly back from Washington for it."

I scoffed. "Why wouldn't he? It's the perfect thing to put his mug in the paper."

"Vicky –"

I didn't let her finish. "Does he know I'm living here?"

"Of course. You mother had to tell him something. He thinks you're helping me adjust." She put air quotes around "adjust" then threw the towel on the stove. "He thinks I'm a delicate old lady who can't do anything for myself. It's the perfect cover."

I nodded and stared at the tiled floor.

"You realize that your mother's upset about all this, don't you?"

"What? Why would Mom be mad at me?"

"She wishes you would've come to her first."

So that was the deal in the bedroom. She wanted to tell me how disappointed she was or angry because I arranged to move in with Grandma before I asked her. I'd already sent in my application to play ball too, but she didn't need to know that.

Besides, I get enough of that kind of crap from my father.

The phone rang in the living room and she hurried past me. "And get dressed," she shouted from over her shoulder. "You're going to the Habitat house with me this afternoon."

I mouthed the words along with her as she added, "It'll look good on your college applications."

Habitat Homes for St. Louis was one of Grandma's first charities. And her favorite. Before Grandpa died, she donated money and helped out at the office. Now, she'd taken over. As soon as we got to the site, she jumped in to help build something while I stood on the sidelines, helpless.

"Hey," a rasping voice said behind me, making the hair on my neck stand at attention. "You're Vic, right?"

Turning to defend myself from possible attack, I pulled my fists up to my chest. They fell back to my sides when I saw one of the guys from the team. "Oh, hey. You're Daniel?"

Of course he was Daniel. He was the only Asian guy on the team. Without the ball cap, his dark hair stood in every direction. There was a hammer in his oil slicked hand and a streak of grease on his right cheek. Instinct told my fingers to reach out and wipe the grease away. Fortunately, my brain didn't let that happen.

He cleared his throat. "Do you need something to do?"

I must have looked totally confused before I realized what he meant. "Oh. I mean, yeah. Sorry, I've never done this before." Now I sounded like an ass for being Habitat stupid. *You go, girl.*

He grinned, showing a chipped front tooth. "I can tell. You have that deer-in-headlights look about you. Not that I've ever actually seen a deer in headlights." He nodded behind him. "Help me over there."

I followed him through the wooden juggernaut. It looked like a bunch of two-by-fours stuck together. No way did it resemble a house. I couldn't even see the grass, and my sneakers were no longer white from all the sawdust. But the smell of fresh cut timber made me swoon. It was clean and foresty like the potpourri Mom had stocked in the bathrooms.

"How long have you been doing this? Volunteering, I mean." *Stupid, stupid, stupid. What is it about him that makes me feel like an idiot?* I tripped and seized what looked like a door frame. "Mother trucker."

"You okay?" He turned around and grabbed my arm to steady me as my hand slid on the rough wood. "Easy, slick."

"Ow, ow, ow." God, I was whining like a baby. I held out my palm and there was a long splinter jammed into the fleshy pad under my thumb.

"Come on," he said, with a shy smile that sent little sparks from my toes to my fingertips. "First aid is over here. And I'll get you some gloves."

I shook off the tingleys as I followed him to a card table with a white cloth draped over it. There were a couple of opened first aid kits scattered with bandages, antiseptics, and bottles of peroxide and alcohol.

He pointed to one of the flimsy folding chairs. "Sit."

The chair tipped to the right and I scooted to the edge to keep from falling to the ground, further exposing my asinine ways.

He sat down with a pair of tweezers and lifted my hand, laying it flat on the table. "This won't hurt."

"Promise?" My thumb brushed over his finger as he lowered the tweezers – *Crap, I shouldn't be flirting. I don't even know this guy. And I have Theo. He's been a good boyfriend. Besides, I'm not going to go out with a guy on my team. No way. Not happening. But I really like how soft Daniel's hand feels. Not good. No, not good at all.*

Then he ripped the splinter out. I yelped at the stinging pain. That knocked out any good feelings I had. The guy was a masochist.

"Hope that didn't hurt." He grinned. All was almost forgiven. Except my hand throbbed in time with the mariachi music playing on the other side of the yard. "Let's get you some gloves."

We walked over to a workbench and he grabbed a pair of well-worn gloves. They were surprisingly heavy and too big, but I slid them on anyway as he led me to the north side of the soon-to-be house. The pounding and yelling were starting to give me a headache. Then the saws started.

Daniel bent over a haphazard pile of two-by-fours and freed a lost bandana. I admit I checked out his perfect rear end. It was way better than Theo's.

"Help me carry these, would you?" Daniel asked as he straightened up.

"Huh?" My head snapped up and the tell-tale flush of guilt crept on my face. He'd caught me checking him out. *Bad, Vic. Think about Theo.*

He walked to one end. "I'll go in the front and lead the way. It's easier if you pull it up and hold it on one side of your shoulder like this."

It wasn't heavy. At first. By the time we'd taken all the boards over to the saws, my arms burned. Fortunately, Daniel didn't talk while we worked. We just moved the wood, doing what needed to be done. It was actually kind of cool. I didn't think about anything for an hour other than "lift, carry, walk," and "look out" or "don't trip."

Daniel pointed to a row of orange water coolers that sat precariously on a wide piece of plywood over two sawhorses. We staggered through the cloud of sawdust. The water coolers were in a much quieter area where the saws were just a buzz in the background. He handed me a paper cup and I sipped the lukewarm water, then drained it. I refilled it two more times.

"Let's sit over there." He pointed to a lone picnic table under an oak tree on the edge of the work site. It didn't look sturdy either, but my body screamed "sit down," so I followed and sat across from him.

I sipped my fourth cup of water and surveyed the site. The saws, hammers, and shouting worked into a melodious rhythm.

"Why play baseball?" he asked, breaking me out of my daze.

My shoulders fell as I faced him. I knew the question would be asked, I just didn't expect it twice in one day. "It's complicated." I looked back toward the wooded maze. From this distance, I could see the shape of a house. Grandma stood in the center with a bright red hardhat, barking orders to a group of guys on the eastern side. "Why do you do this?"

He shrugged. "Just do. I like working with my hands." He pointed to a tall Asian man in a blue polo with blueprints in his hand. He was talking to a big guy who looked more like one of the lumberjacks from reality TV. "Dad's an architect and helps design the Habitat houses. Ever since I can remember, we've been working on them." He paused and half smiled. "It sounds cheesy, but I like that someone is going to live here. I can picture it. I can see some kids running in the yard. And it's cool knowing that I helped."

"That's really nice." *Of course it's nice. He* has *to be hot and nice.*

"Tell me why baseball."

"What if someone told you that you couldn't do this anymore because you're a boy?" I waved my hand dramatically around the work site. "Not because you aren't a good worker or because you made a bad call or a major mistake, but because you have the wrong sex organs. How'd you feel?"

15

His eyebrows shot up into his hairline. "So this is a girl versus boy thing?"

"No, not at all." I watched him for signs of disbelief. He looked interested. It didn't seem normal. "I love baseball. When I was little, I played all the time. Then they kicked me out of Little League and told me to play softball. That's all fine, but it isn't the same. I know that you guys will all think I'm trying to make a point that girls can play as well as boys, but that isn't the case. I honestly just want to play baseball. This is my last shot. After this year, I'm not eligible for the summer programs. Then I'll be in college. I just want to be on a team again. That's all."

"Softball teams aren't good enough?"

I laughed. "Wow, I'm going to say something totally anti-feminist right now. Have you ever played on a team with a bunch of whiny girls? The summer leagues don't cut anyone. You know that. The district I lived in had a bunch of girly girls who only played because they thought they'd meet boys. I bet other leagues are different, but not mine.

"And my school doesn't have a softball team. Just volleyball and basketball. Plus the guys I know take the competition more seriously." I dropped my head to my chest. "God, that sounded more horrible than I thought."

"Yeah, that is kinda anti-feminist."

We laughed like we'd known each other our whole lives. He was too damned easy to talk to. "Daniel, I am seriously not trying to make any statement. I just want to play baseball."

He stared at me for a minute before smiling.

"Can I ask you a question without offending you?" I crumpled my cup.

"Probably not, but you can give it a shot."

"Where are you from? Your family, I mean."

"St. Louis born and raised. So is my dad. Mom's from Chicago, but don't worry." He glanced around and leaned in. "She's not a Cubs fan." He started laughing in his light tenor voice again. "But seriously, my great-grandparents on my dad's side are from Korea. They immigrated just before Grandfather was born."

I was suddenly worried that I'd made an ally to only piss him off. "I didn't offend you, did I?"

"Nah, I get that all the time. Just comes with being a hot Asian guy." He took my crumbled cup off the picnic table and tossed it in the trash. "Come on. I'll teach you how to hammer a nail, Korean style."

"There's a Korean way to hammer a nail?" I asked as I stood up.

"Nope, but I figured you'd fall for that."

The rest of the afternoon, Daniel and I hammered nails into boards and connected them to other boards. I didn't have the slightest idea what I was doing. By the time we finished, we'd put together a wall. Well, part of a wall. A couple of the guys came over and took it away from us. They carried it carefully up the stairs that weren't there this morning and hammered it in place.

He stood over my shoulder and I was totally aware of it. Daniel was a couple of inches taller than me, which was nice for a change. "Cool, huh?" he said.

It was hard not to lean back and inhale his soft sandalwood scent I was all too aware of. "Very. I can see why you do this."

"Yeah, but you're gonna feel it tomorrow."

I looked over my shoulder at him. "What do you mean by that?"

He laughed and the corners of his eyes crinkled. "Just wait."

"Time to go, Dan," his father said, coming up behind him. He was taller than I'd originally thought. His skin was darker and his hair was combed. Other than that, he looked just like his son.

"Hey, Dad. You know that girl I was telling you about that's gonna play baseball this summer? Well, this is her."

Mr. Cho looked me up and down then offered a thin hand. "Nice to meet you. Daniel tells me you aren't a bad player."

I forced back a proud smile. "Thank you, sir. It's nice to meet you too."

"Are you here with anyone?"

"Oh, my grandmother." I pointed to her. She waved at me before a construction worker scooped her up in his arms. I never heard Grandma squeal like a teenager before and I wasn't too sure I wanted to hear it again. She was loud enough people could hear her down by the Arch.

"Charles should be more respectful." He looked between me and Grandma for a moment. "You're Mary Falls' granddaughter?"

As I nodded, I saw a hint of recognition in his eyes. I didn't want to jump to conclusions, but something told me he knew who I was. It wasn't like I was trying to have a secret identity, but I wanted to be a normal girl. One that played baseball but was otherwise normal. I wanted to spend one summer of my life not being Victoria Hudson, daughter of U.S. Senator Warren Hudson, potential presidential candidate.

Then it dawned on me that he used Grandma's maiden name. And she probably never talked about the Senator's politics around here. Maybe he *didn't* know.

"Come on, Daniel. Your mother's making mango curry." He bowed slightly to me. "Nice to meet you again, Miss Hudson."

Yeah, he didn't know.

"See you tomorrow, Vic," Daniel added as he followed his dad.

Grandma's eruption of laughter stopped me from responding. One of the other guys had taken a water cooler and dumped the cold water over her head.

"That's what you get for dumping ice down my back, Mary," he laughed.

Shaking my head, I walked toward her. Sometimes grandparents can be just as embarrassing as parents.

TOP OF THE 2ND

The charity event was a thousand dollar a plate dinner with a silent auction followed by dancing. Since Grandma organized the entire thing, she'd be on her best behavior. She definitely wouldn't act like she had at the Habitat house early in the week.

The car pulled up at six-thirty with Theo. He looked sharp in his tux. Theo was handsome, plain and simple, but he'd combed his hair into a side part and gelled it down so it wouldn't move in a hurricane. It was a bit over the top.

Theo lifted my hand, kissing the tip of my thumb. My thoughts drifted to Daniel for a moment and the way he'd removed the log of all splinters. Theo's fingers felt cold in comparison. His rich dirt brown eyes glowed golden flecks with mischief, unlike Theo's serious green ones. I shook my head to get Daniel out of my mind.

I smiled at Theo, but he didn't notice. The Senator was telling him something about Capitol Hill that didn't and wouldn't interest me. Theo acted like a puppy getting a treat.

We rode along in the limo while my father continued educating Theo about all things Senate related. Mom interjected her two cents here and there, but Theo was mesmerized and gave my father his undivided attention.

I was bored.

The Palace Renaissance Hotel was the epitome of elegance. The valets wore black slacks with white shirts and red sateen vests and stood at attention outside the entrance to the lobby. The Senator exited first, then Mom, me, and Theo. I must have slouched too much for my mother's taste since she prodded my lower back. I stood straighter and linked my arm through Theo's. Once we entered the hotel, the press would pounce.

"Ready for this? I asked him out of the corner of my perfect smile.

"I've been to charity events before, Victoria."

I suppressed a laugh. If he was going to get all cocky, I wasn't about to warn him about the impending press attack.

We followed my parents inside, and Theo was immediately blinded by a photographer. He pinched his nose between his fingers, squeezing his eyes shut. I let out a very unladylike laugh as I led him toward the ballroom. A society reporter from the Ledger named Wakefield asked me a question I ignored. Mom talked to him at every opportunity, but he gave me the creeps.

Grandma stood at the head table with the mayor and several members of the city council. Everyone shook the Senator's hand, even if they didn't agree with his political agenda.

Theo started to comment on the room, but I shushed him. Rule number one with my father: don't talk to someone you're with while shaking hands with other people. It's rude and you can talk to your companion later.

By the scowl on his face, Theo didn't like to be shushed.

He'd have to get over it.

When we finally made it to our table, Grandma tapped on the mic at the podium. She talked for a minute about how we needed to fight cancer and win. Then Grandma introduced somebody. I wasn't listening, but I smiled like I was, as the guy blabbered on about research progression. Everyone clapped.

Grandma took the podium once again and introduced my father. Now I had to listen, or at least half listen. If he said my name or pointed me out, I needed to be ready for heads to turn my way. My name came up in the first minute as he talked about Grandpa and his battle with cancer.

Apparently, I was the sad survivor who never knew her grandfather because of this horrible disease. I hadn't planned on that angle. I forced myself to look sad and heartbroken, which is a lot harder than it sounds.

Twenty minutes later, it was over. Finally.

"I'm starving," I whispered to Theo.

"Oh, so I can talk now?"

I stopped myself from rolling my eyes. "Of course."

"Good to know. Are there any other things you forgot to tell me?"

"Beside the picture in the society section of tomorrow's paper? No, not that I can think of."

"As long as it isn't the one of me throwing my hand up in shock, I don't care." He pulled at his vest as he sat straighter. "After all, I'll be in a photo with Senator Hudson."

I rolled my eyes. "Whatever. It isn't all that. Believe me."

"Your dad's speech was great," Theo said as I spotted Andrea Hoffpauir in a corner with her parents. I resisted the urge to wave. Unfortunately, the Perday family sat at the same table. The night was already full of suck without Erik Perday around. On Andrea's first day at Xavier, Mr. Landerson stuck us on a science project and that was that. We became inseparable, much to the chagrin of my former best friend, Erik Perday. Andrea was interesting and listened to me like what I said mattered. Erik had taken to hitting me in the arm like I was his personal punching bag.

The first course arrived, carrot fennel soup. Why couldn't they serve burgers and fries at these things?

"I really like the point he made about smoking bans." Theo polished a spot from his spoon.

"What point?" I stared at the soup. It looked like baby poop, and I wasn't *that* hungry.

Theo shook his head. His hair didn't move. "I don't understand you, Victoria. You father is one of the most powerful men in Washington –"

"Politics don't interest me."

"And yet you do the most political things –"

"Like what?" I didn't like where this conversation was going.

"Well for one, the baseball thing."

I grabbed his arm. "Shush it, Theo." I glanced over and the Senator was deep in conversation with the mayor. No way he heard the loudmouth boyfriend. "Why do you insist that it's political?"

"I just don't understand. You could play softball like you have every summer. You could go to Europe with the rest of us. You could visit colleges. You could go to a spa –"

"Baseball's not 'girly' enough for you, is that it?" I snapped.

"That's not what I said – "

"Just stop." I shook my head. God, he was pissing me off. "Like I've said before, I don't want to play softball. I've been to Europe. I'm going to Mizzou. And I don't like spas. Does that clear everything up?"

He reached for my hand. "I don't want to fight. I just don't want to go a month without seeing you."

I nodded like I knew he was sincere. But he wasn't. Something told me he was lying and it nagged at me as the waiter set a salad plate in front of me. It dripped with oil and vinegar. Gross. My stomach rumbled loud enough to get Mom's attention. She handed me a roll. Theo started chatting with the man on his left, a city councilman on his way out of office. I nibbled at the roll until the main course arrived. Duck. Great. I'd be raiding the kitchen later.

As soon as the meal was over, I motioned for Andrea to join me in the restroom.

I collapsed on the tiny couch in the most unladylike fashion with my head resting against the cheap pleather. Mom wouldn't be happy with me and that thought made me smile.

"Theo still mad at you?" Andy asked as she sat properly beside me.

I rolled my head to face her. "He hasn't said so, but …"

Andy glanced around before whispering, "He told Colby Bender that he couldn't wait to get you alone in a hotel in a foreign country before you dropped the baseball thing on him."

"What?" I bolted up, staring at her like she'd grown a third head. "We've only been going out for three months. You seriously can't mean that he thinks he's going to get laid just because we're in freaking France."

"Who knows with boys." She flipped the flap of her clutch open and closed. "Colby said Theo's getting a little tired of being teased."

The weight of the past few months fell on my shoulders. It explained so much. "Oh good God. How does he think I'm teasing him?"

Andrea gave me the look that said everything.

"One little indiscretion and I'm doomed for life."

"I told you to stop drinking like a million times that night. *You* didn't listen."

The door opened, ending that part of our conversation. While

Andrea and I touched up our makeup, she asked about my practices.

"Coach Strauss is a hardass, but pretty cool," I said after gliding lipgloss on.

"Any hotties on the team?" She wiggled her eyebrows up and down.

I laughed but stopped when Daniel's face floated into my head. "How would I know? I'm spoken for, remember?"

Andy scoffed. "Just because you've got Theo doesn't mean you can't look at the merchandise, Vicky."

She tossed her hair over her shoulder and strolled out of the restroom. I followed her as we headed back into the ballroom. Erik stalked toward us with a sneer creeping over his lips. I was about to turn and run the other way when someone gripped my elbow, spinning me around.

"Victoria, I don't believe you've met John Barton." My father beamed as he motioned toward the city councilman.

Of course I'd met him like five freaking times in the last year. I smiled like a good daughter and shook my head no as I shook Mr. Barton's hand. Andrea scooted away toward her parents and Theo.

"Ms. Hudson, so nice to see you." Mr. Barton gave my hand a slight squeeze.

"I believe you have a son about Victoria's age." The Senator chuckled like he knew something the rest of us didn't. "Doesn't he attend St. Pius Academy?"

"Yes, he'll graduate in December." Mr. Barton smiled with pride. "A semester early. We've arranged for him to take a few classes online until he starts at Mizzou in the fall."

"Victoria's going to Mizzou." He was in full political mode now. The gears in his head were churning.

What am I even doing here? I forced myself to smile. Even the waiter could see it was fake. He raised his eyebrows at me as he scooted by with a tray of champagne. I glanced around quickly. Andrea and Theo were on the dance floor. Erik sat with his parents, glaring at me. *This night just keeps getting better.*

"Maybe we should introduce them." My father chuckled. Mr. Barton joined in.

Yeah, *that* was going to happen. I laughed anyway, playing the role of the perfect daughter. Totally nothing like the real me, but I come from a long line of fakers. And I acted like them for the rest of the night.

My body still ached from practice and working on the Habitat house, but not to the point where I couldn't play for our first game on Tuesday. I showed up at the field ready to ride the bench anyway. Coach Strauss didn't give me any indication that I would start, much less play. It was easier to have no expectations.

I dropped my bag at the far end dugout and laced up my cleats. A few of the boys were warming up. I hustled out to join them passing Coach as he hung the lineup card on the fence. I didn't dare peek. When I headed back to the dugout with Adam in complete silence, I expected the worst.

The guys huddled around it, but none of them said a word as they got ready to play. I tripped over a bat to get a glimpse. Not only was I starting at third, I was leading off. Daniel stood behind me, looking over my shoulder. His sandalwood scent had become all too familiar after just a few practices.

"Huh," he huffed.

"Surprised?" I asked as I peered over my shoulder at him.

"Nope." He ran his hand through his disheveled hair and pulled on his catcher's mask. "Come on, Hudson. Get on the field. We're the home team."

I forced back my smile as we ran out. Jayden tossed me some hard grounders from first. I bobbled the first two but settled down. Adam warmed up on the mound. Everyone was in game mode.

Then the umpire yelled, "Play ball."

My heart jumped into my throat before sinking to the pit of my stomach.

It's like any other game. Nothing to be nervous about.

I took three strides off the third base line and crouched low. When Adam threw the first pitch, I balanced on my toes, ready to move left or right, up or down.

The first batter struck out swinging. The next one grounded to T.C. at short. A fly ball to left center ended the top of the inning. I headed toward the dugout when their third base coach stopped me.

"You're a girl," he said obviously surprised.

"Good observation skills you got there." I slapped my glove on my thigh and kept going. *Good idea. Piss off the other team's coach.*

I grabbed my bat from the dugout and took a few warm up swings. My eyes were locked on the pitcher: the way he stood on the mound, the way he threw the ball, where his release point was. There was no way in hell I was going to strike out in my first at bat.

"Batter up!" the ump bellowed.

I made my way to the plate. The guys shouted for me.

"Get us started, Vic."

"Come on, Vic. Let's go."

"WooHoo. Alright, let's go, Vic," Daniel yelled, followed by an ear-piercing whistle. Other than Daniel, I had no clue who said what. Didn't really care, either.

Lock in. Don't take your eye off the ball.

I dug into the batter's box. The pitcher leaned in to get his sign, and then jolted upright. I winked at him. Cheesy, but I couldn't resist. He took another signal from his catcher and threw a fastball right down the middle.

The pitch had more heat than I anticipated. I fouled it back, which was already more contact than their lead-off guy.

I reset myself in the batter's box. The next two pitches zoomed too close to my knees.

Two and one.

There was no way he wanted to walk me. One, because I'm a girl, and two, because you just don't walk the lead off hitter. That's not how you start a game.

Fastball. Has to be. He won't go down the middle. As soon as he threw it, I realized how wrong I was. His curveball caught the outside corner.

Two and two.

The brim of my helmet shaded my eyes from the afternoon sun. Since I didn't even swing, he might throw that again. Or a fastball. I knew one thing for certain. He would come at me inside. I waited.

The ball hurled toward me in slow motion. It inched toward the inside and I turned on it, ripping it over the third baseman and down the line. I sprinted around first on my way to second, finding the ball as it rolled toward the left field fence. The outfielder chased after it, but I knew I could get to third. My feet pounded into the hard infield dirt as my heart thudded the same rhythm in my ears. I rounded second and caught Coach Strauss.

He held up both hands, and I skidded to a stop, hurrying back to second. The throw hit the cutoff man.

I had third. It was mine. I glared at Coach Strauss, but he focused on Ollie, giving him the signs to hit away. I kicked the dirt and took a decent lead. Coach rubbed his thighs and tapped his elbows: the steal sign.

The catcher set up on the inside. There was a good chance the pitcher would toss a fastball to Ollie. The catcher extended his leg. There was no way he'd throw me out from that position. He didn't think I'd steal.

Talk about insulting.

You're gonna regret this, Bubba.

The pitcher began his windup, and I was off. I slid into third without a throw. I should've already been there, but that wasn't the point. My first hit. My first stolen base. The day was going great so far.

I took a shorter lead from third. Ollie grounded out hard to second. I stayed put. Jayden brought me home with a long fly ball into right center. By the bottom of the first, we were up two to nothing.

The rest of the game went just as well. I fielded a few grounders at third, making the plays without an error. We were winning six to one in the bottom of the eighth. Freddie hit a soft grounder to short, but the shortstop threw wild and Freddie ended up at second.

Coach gave me the signal to swing away before I stepped into the batter's box.

Their reliever looked more like a linebacker for a professional football team than a high schooler. He also had a massive unibrow, which was very distracting. I'd seen pictures of prettier Neanderthals.

That should've been my first clue.

The first pitch whizzed over my ear as I dropped to the ground. I jumped back up as fast as I went down. The guys in the dugout shouted that it was intentional. Coach stepped out of the dugout, but I shook him off. This battle was between me and Brutus. If he hit me, I'd get first. If he didn't hit me, I'd get on base somehow.

Keep your head in the game. Don't let him win.

He threw three outside, all of which I fouled off.

Then he came back inside again. I moved, but not fast enough. The ball smashed into my ribcage. I crumbled like a paper doll.

As I sucked in my breath, bursts of pain splintered through my upper back.

"You're outta here," the ump shouted.

Good. He deserves it. He hit me on purpose. An anvil ground into my back. *God this hurts.*

I got to my feet with pure determination and found Brutus backing toward his dugout. He smiled and blew me a kiss.

You're not beating me, dickhead. Any pain I felt disappeared. *Not even my father blows kisses at me.*

Adrenaline cleared my mind and I ran at him, knocking his bulk into the fence. He really was pure muscle. I bounced off, landing on my ass, reminding me of the huge bruise that was forming on my back.

"You stupid bitch," Brutus yelled as his hand cut into the metal fencing.

I scrambled to my feet again, filled with the rage bulls must have in Barcelona. Brutus was my red scarf. Before I got my balance, Daniel and Coach grabbed my arms to drag me away. I didn't get a chance to throw a punch or a slap. I tried to kick him, but Coach yanked me back hard. Daniel, however, ran at Brutus. I grabbed his arm before he got by me. If I couldn't beat on the jackass, I wasn't about to let Daniel take a swing.

"Come on, Ali. Onto the bench," Coach said. He pushed me toward the dugout.

"He hit me. I get first."

"Yeah, if you were still in the game. You got booted, kid. Now pop a squat."

I fell to the bench and watched Shane take my spot on the bag. I'd never been kicked out of any game before. Never. I almost did the most girl-like thing there is. I wanted to cry.

How could I get kicked out?

It didn't help that my back began to throb with its own heartbeat.

The game ended without any more drama. We won. They lost. I stayed on the bench, licking my wounds when Coach Strauss raised his voice during a conference at the plate.

"It ain't against the rules, Chuck," Coach Strauss bellowed.

Their coach equaled ours in yell capacity. "Damn it, Bernie. She attacked John –"

"After he beaned her. He threw at her head, for cryin' out loud."

"Guys, calm down," the ump intervened. "I had a look at the rules before the game. There isn't anything that says she can't play."

"Then she needs to be suspended for attacking John –"

"As soon as John gets the boot for throwin' at her head then hittin' her in the back."

"Stop it. Both of you." The ump yanked on his thick silver hair. No wonder he was balding. "Here's what I'm going to do. Both get one game suspension and both teams get a warning. It happens again and they're both gone. Got it?"

The coaches grunted and walked back to their dugouts. I kept my head down, waiting for the barrage of expletives only a Marine would know. When Coach Strauss didn't say anything, I couldn't stop my own mouth from running.

"I'm sorry." I sucked up the embarrassment. "It was stupid. But I was just trying to protect myself. He thinks he can throw at me and I'll quit. That's not going to happen. I mean, I'm not some wussy little girl that's afraid of a stupid baseball."

"Just shut up, Hudson. The little bastard had it coming. Girl or not, he didn't need to throw at you." He sat by me on the bench. The weathered wood groaned under his size. "Kid, you did good. I'm impressed. You hit well, played well. Don't let that idiot get under your skin. Besides, we play 'em again."

"I … um … I …" I sighed. "Thanks, Coach."

He nodded and stood to collect the rest of his bats, dismissing me.

Daniel leaned against my car as I made my way through the parking lot.

"Hey, how's your back?" he asked when I got close enough to hear him.

I looked over my shoulder to see if anyone might overhear me. "It hurts like hell."

"Don't doubt it." He grinned. "You mind giving me a lift? Ollie brought me, but he took off right after the game."

"Yeah, no prob." I unlocked the doors with the remote. "Get in."

He rattled off the directions, half of which I forgot almost as soon as they left his mouth.

"Thanks for the ride," he said after I passed the first turn.

I shrugged and regretted it. The pain snaked up my back and into my head. Before Daniel could comment, my cell rang with the distinctive song, which made me grimace even more.

Theo.

"Isn't it like two in the morning or something?" I asked instead of bothering with a hello.

"Something like that. Paris never sleeps," Theo slurred.

"I take it you're having fun." I wondered how much he'd been drinking. Theo's not much on alcohol or drugs, but he's been known to have a beer or a joint on rare occasions. Not since we started dating though.

"Absolutely." He laughed then added, "Andy got toasted last night. I had to fish her out of a fountain."

Andy?

"Turn left here," Daniel said as we approached the light.

"Who's that?" Theo asked, sounding less drunk than he had a minute ago.

"Daniel. He's on the team." When Theo didn't respond, I added, "I'm giving him a ride home."

"A ride, huh?" There was no mistaking the annoyed tone in Theo's voice. "Well, I better get going. I'll call you later." He hung up before I could say another word.

What did I do now?

"Boyfriend?" Daniel asked, interrupting my thoughts.

"Yeah." I slowed at the stop sign and faced Daniel. "He's in Paris. Senior class trip."

Daniel snorted. "Nice class trip." He glanced out the window then back at me. "Why didn't you go?"

I rolled my eyes and pulled through the intersection. "I wanted to play ball."

He stared at me for longer than necessary. "Where do you really live, Vic?"

"With my grandmother. In this district." I glanced over at him. "I moved in to help her over the summer. Why?"

He raised his eyebrows and fought back a grin. "But where do you live the rest of the year?"

I stopped at another stop sign. I didn't like where this was going, but I answered anyway. "Hillside."

"Ah." He turned away, staring out the passenger window.

"Ah, what?" My hands were starting to hurt since I gripped the steering wheel too tight.

He paused until a car horn sounded behind us. "Where do you go to school?"

You knew this was going to happen eventually. "Xavier."

"Brainiac, rich kid school." He pointed to the upcoming intersection. "Turn right. My house is third on the left."

I followed his directions and parked in front of a three-story brick house. The place was at least a hundred years old. The simple concrete steps led to a dark oak door with a stain glass window. A large bay window looked out onto the street with a petite blonde woman peeking out from behind the heavy curtains.

"That's my mom," Daniel said, pointing to the window. "She gets nervous when a strange car stops in front of the house. Especially a Beemer." He opened the door but didn't jump out. "Can I ask you something else?"

"Yeah, sure. What?" I gripped the wheel tighter.

"You didn't mention the game. Did the boyfriend even bother to ask?" He slid out of the car and ran up the steps without waiting for my answer.

He was right. Theo didn't ask. Theo knew the schedule. I'd emailed it to him as soon as I'd gotten it. And he knew Daniel was in the car. I told him Daniel was on the team. But then again, I didn't offer up any information either. I turned to look over my shoulder before merging onto the street. The pain returned like a lightning bolt. When I got to Watson Road, I made a left instead of a right and got on the highway.

The Jacuzzi tub at Chez Hudson called my name.

BOTTOM OF THE 2ND

Wednesday's practice was laid back compared to the week leading up to our first game. Coach didn't ask how I was and I didn't expect him to. The bruise on my back was about the size of Mom's silver turkey platter. Tossing the ball was difficult and I avoided batting practice. Coach didn't say a word.

Shane got a full workout. Coach put him at every spot in the diamond. He suited up with a chest pad and helmet to catch toward the end of practice. I watched from the dugout as Adam pitched to him, throwing harder as Shane's confidence grew. He was pretty good at blocking the ones in the dirt, but he didn't have any clue how to call pitches.

I put my foot on the bench to tie my cleat.

"Hey, Vic," Reggie said as he slapped my back in the wrong spot.

My knees buckled and I dropped to the bench before crumbling to the ground.

"Oh, man," he said. Then he screamed, "Coach, Vic's hurt."

Stars burst in my vision. My entire body groaned with the dull throb that originated in my back. I curled into a fetal position, hiding my head under the wooden bench. Coach knelt beside me with pairs of cleats surrounding him.

"From when he hit you?" Coach asked.

I whimpered, "Uh-huh."

"Can I see?"

This time I nodded.

He gently pulled my shirt up. Boys don't gasp. Not usually. I knew I was trouble when I heard them do it simultaneously.

"Vic," Coach began, "this is gonna hurt a bit, but I need to determine if you broke a rib or three."

His big hand was cold as he pressed on the bruise. I didn't cry. I didn't scream in pain. But I wanted to. There was no way I was going to let the guys see me wuss out and cry. I bit my lip, tasting blood. Coach sighed and pulled my shirt back down. He grabbed my arms and helped me to my feet.

"I don't think you broke nothing. Just a nasty bruise. If you want, I'll take you to the ER, but it would be a waste of money if you ask me." He squeezed my shoulder. "Take some aspirin and stay off your feet. Alternate ice and heat."

Again, I nodded.

"How you gettin' home?"

"I can drive," I snapped. I wasn't completely incapacitated.

"I'm sure you can, but you ain't."

Daniel stepped next to Coach. "I'll take her. Come on."

He grabbed our duffels and looped his arm around the good side of my waist to keep me from falling over. His hand was warm and I leaned into him more than I needed to.

"How're you going to get me home?" I grunted as he led me to the parking lot.

"I've always wanted to drive a Beemer," he said. My head snapped up. He smiled and I could see the concern behind the playfulness. "Cough up the keys, Hudson."

We stopped by the passenger side. Daniel's arm was still wrapped around my waist and our duffels were in his other hand. I leaned across him and he tightened his grip on me. I yanked on the keys from one of the outer pockets of my bag, fully aware of his warm breath drifting across my neck. I swung the keys around my finger and smiled.

"Don't speed. That's the last thing I need." I dropped the keys into his hand and slid into the passenger seat. After Daniel got behind the wheel, I asked, "How will you get home?"

He smirked and started the engine, giving it too much gas. "Don't worry about me. I'm crafty. I know how to use a phone."

My cell started ringing before I could get enough energy to smack him. Even Daniel knew it was Theo.

"Hey," I grunted, trying to keep the pain out of my voice.

"Rome is ah-mazing." The childlike excitement in his voice made me smile. "You should see it, Victoria. I would love to live here for a year."

"Except you don't speak Italian." I clicked my seatbelt. Even stretching it across my chest hurt. How I got through the day so far eluded me. A small groan escaped my lips.

"True. You doing okay?" he asked, but he didn't really sound concerned. No reason to make him worry.

"Fine," I said through gritted teeth.

It was Daniel's turn to grunt. Theo didn't hear him since he'd started talking about the architecture of Rome.

"This entire city is like a museum. I cannot believe people live in these ancient houses. We met this one guy in a piazza and talked for an hour. He invited me and Andy back to his apartment. We walked down this narrow alley to his building. It was two rooms total."

My head started pounding, but I didn't miss the mention of Andrea again.

Daniel leaned over and whispered too close to my phone, "Where to, Vic?"

"Who's that?" Theo asked. He didn't even try to mask his irritation. Whether it was because of Daniel or because he hated to be interrupted, I wasn't sure.

"Hold on." I put my hand over the phone and shot Daniel eye daggers. He didn't seem to care. "Take me home."

"Love to." He grinned and said as loud as he could without shouting, "Yours or mine?"

"My mom's in Hillside. Just get on the highway. I'll tell you from there." I took my hand off the phone. "Sorry, Theo. I …"

He'd hung up. I sighed and closed my eyes, leaning back against the leather headrest. I wanted to be angry with Daniel, but I didn't have the energy.

"Vic, you know you have a GPS in this thing, right?"

"Um, yeah."

"If I hit 'home', will that take me to your mom's?"

"Oh, of course." I raised my head and looked at him. "I never use it."

"I can see that. There's only one address programmed into it." He started pushing the buttons on the stereo as he pulled out of the parking lot, following the computerized voice's directions.

Once we hit the highway, he asked, "Did the boyfriend hang up or something?"

I stared at him. He kept his eyes on the road. "We got disconnected."

"Is he the jealous type?" he asked, glancing at me out of the corner of his eye.

I couldn't read his expression. "No, why?"

"Just asking." He checked over his shoulder before merging into another lane.

"Well, is your girlfriend the jealous type?" I huffed.

He half-smiled when he glanced at me. "Don't have one."

"Turn right in one hundred meters," the GPS voice said.

"As you command, sexy voice," Daniel said.

I closed my eyes again and rested my forehead on the passenger window. The pain in my back had turned into a dull ache. Mom probably wasn't even home right now. I'd have to call Grandma later and tell her where I was and why. Wasn't looking forward to that. The car rode so smooth that I drifted off.

"Hey, Vic, wake up." Daniel nudged my leg. "I think we're here. At least the sexy voice said we were."

Daniel helped me climb out of the car. I couldn't have dozed for more than fifteen minutes, but that was enough to tighten every muscle in my body. He wrapped his arm around my waist again and led me to the front door. I leaned against him, comforted by his presence and the odd mix of sandalwood and sweat that tickled my nose.

It felt like a train had hit me. Last night, my back hurt a little. It was sore this morning too, but after Reggie's friendly slap, I could hardly walk. The bruise pulsed and spasmed worse than after the ball hit me.

The front door opened and Lilly came rushing out.

"Victoria," she said with her slight Cajun accent. She'd been my nanny since I was six and opted to stay on as a maid when I didn't need her to babysit anymore. "Why are you coming in the front door?" She stopped when she noticed Daniel and the way he held me upright. "Child, what happened to you?"

"It's just a bruise, Lilly." She backed into the house as Daniel helped me inside. "Is Mom home?"

"No, she went to the Tea Room to meet with the ladies from the foundation." She kept her eyes on Daniel while she talked. Lilly was five feet nothing and a very protective mother hen. "What do you need me to do?"

"Can you bring some drinks to the rec room? And some lunch?" I asked.

"Where's the aspirin?" Daniel asked. His eyebrows creased with worry.

Lilly stared at him for longer than necessary. "I'll bring it." She nodded and hurried away in her silent shoes.

"I never know where she is in this house," I grumbled as I tried to straighten my back. Daniel squeezed me closer to him and I suddenly didn't want to be alone. "Can you stay? I mean, do you have to be somewhere?"

He grinned. "I'm all yours. Just let me call my dad."

"Thanks. I could use the company." I pulled away from him and lurched toward the back of the house. "I'd give you a tour, but I'm not really feeling up to it at the moment."

Daniel ooh-ed and ah-ed behind me. I kept shuffling my feet.

"This place is huge." He said as he slid his arm back around my waist when I stumbled over nothing but my own two feet. I let him hold me up even though it felt wrong. And oh-so right.

"It's too big. We only use about a third of it."

Joba came bounding up to me. He jumped and pushed me into the wall, putting his oversized lab paws on my shoulder and his tongue on my face. Thank God for the wall, or I would've kissed the marble floors. Once he was done with me, he made his way to Daniel, who laughed at the golden retriever's enthusiasm. We walked out the patio doors with Joba leading the way. The pool glistened in the midday sun. I wanted to dive in but knew I wouldn't be able to get back out.

The rec room was in the pool house. The Senator decided it was best to keep the games away from the real world. When I was ten, I ran away from home and moved there for a month. He never even knew.

I slid open the patio doors and flipped on the lights. The pool house was basically a one room building. There was the small bar/kitchenette and an oversize fireplace. Beside that stood the entertainment center, complete with a sixty-inch flat screen TV and three different gaming systems. One wall was nothing but windows overlooking the kidney shaped pool. Scattered about the rest of the room was a pool table, foosball table, and an air hockey table. It was a gamer's dream.

In the large bathroom, I grabbed a heating pad from under the sink. Joba and Daniel waited for me on the couch while I tossed it in the microwave as Lilly came in with a plate of sandwiches, a pitcher of fruit punch, and a lifetime supply of aspirin. She sat them on the coffee table and started straightening up the room, watching Daniel out of the corner of her eye. She finally left when there wasn't anything left to clean.

"I can't believe your family room is in a completely different building," he said as I sat beside him. But not too close.

I laughed, harder than I should have. "Don't make me do that. It hurts."

"Sorry." He pushed me forward and adjusted the heating pad.

The heat made my eyebrows sweat. "Will you do me a favor?" I asked. "Will you keep all this between us? I don't want the other guys to think I'm some rich bitch looking for a cheap thrill."

"Says the girl who drives a Beemer."

I rolled my eyes. "Point taken."

Daniel leaned back into the plush leather sofa and put his feet on the table. "Don't worry, Vic. I wouldn't want them trying to hoard in on all this anyway."

The TV remote was just out of my reach. I pointed at it, but, like most guys, he snatched it and started flipping through the stations. Daniel found the Cardinals pregame show. I'd watch baseball twenty-four seven if I could. Grandma was tired of the games already, but that wasn't going to stop me.

"Hey, Daniel," I said, drawing him away from an interview with a just-called-up minor leaguer. "Can I ask you something?"

He shrugged and kept his eyes on the TV.

"Will you be honest with me?"

He looked at me then muted the TV.

"How bad did it look?" I already knew how bad it looked to me, but I wanted his opinion.

"Pretty nasty."

My stomach sunk into my knees. "Great. I bet the other guys think I'm a wuss."

36

This made him laugh for some reason. "They think you're crazy, Vic, but not a wuss."

"Crazy?" I didn't know if I liked the sound of that.

"For going after CroMag man. For trying to practice hurt. For playing in the first place. Most of the guys think it's kinda cool you're on our team." He lifted the remote to turn the sound back on.

"Most? Who's the exception?" Each guy's face passed in my mind. But I knew the answer.

He sighed. Loudly. Then put the remote back in his lap. "Do you really want to know?"

"Yep."

"Jayden thinks you're making a mockery out of the game. His words, not mine."

I nodded. "He's pretty intense, isn't he?"

"Yeah. His mom works two jobs to stay in the neighborhood. His dad's out of the picture. Most of us, including you, aren't going to have a problem getting into college. Jay's depending on a scholarship."

"There are other ways —"

"He's not the sharpest guy with the books. He tries, but he knows his GPA isn't going to help. Don't get me wrong, he isn't stupid. He works hard to get okay grades. There's no way he can get any academic scholarships. It'll have to be athletic."

We sat in silence. I'd never thought that one of the guys might *need* baseball. The heating pad had cooled off and the throbbing in my back ached. "Is that why he never talks to me?"

"Pretty much." He glanced at the TV then back at me. "Okay, my turn."

I waved my hand at him and closed my eyes.

"Why'd you ask me to stay?"

It was a valid question. Why did I ask him? It's not like I don't spend plenty of time alone. I shook it off and grabbed the nearest game controller.

"To kick your ass at 'Swords of Fury', of course."

"Oh, game on." Daniel smiled and reached for the other controller. He turned on the game console. "You aren't the only one with this game, princess."

We played until the game came on. Daniel would warm up the heating pad for me. A couple of times, I hated to admit this, I would cheat and kill his avatar. That only made the competition worse. He started bumping into my arm and I'd give it right back to him. I even faked pain in my back to get him to stop. He caught on to that pretty fast though.

Then he elbowed my arm too hard and I lost my balance. Daniel did too and landed on top of me. We both forgot about the game. His breath smelled like cucumbers and mayo from the sandwiches Lilly had brought us. He stared at me for a moment then pushed himself back into sitting position.

I laid there in shock before forcing myself to sit back up beside him. He gripped my arm and helped pull me up. My skin burned where he'd touched me. The throbbing in my back had increased with the added pressure of Daniel's weight.

"I think I better go." He stood up, stretching his arms above his head. His shirt rose to expose his thin stomach and the black band of his boxers. Not that I'd normally notice such things. He dropped his arms with a scowl souring his face. "Great. I forgot to call Dad."

I opened my mouth suggest calling a cab when a car pulled around the back of the house. Mom used a service when she went to the Tea Room just in case she had too much "tea."

"Come on. I know how you can get home." I brushed by him and immediately regretted it. He might think it was intentional. Whatever just happened between us, I didn't need to encourage it to happen again.

Mom stood in the driveway while the driver took her shopping bags from the trunk. She eyed Daniel with clear suspicion. In a matter of minutes, Daniel was gone.

Before Mom could play Spanish Inquisitor with me, I took off to my room and closed the door. It may have been princess era hell, but it was still mine. I checked out my back before climbing into the four-poster bed. The swelling had gone down even though it looked greener than before. Within twenty minutes, I was asleep and dreaming of a Korean boy.

The next two games were uneventful. I was suspended for the Thursday game, which we won by one run. For Saturday's game, I expected to be back in the lineup. My massive bruise still scarred my back, but it looked uglier than it felt. The lineup card did not have my name on it. Hiding my disappointment, I warmed up with Shane and T.C. It felt good to stretch and loosen up.

It was the bottom of the ninth with one out and our team down by one run.

"Hudson, you feelin' up to hittin'?" Coach growled.

My response was to grab my bat and batting gloves.

"Just get on the bag. And for God's sake, get outta the way of the ball." He trotted back to the coach's box at third.

A couple of the guys laughed as I stretched again and eyed the pitcher. My back was too tight to turn on a pitch. I'd have to loop it to right field. And I knew the pitcher would offer up a fastball down the middle. Boys never learn.

He didn't smile at me or acknowledge me in anyway. The fastball I so cockily expected ended up as a curveball on the outside of the plate. And I totally missed it by swinging over the ball. It had great curve. No wonder this guy was the closer.

I stepped out and looked for my sign. Coach nodded. I was on my own.

Bunt.

They were playing me to hit but not hard and not too far. They weren't playing me to bunt. If I laid it down the third base line, I could beat it out. But if I faked a bunt, I could draw them in and then pop it into right.

I squared.

The first and third basemen moved in and everyone adjusted.

The wind up. The release.

I pulled my bat back then slapped the ball over the second baseman's head. If I'd been at full strength, I could've turned it into a double, but I stayed at first. Coach sent Freddie in to run for me. High fives went around the dugout from everyone but Jayden. Daniel grabbed my hand for a second too long. His face started to turn pink and he let go, walking to the other end of the dugout. Thankfully, none of the guys noticed. That would've been awkward.

My cell rang in my duffel. I looked over at it and shook my head.

"Gonna pick that up?" Daniel asked, sneaking up behind me with a sneer on his lips. He knew it was Theo. Stupid ringtone.

"Of course not. I'm a little busy at the moment."

He smirked as I brushed by him to rattle the fence and annoy the other team. Daniel joined me. I was all too aware of how close he was. Even if I wasn't with Theo, I couldn't go out with Daniel. It would mess with the team.

Freddie was at third now with Jayden coming up to the plate. If they were smart, they'd walk him with first base open. They didn't, and he made them pay. One pitch and Jayden jacked it out of the park in dead center. We greeted him at home for the walk-off celebration, jumping up and down like we just won the World Series.

During the mandatory round of handshakes with the other team, their pitcher grabbed my hand and held onto it for a moment. Daniel stood too close behind me and I felt him tense up. The pitcher grunted.

"Nice hit," he said. Then he moved on.

Smiling like a moron, I almost skipped back to the dugout.

"What did that dude say?" Daniel asked, hurrying to catch up with me.

"Why?"

"He looked like a dick. What'd he say?"

I stopped and glared at him for a moment. "He told me I had a nice ass."

He scowled. I could've sworn that was smoke coming out of his ears. It was both flattering and annoying.

"What would you have done if he'd called me a bitch? Beat him up for me?" I snapped. "I can take care of myself, you know." I threw my glove into the dirt. "God, don't be such a –"

"A what?"

"A guy!"

He glared down at me and I could've sworn the imaginary smoke was real.

"What's your problem, Daniel?"

He shook his head and strode to the dugout. I bent down and grabbed my glove, not entirely sure of what just happened. Daniel didn't turn around or even glance at me as he took off to the parking lot. It bothered me more than it should have.

I stomped into the dugout and plopped on the bench.

"Damn, Vic. Why you gotta be so hard on him?" Reggie asked as he threw his glove into his bag.

"What are you talking about?" I yanked my cleats off without untying them.

"You're an idiot." Adam sat beside me, draping his arms across the back of the bench. "He likes you. Everyone knows it."

I shook my head. "No, you're wrong. Daniel knows I've got a boyfriend."

"And you think that stops a guy from liking a girl? What the hell is your momma teaching you?" Reggie laughed. "Get serious, Vic. The guy's got the hots for you."

My cell rang again.

"And you better turn that off next time or Coach'll have your head," Adam said as he stood up and grabbed his own bag.

Theo's smiling face on the screen made me want to chuck the phone onto the field. I didn't want to deal with him. Not now. I pushed the button to silence the damned thing and dropped my head into my hands.

I didn't need this.

TOP OF THE 3RD

Coach gave us Sunday off. Instead of heading with Grandma to beautify some neighborhood garden, I went over to Chez Hudson. Grandma didn't push it, but she did give me her patented stink eye. The conversation with Reggie and Adam weighed my thoughts. It hadn't occurred to me that one of my teammates might *like* me like me. It hadn't crossed my mind that I might like one of *them*. The other thing that hadn't crossed my mind much lately was Theo.

He called me a couple of times since he left. I only called him once, but I'd emailed him details of the games he never asked about. He never mentioned them or responded to the emails.

After swimming a few laps in the pool, I called Theo like a good girlfriend should.

"Hello?" a groggy voice answered. It sounded somewhat familiar and was most definitely not Theo's. Or male at all for that matter.

Uh-oh. I also hadn't thought about what time it was there. "Is Theo around?"

Whoever it was dropped the phone. I heard it hit the floor.

"Victoria? Do you have any idea what time it is?" Theo sounded quite clear and quite awake.

"Yeah, it's around noon." The tone in his voice made me squirm on the chaise lounge.

"I mean here."

"No, Theo, I don't know what time it is there." I sighed so he would hear me. "You called yesterday. I was just calling you back.

That's all."

Something shuffled in the background. Papers? Maybe.

"Look, I'll just talk to you later," I added. The shuffling continued and curiosity got the best of me. "What're you doing anyway?"

"We're on a train heading back to Paris." A girl giggled near him. "Why didn't you answer your phone yesterday?"

"I was in the middle of a game. Who's with you?"

He paused. "What?"

"Someone else is with you. Someone else answered your phone and it was a girl. Who's there?" Something was wrong. I could feel it in the pit of my stomach.

"That's Stacey. You remember her, right? She was in our poli-sci class last spring." He tried to keep his voice casual, but it cracked on her name. "Rod and Leslie are in here too, but you didn't wake them up when you called."

"And why did she answer your phone, Theo?" I was seething inside. That's why I knew the voice. Stacey had been chasing Theo since the minute he asked me out.

"I don't know. Her phone looks the same as mine –"

"Don't pull that crap with me, Theo. I can see through it. Just …" I took a deep breath. "Tell me the truth."

I heard the sound of the door sliding open then close.

"Victoria, it's not –"

"Don't patronize me either."

"She's a friend –"

"Who's sleeping in your compartment?"

He didn't say anything. I could almost see him leaning against the doors to his sleeping compartment and staring out the window of the train, northern Italy flashing by outside but barely visible.

"It's not what –"

I hit end. It was the oldest song in the book and I didn't want to hear it. I fell back onto the lounge chair and waited for the tears to come.

They never did.

Practice on Monday was tense. At least for me. Daniel wouldn't talk or even look at me. Not once. Reggie and Calvin made fun of my "owie." Now that it no longer hurt, it was acceptable to insult me. Ian and Reid jokingly ducked whenever I threw the ball from third to first. Apparently, I grunt when I throw. I didn't realize that until Adam pointed it out. Ollie and I chatted about pulling the ball. T.C. helped me work on bunting. Jayden ignored me.

When practice ended, some of the guys started talking about going to get lunch.

"Hey, Daniel, we're going to Hansen's for a burger," Adam shouted as Daniel hurried toward the street. "Want to come?"

He shook his head no and kept walking.

"What's up with him?" Delvin asked.

Adam, Walter, and Reggie looked my way.

"What?" I snapped. "You seriously can't blame this on me."

"Just go talk to him, Hudson," Walter said.

"And what am I supposed to say?"

Reggie slapped me on my shoulder. "I'd start with 'hi' or 'what's your problem, Cho.'"

"Whatever you tell him, go easy on the guy," Walter added.

"Yeah, the last girl that broke his heart put him in a slump of monumental proportions," Adam said. "Personally, I don't think I could deal with that again. Plus, we've got a real shot at the city championship this year."

"It won't do anything to the team," I whined like a five-year-old girl. This was not looking good for me.

"Of course it will. He couldn't hit worth his weight in coal last year after Shelby dumped him." Reggie tossed his bag over his shoulder. "And he was an ass to be around."

"What affects one of us, affects all of us. It'll mess with the team, Vic. You know that already," Adam said. He smiled with a hint of sadness. "Man, I was so sick of hearing about Shelby. Every time I pitched, I wanted to throw at Daniel's head and knock some sense into him. It wasn't good. Just talk to him. Then come over to Hansen's so we know what to expect tomorrow."

They walked to the parking lot in a group. I stared down the street where Daniel disappeared. This wasn't going to be pretty, but the guys were right. I needed to make my intentions clear. No dating my teammates. I didn't need any distractions, especially with my relationship with Theo up in the air.

Daniel had made it to the entrance of the park when I pulled up beside him and honked. He stopped but didn't look my way. It took all my power not to honk again or to get out and yell at him to stop being a douche.

I waited. He turned and got into the car without looking at me.

"Wanna go to Hansen's?" I tried to figure out what he was thinking. His face was expressionless. "Or we could go –"

"Hansen's is fine."

"Okay, cool. Where is it?"

He laughed. For a moment, I thought everything would be okay. Then he said, with as much sarcasm as he could, "How's the boyfriend?"

I so did not want him to think that I was available just because Theo and I weren't on the same page. This was not the time for the truth about *that* to come out. I put the car in park and turned to face him. "Last time I talked to him, he was heading back to Paris." *With Stacey.*

"He doesn't treat you right."

I couldn't argue that, but I tried. "You don't even know him."

"I know his type. You aren't important enough. He never asks about what you're doing. He only talks about himself. Right? He treats you like a trophy."

"Don't. Ever. Call. Me. That." The calm in my voice frightened me. I punched him as hard as I could in the arm. He winced, but I didn't give him a chance to complain. "I'm nobody's trophy. And you based your opinion on two partial conversations you overheard. You don't know what we are really like together." I slammed my hands on the steering wheel. I couldn't stop myself from getting more and more pissed.

"You deserve better," he said quietly.

I closed my eyes and rested my forehead on my battered steering wheel. I didn't know what to say. I needed to get the focus off me and off Theo. "Tell me about Shelby."

"Who told you –"

"Does it matter?" I sat up and stared at him. "Reggie, Calvin, Adam, Reid, take your pick. They're afraid you're gonna mope like you did last summer. So what happened?"

He stared out the passenger window. I waited.

"Never mind. It's none of –"

"Last summer, I caught her with a dealer. She was blowing him for meth." He rubbed his hands together. "We'd been together since freshman year."

I reached toward him then thought better of it, letting my hand fall to my lap.

"Worst part was that she blamed it all on me. Told me that I never paid attention to her. I never asked her about her stuff. Said all I ever did was talk about baseball or cross country or college." He finally looked at me with dull eyes. "And she was right. But she was wrong too. She didn't have to cheat on me. She didn't have to smoke meth and weed. I didn't notice her falling into drug abuse, but she didn't try to stop herself." He almost smiled. "See, I told you I know Theo's type."

I didn't know what to say. He leaned over to close the gap between us. I blurted, "We can't do this, Daniel. Regardless of how you think Theo treats me, he's my boyfriend. I didn't sign up for the team looking for a new one either." I sighed, wishing I could close the gap between us and knowing I couldn't. "Can't we just be friends?"

He sat up fast and nodded. "Yeah, friends."

I started the car and put it in drive. "Daniel, I do like hanging out with you –"

"Me too," he interrupted.

"So," I said, pulling out onto the street. "Where's Hansen's?"

We chatted about the weather on the way. The part of me that liked Daniel too much was mad at the part of me that didn't want to get involved with anyone on the team. Talk about an inner battle of wills. On top of my own issues, Daniel's problems with Shelby circled in my head.

I found a spot half a block from Hansen's. It was a soda shop not far from the park. The booths and chairs were white with red vinyl seats like it was the 1950s. The floor was even made of white and red checked tiles. Daniel waved at the guys who took up two booths and a table in between. "Teen Angel" blared from the old-fashioned jukebox in the middle of the room.

"Hey, did you guys kiss and make up?" Reggie shouted, making the other guys laugh.

I felt the blood rush to my face. Sometimes it sucks being a girl.

"Don't be a dick, Reg." Adam slapped Reggie on the back of the

46

head. "Come on, guys. Get an ice cream high like the rest of us."

They raised their various glasses in a toast. Daniel and I joined them, sliding into a booth. It was a tight fit and Daniel's side pressed into mine.

He smiled and mouthed "sorry."

I knew he wasn't. He didn't even try to scoot over an inch. But it was okay. I had made my feelings clear. I hoped.

We started joking and I relaxed. It was nice being just one of the guys.

Tuesday's game was a blowout. Coach gave me the start, but he batted me eighth. The other team never hit the ball toward third, so I had zero chances in the field. And I went oh-for-two at the plate with a walk. Not my best day. Not my best game. Regardless, we won by eight runs.

During the game, I decided to get Jayden to talk to me somehow. I stood before him in the dugout after the final out.

"Good game, Jay," I said with my hand up for a high five.

He stared at my hand and then walked around me.

"What the hell?"

Daniel shrugged.

"No, no shrugging." I pointed at Reggie and Calvin. "You guys didn't want me and Daniel fighting because of team unity or whatever, but jackass Jayden can treat me like a ghost and it's no big deal? That's such a load of puke."

"He's..." Reggie didn't finish.

"It's just that..." Calvin seemed to have the same problem as Reggie.

I turned to Daniel. "What's your excuse?"

"I already told you why he won't talk to you. I can't make him do it." Daniel tossed his glove in his bag. "If you haven't noticed, he doesn't really talk to the rest of us much either."

"Just Adam," Calvin chimed in.

"Did I hear my name?" Adam said as he strolled into the dugout.

"Vic wants to know why Jayden's a jackass," Calvin said, ducking as I took a swing at him. He didn't have to shout it for the entire park to hear.

Adam smiled. "He's not. He's actually a good guy but doesn't trust a lot of people. And he just doesn't like you, Vic. Thinks you're doing this for some kind of feminist glory."

"I've told you a million times, I –" I began.

"Just want to play baseball," they finished my sentence for me. In unison, no less.

"We know," Daniel added. "But he doesn't see it that way. No matter how many times you say it, he won't change his mind. Believe me, we've tried to convince him that you're innocent."

Reggie smirked. "Well, somewhat anyway."

Daniel smacked him on the arm with the back of his hand.

I smiled, faking sweetness. "And what exactly does that mean?"

"Nothing, it was just a joke," Reggie said, holding his hands up in mock surrender.

"Just let it go, Vic. Jayden will come around eventually." Adam walked toward the bleachers where a girl with bouncy blonde hair waited.

"Who's that?" I asked whoever was listening.

Daniel tossed his bag over his shoulder. "Adam's new girl. Think her name's Heather." His eyes narrowed. "Why?"

"Just never seen her before." I picked up my bag and watched Adam kiss Heather like he'd just gotten back from war.

"Not crushing on Adam now, are you?" Daniel snapped.

I dropped my bag and pushed him onto the bench, jumping on top of him. Then I started punching him in the soft part of the upper arm. "Take it back."

"Okay, okay," he laughed. "I take it back."

I let him up and he rubbed his arm.

"You hit like a girl, Victoria."

"No kidding, Cho. I *am* a girl."

He bent down to get his bag and mumbled something I pretended to ignore, "Believe me, I know."

"Need a ride?" I asked over my shoulder as I headed toward the parking lot. I shouldn't have, but the game of "Punch Daniel" was too much fun and I liked hanging out with him. Friends do that.

He took two strides and fell into step beside me. "Well, here's the thing. If you give me another ride home, you're gonna have to meet my mom." He cleared his throat. "She kinda thinks you're my girlfriend –"

I raised my arm to hit him again.

"Wait, wait, wait. Hear me out. I didn't tell her that. She made an assumption."

I let my hand fall and crossed my arms, giving him my version of Grandma's stink eye.

He smiled like his words hurt. "I kinda let her believe it." When I didn't smile back, he added, "She's happy about it. It was easier than telling her the truth."

I raised my eyebrows. "Fine. If you want me to be your pretend girlfriend, you have to buy me a real dinner first."

He threw his arm over my shoulder. "No problem. How about you just come over tonight? Eat with the family. You've already met my dad. You'll make my mom's day. And my little sister desperately wants to meet you."

"Wait." I stopped before we got to the car. "You have a little sister?"

He smiled and walked to the passenger door. "Yeah. She's fascinated with Xavier. And she's brilliant too. Dad's hoping she can get in next year."

"Seriously?" I unlocked the doors and opened the driver's door.

Daniel got in and immediately started adjusting the seat. "Yeah, she's already skipped a grade –"

"No. I mean about having dinner at your house."

"Of course." He reached over and turned the key for me. "You'd be doing me a huge favor."

"And you understand that you will owe me big time."

He smiled widely and leaned back into his seat. "I know."

BOTTOM OF THE 3RD

Living with my grandmother was almost like having my own place. Her calendar was more extensive than my mother's. Besides the social obligations she kept up after Grandpa died, she volunteered the majority of her time. There were gardens to tend to all over the neighborhood, the Habitat house and its office, and walking door-to-door collecting clothes for a nearby homeless shelter. On the odd off day, she'd work at a woman's shelter. Her energy amazed me.

Of course, this meant she was home the one night I was going to Daniel's house for dinner.

"Tell me about him," she asked. She sat at the kitchen table with her hand curled around a cup of tea.

I pulled the carton of milk from the fridge. "You know him already. He works at the Habitat house."

Her eyebrows scrunch while she thought about this. "The Cho boy?"

"His name is Daniel." I chugged the milk and put the glass into the sink. Staring out the window with her in my peripheral vision was easier than looking at her head on.

"Good family." She sipped her tea but didn't take her eyes off me. "What does Theo think of this?"

I hadn't told anyone that Theo and I were on the rocks. The one person I would've discussed it with was in Europe with the maybe-cheating boyfriend. "Theo doesn't know."

"You didn't tell your boyfriend that you're having dinner with another boy and his family? Do we have something to hide?"

"No, 'we' don't." Three birds hopped around the birdbath chirping at one another in the back yard. I wished I could be that carefree.

"Then why not tell Theo?"

I closed my eyes. Why didn't I just tell her? "Because it's more trouble than it's worth. I'm doing Daniel a favor to get his mother off his back. That's all."

"By pretending to be his girlfriend? Honey, are you sure this is a good idea? Daniel likes you. Anybody can see that." She snuck up behind me and hugged my shoulders. "You may do more harm than good."

"You sound like Mom."

She laughed then let go. "Your mother is much wiser than I realized."

My cell rang in my pocket. Theo. Grandma cleared her throat and went back to the crossword puzzle she'd been working on. I walked down the hall, staring at the flashing screen. Why was he even calling? I flipped it over on the bed so I couldn't see his smiling face and surveyed my little room. This felt more like home every day.

After showering, I dug into the closet. It was crammed full of the clothes that I hadn't even worn or looked at. My daily attire had been shorts and a t-shirt or my baseball uniform. I had nothing to wear. I sat on the bed to think it out. If this was my family dinner, I would have to wear a nice dress with heels. That didn't seem right. What would the Chos wear? Jeans? No, too casual.

Then I spied my simple white skirt sticking out in the back. My legs were tanned sufficiently and would only appear more so. I pushed around and found a black v-neck tee. Perfect. It was casual but dressy enough for a girl meeting a boy's parents for the first time.

I tied my hair into a low ponytail and swiped some mascara over my lashes. Simple and classy. I slipped on a pair of black flat sandals to complete the ensemble.

"You look … nice," Grandma said as I hurried to the front door.

I stopped. There was a hidden meaning in that statement. I turned to face her.

She put her hands up. "I didn't mean anything by that."

51

There wasn't any point in arguing. I shook my head and left the house. When I got to the car, I realized what she implied.

Why did I agree to this? This is stupid. I'm not his girlfriend. God, I'm an idiot.

It was too late to back out gracefully. Feeling guilty for what I was about to do, I called Theo on the way over. He didn't answer.

Andrea did.

"Vicky! I miss you. Europe is so awesome." She giggled like she did whenever she was nervous.

"I miss you, too. What's going on?" It *was* great to hear her voice. "I'm surprised you haven't called me earlier."

"I know. I keep meaning to." She laughed again. This was odd. "We've been like everywhere. The Louvre was so incredible. We spent two days in Paris. Oh, and the Eiffel Tower was muy romantic."

My eyebrows shot up. "Did you hook up with someone?"

"Vicky, you're so funny." She giggled and I knew she was lying. "Did you get my email? I sent you a ton of pics."

"No, I haven't checked my mail." It was partially true. I'd seen it on my phone but hadn't bothered to open the attachments.

Someone shouted "let's go" in the background.

"I'll tell Theo you called. We're heading somewhere … Oh, I don't even know where we're going now. I think another club. There is so much to do in Amsterdam. I can't wait to see you. Bye."

She hung up.

Less than ten seconds later, Theo called me back. I was turning onto Daniel's street and didn't feel like answering. The conversation with Andy bothered me. Why did she answer Theo's phone to begin with? Why was she laughing nervously? Something was going on. For the first time since we'd become friends, it felt like there was more than an ocean between us.

I parked in front of Daniel's house and double-checked my make-up in the rearview before sliding out of the car. I couldn't dwell on Andrea's odd behavior, or Theo, at the moment. There was a more pressing problem at hand. I needed to tell Daniel that this was not a good idea. In fact, it was a very, very bad one.

The sun had started to set as I strolled up the sidewalk. The pink and orange hues stretched across the sky like fingers reaching for the night. I stopped before the steps, staring at the imposing front door for a moment. I hated to admit it, but I was nervous. It'd been a long time since I'd met a guy's parents. I had known Theo's mom and dad for years so this situation was unprecedented. For once I wanted to be more like my parents. They were masters of self-introduction. Here I had to make conversation that didn't revolve around Senator Hudson or the state of the nation.

I reached for the doorbell just as the door opened. Daniel smiled, and his eyes slid down to my legs as I stepped by him.

"Hey," he said as if he'd run to meet me at the door.

The house was much larger than it appeared. To the right of the door was a large staircase that wound up to the second floor. On my left, a set of pocket doors were opened to a parlor. A hallway stretched out before me, leading to the kitchen where the smell of roast and potatoes clogged the air.

Daniel leaned against the banister, staring at me. "Want a tour?"

I smiled, remembering how I hadn't given him one of Chez Hudson. "Yeah, sure."

"Um ... okay." He walked into the parlor. There was a light gray sofa and loveseat arranged to face a corner fireplace. "Well, this is the living room. That," he pointed through another set of pocket doors where a long cherry table sat beneath an elaborate chandelier, "is the dining room."

Back in the hallway, he pointed out the kitchen, bathroom, and stairs to the basement. His mother peered down the hall and waved.

"Dad's not home yet. Mom's cooking like she's going to feed the entire neighborhood." He glanced back to the kitchen where his mother's head disappeared. "Let's go upstairs."

I asked in the universal language of the raised eyebrows, "Are you serious?"

He smiled and bent close to my ear. "My sister's in her room. She's dying to meet you, remember? I'm surprised she didn't run down the minute I opened the door."

He led me up the stairs. I couldn't keep my eyes off the walls. There were photos everywhere. All of them were family; that was obvious. Pictures of Daniel and his sister covered the lower part of the walls, but older images drew me in. They were orange with age.

The faces were all Korean. Daniel must have seen me staring at them because he stopped suddenly. I smacked into his backside. My hands grabbed his thighs to keep from falling back down the stairs.

He looked a little flushed when I let go.

"That was taken in Korea," he said, pointing to a picture of a man and woman standing in front of a cart on a dirty road with hills behind them. "They moved south to get away from the combat."

I stepped up between Daniel and the photo to get a better look.

He leaned over my shoulder and pointed at the cart. "See that little guy there. He would've been my dad's uncle."

"Would've been? What happened?" All I could see was a tiny face wrapped in thick blankets.

"War." He breathed the word onto my neck.

I shivered. I didn't know if it was the way he said "war" or how his hot breath caressed my neck.

He walked up the rest of the steps and waited for me. I stared at the picture for another moment before joining him. The upstairs hallway contained even more photographs. Some were more recent, like Daniel and his sister by a river somewhere. Some were older, but these were of Daniel's mother and her family.

We walked by an open door with a full-size bed and a chest of drawers. He didn't need to tell me that it was his parent's room. Daniel knocked on the first closed door to his left.

"Go away, Mom," a girl squeaked.

"It's not Mom, idiot," Daniel snapped as he wiggled the door knob.

I slapped his arm. "That's not nice."

"You don't know my sister."

She opened the door with a major scowl on her face that disappeared when she noticed me.

"Omigod, you're Vic. You have to tell me everything about Xavier." She grabbed both of my hands and pulled me into her room, kicking the door closed at the same time.

"Hey," Daniel yelled as he pushed his way inside.

"You aren't invited to this conversation," she snapped. "Nor are you allowed in my room without my permission."

"Becca's trying to impress you with all the fancy talk." He plopped on her bed. "And I can go where I want."

"Why are you dating him?" Becca looked more like her mother

with a heart shaped face and high cheekbones. Her eyes were a striking golden color that I didn't think was humanly possible. "He's such a loser. I bet there are much smarter and better-looking guys at Xavier."

The blood rushed to my face and I glanced away from her. "Smarter, yes."

"Not better looking?" Daniel asked with a cocked eyebrow.

"Gross," Becca said as her brother pushed off the bed to stand beside me.

Daniel's hand snaked into mine. Heat swept up my arm like a California wildfire. He squeezed and pulled me out of the room. "Come on. I'll show you our game room. Becs, quiz her later."

Becca huffed and muttered to herself. Once we were in the hall, she slammed the door. Daniel let go of my hand, leaving it cold.

He pointed at a different closed door as he walked down the hall. "That's my room."

"Wait a minute," I said, grabbing his arm.

He looked down where my fingers curled around his wrist.

"Doesn't your 'girlfriend' get to see all your little secrets?" I yanked him back toward the door and opened it to the biggest mess I'd ever seen. There were DVDs, magazines, and books scattered everywhere and a life-size skeleton wearing a blue plaid shirt and cargo shorts. The bed, once I figured out exactly where it was located, was a pile of comforter and sheets and clothes. "This is beyond disgusting."

"You're the one that opened it." He slid his fingers through mine and tugged me toward the other end of the hallway. "Come on."

"Why do you have a skeleton in your room?" I said, staring at the mess. "And I thought I saw a massive computer system in there."

He tried to drag me away, but I let go of his hand. Daniel teetered, and I stepped into the room. At least there wasn't an odd smell. On the same wall as the door was a computer desk with a huge flat screen monitor. This was the only clean spot in the room.

I turned it on.

"Good evening, Daniel," a computerized voice said.

I started laughing. "Holy crap. That's awesome. Where'd you get that voice?"

"Nowhere." He turned a pale pink. "It's just a program."

"Where did you buy it?" I sat in the chair and felt him directly behind me.

"Didn't." He spun the chair around and knelt before me. "I created it in a programming class I took last year."

He started to explain code and it went over my head. So far over my head, my eyes must have glazed over.

Daniel laughed. "This is boring you."

"No, really it's not." I smiled like I was Grandma at a benefit, interested even if I really wasn't. "It's cool. I'm just not that big into computers or anything. How do you know so much?"

"The usual. Books, magazines, internet. It's not that complicated."

"For me it is. You might as well be talking Klingon."

"Okay, come on." He pulled me to my feet until we were chest to chest. "Let's move on before you fall asleep."

I didn't even try to move away. "Why do you say that?"

"The look of death on your face."

"Stop. I'm not bored." Then it hit me almost as hard as that pitch I took in the back. "Shelby didn't like any of this stuff, did she?"

He shrugged and took a step back. "No."

"Not everybody is like her, you know." I reach out. My fingers skimmed over his forearm. I shouldn't have touched him, but I wanted him to know *I* wasn't like her. "Don't let one idiot ruin you."

He stared at me, leaning down slowly. I tilted my head, wanting him to kiss me. And I hated myself for it.

"Daniel, please come downstairs," a sweet voice screamed up the stairs.

He turned away, breaking the moment. "Coming."

With a sheepish grin, he headed out of the room with me behind him. He stuck his hands in his pockets.

Don't do this. Don't fall for Daniel. Don't, don't, don't. He's still hung up on Shelby. And I'm still with Theo. Why else would I call him on my way here? Don't fall for Daniel. Think of the team. But I wanted to take his hands from his pockets. I wanted him to feel them warming mine again. I wanted him to stand so close I could feel the heat from his body and hear his heart beating.

And I wished like hell he would've kissed me. I wanted him to kiss me.

I didn't know what to do.

Becca peppered me with questions about Xavier during dinner. She was a nonstop whirlwind of conversation. Daniel's parents sat back and broke in only when she took a breath. When Mr. Cho asked what my father did for a living, I told the truth. Mostly. "My father is a lawyer and a partner in his firm." I just left out minor details. Like that he wasn't practicing and that he's a U.S. Senator, for example.

I realized a few minutes later that it had been wise not to bring up my father's political life. Daniel's parents started talking about the new immigration bill going through the House. My father opposed it as too liberal. Daniel's dad thought it wasn't liberal enough. I kept my mouth shut.

Becca tried to drag me to her room after dinner, but Daniel peeled her off me.

"I didn't get to show you the game room. Up for a round of racing?" He smiled, but it didn't reach his eyes.

"Only if you want to get your butt kicked."

He stuck his hands back into his pockets and we went back up the stairs. My thoughts raced with the all too recent memory of grabbing his tight thighs.

Stop it. Stop it. Stop it.

We walked toward a door at the end of the hall. Daniel opened it and led me up another flight of stairs into a large attic room. A flat screen hung on one end with an overstuffed ocean blue sectional in front of it. The other side of the room had a drafting table, a computer, and three large bookshelves.

"It's also Dad's office," Daniel explained when he saw me looking at the drafting table.

He walked over to the TV and turned everything on. I sat on the couch, tucking my legs in and grabbed a game controller. Daniel plopped beside me, making me roll into him. He wrapped his arms around my waist to keep me from falling off the couch. I stiffened, but not because I was uncomfortable.

"Sorry," he said. "I should've warned you about that."

He didn't let go. I didn't make much of an effort to get up either. Again, I thought he was going to kiss me. Then Becca burst into the room.

"Daniel, Mom wants to know …" She stopped as she saw us struggling to sit up. "I'll just tell her no."

I stared at the door, horrified. At my behavior. At being caught … doing what?

"I better go," I said, standing up too fast and losing my balance. Daniel put his arm around my waist to steady me. "Please don't."

He stood up, keeping his arm around me. "Don't what, Vic?"

"I have …" I didn't finish. He knew what I was going to say.

He leaned down toward me. The boy was determined.

"What about the team?" I whispered.

"Screw them."

I tilted my head to meet him but looked away when I felt myself leaning in. This wasn't right. "I can't."

He put his forehead against my temple.

"I should go," I forced through the breath I held.

I said good night to his family. Daniel walked me out to my car. We stood in that awkward silence that always shows up right after something romantic almost happens between two friends. A feeling I knew all too well lately.

"I'll see you tomorrow," he said, turning back toward the house.

"Daniel, wait." I closed my eyes. I couldn't leave it like this.

"Yeah?" He leaned against the hood but didn't look at me.

"I'm sorry."

"Didn't we already go over this upstairs?"

I sighed. "Yes. And no. I just …" I started crying like a princess who lost her tiara.

He looked to the sky. "Get it out of your system, Vic. You think I'm a nice guy but not 'The One.' You have a horrible boyfriend and would like to keep it that way –"

"Shut up. Just shut up." I smacked my hand on the roof my car as hard as I could. "I don't have …" I paused to figure out how to say it. "I don't know for sure, but I think Theo's cheating on me."

He whipped around to face me.

"I'm sorry I didn't tell you. I just … I didn't want it to mess with the team. And I really didn't want to get all romantic with …" I wiped my cheeks. *Damn it. Stop crying like some little girl.* "But I like you too much –"

He rushed at me. I stepped back into the front quarter of my car to get out of his way. He cupped my face, pulling my lips to his. His kiss was angry and hungry at the same time. He relaxed when he realized I wasn't fighting, but kissing him back with the same intensity. I put my hands over his to steady myself. My knees buckled. The aftershave he barely wore filled the air. He pulled back, kissing my nose. The warm night air felt cool against my lips. Theo never kissed me like that.

Theo.

"Victoria –"

The way he said my full name reminded me of the last person I wanted to think of. It didn't matter that I liked the way Daniel said it.

"I have to go." Guilt choked the words in my throat.

I jumped into my car and raced to Grandma's. Theo and I hadn't broken up exactly. I mean, it was implied when I hung up on him. But then he called me. And I called him back. I liked Daniel way more than I should, but I needed to clarify my relationship with Theo. What if Theo came back and we made up?

My head hurt from all this.

Too many what-ifs and not enough answers.

TOP OF THE 4TH

It goes without saying that things were uncomfortable during the game on Thursday. Again. We lost by a run. I went oh-fer again, and I made my first fielding error of the year. Coach said they ruled it a hit, but it was an error in my mind. Their first baseman smacked a line drive over my head. I jumped and knocked it down, but I should've had it clean. My leap was a millisecond too late. It cost us the game.

Daniel tried to act like nothing had happened. Like he hadn't kissed me. Like I hadn't run away. Whenever he headed toward me, I went the opposite direction. Not easy to do in a crowded dugout.

After the ninth inning, he was the first to leave. He didn't try to say another word before he left with his mom and Becca. Coach and I were the last ones in the dugout.

"Word must've gotten out that we've got a girl on our team," Coach growled as he sat on the bench next to me. "Stands keep gettin' more crowded."

I shrugged.

"Look, Vic. I dunno what's gotten into you, but snap outta it. This team could win the district. Hell, we can make a run at the city championship. So whatever's got you outta sorts, get over it and get back in line."

"Easier said than done, Coach." I stopped pretending to fix my cleats and grabbed my gear. It was a long walk to the car. When I climbed in, I glanced at the empty passenger seat.

I never should've kissed him. He'd be here now if ... I couldn't think about it. I drove home and cleaned out Grandma's basement.

Daniel ignored me the next day at practice. It was fair. I deserved it. After all, I'd done the same thing to him the day before. So we kissed, big deal. I never wanted to go out with a guy on the team anyway. At least, that's what I repeated to myself whenever a pang of hurt filled my chest. The rest of the team kept giving me odd glances here and there. As soon as practice ended, Daniel high-tailed it out of the park. And I cornered Reggie in the dugout.

"What's going on?" I asked in my sweetest voice.

Reggie didn't look at me. "What do you mean?"

"You know what I mean. I saw you talking to Daniel. What's going on?"

He shook his head. "You do *not* want to hear this."

My heart fell to the soles of my cleats. "Yes, I think I do."

"You really don't, Vic."

"Damn it, Reggie. Tell me." I stomped my foot on his.

"Ow, fine. But don't say I didn't warn you." He sat on the bench and motioned for me to join him. This had to be really bad if it required a sit down. "Shelby showed up at his house last night after the game. Apparently the guy she'd been seeing got a little violent. He beat her sober." Reggie shook his head. "Her parents kicked her out. She's hiding at Daniel's house. She didn't have any other place to go."

I struggled to get my mind around this. Shelby broke Daniel's heart into a million pieces and now she was back. Where did that leave me? And why should it bother me so much? "Why didn't he just tell me?"

He shrugged. "You'd have to ask him that. Besides, you were doing your best to avoid him yesterday." Reggie clamped his hand on my shoulder and squeezed. "I'm sorry, Vic."

Grandma insisted I go to the Habitat house with her that afternoon. The more I protested, the more she demanded that I go. When we pulled up to the site, my hands shook uncontrollably. I stuck them into my pockets before Grandma could see them.

We walked toward the house in the same deafening silence that we held onto in her car. I kept my head down, scanning the site for any sign of Daniel. I didn't want to run into him, but I wanted to know he was okay.

He wasn't there. Neither was his dad. I wasn't really surprised considering what Reggie had told me. Charles, one of the foremen, took me into the house and put me to work. I learned how to spackle. It was something I hoped I'd never have to do again since I totally sucked at it. Fixing my mistakes only made me feel worse, which was pretty much the entire day of feeling like crap. By quitting time, I was too tired to think about Daniel, Shelby, or Theo. I needed a hot bath and a good night's sleep before the game the next day. It promised to be our toughest yet. The Robins shared the same record as our Wolverines.

At least we had a scarier name.

When I got to the field, I noticed the stands were pretty full. I didn't believe I was the cause of that even if Coach and some of the guys thought so. I wasn't the first girl to play baseball. The regulars were in their usual spots, like Adam's girlfriend and Reggie's parents. Then I spotted someone I never thought I'd see.

My mother. In jeans. And one of my baseball hats.

She looked so out of place sitting on the cheap metal stands. I dumped my stuff in the dugout and ran up to her.

"What're you doing here?" I asked not bothering to withhold the shock in my voice. "And where did you get those jeans?"

"From your closet." She struggled to get comfortable, wiggling back and forth with her hands daintily in her lap. "I thought I'd come watch. Is that okay?" She had to have come from lunch at the Tea Room. I could smell the Earl Grey on her breath masking the hint of brandy.

"Yeah, I guess." I shrugged and stared at her for a moment. This didn't make any sense. The last time she showed up at anything — sports, debate club, trivia bowl — was when I was fifteen, unable to drive, and the service didn't have an available car.

Reggie's mom cleared her voice two rows down and glanced up at us over her shoulder. She smiled, moving over enough that I'd get the hint.

I figured it couldn't hurt anything and Mom would have someone to talk to during the game. "Come on. I'll introduce you to some other parents." In a soft voice only she could hear, I added, "And your husband is just a lawyer, okay?"

Mom shot me a look that would melt glass before climbing down the steps. I introduced her to Reggie's mom and they immediately fell into conversation. I knew she'd be fine. She shined in awkward situations.

"Hudson, is that your mom?" Reggie asked when I got back in the dugout.

"Yeah. Stands out, doesn't she?" I glanced back at her as she laughed her fake that-was-funny laugh.

"Just like you do," Adam said, smacking me on the shoulder. "Come on, let's warm up."

I looked to the field. Daniel was already there in his gear, throwing with Calvin. I wanted to run up to him to kiss him and smack him at the same time. Instead, I jogged to the opposite end of the field and stretched with Adam and Reggie.

We started the game off on the right foot. Their pitcher threw at me and grazed my jersey. The crowd booed. Even my mom got into it, yelling at the ump to throw the guy out. That made me smile. Maybe a little too wide.

"What're you smiling at?" the first baseman asked.

"Your pitcher just gave up a run. What's not to smile about?" I tugged on another batting glove in case I needed to slide.

Then I stole second. It was damned close though. I got my hand on the bag a split second before the tag. No way I'd take third off this catcher.

Ollie got a nice hit over the second baseman's head, moving me to third.

Then Jayden did what he does best. He crushed a double into left center. Ollie and I both scored. We took the lead. The game kept going back and forth. Delvin wasn't his sharpest on the mound, but neither was their pitcher. At the end of the ninth, we were on top ten to eight. It was a good win.

Daniel started to take off right after the last out. I caught him in the dugout.

"Hey, wait a sec," I said, grabbing his arm. "Will you stop and talk to me?"

"I can't right now, Vic."

He pulled away and hurried toward the stands. An Asian girl with stripes of hot pink in her hair waited for him. She was petite with a smirk on her face that was part mischievous and part all-knowing. I hated her instantly.

"That's Shelby," Calvin said over my shoulder.

"Yeah, sorry, Vic. But that's her." Walter slapped my shoulder. I felt a couple more hands slap my back.

"He's an idiot," Jayden added before walking away.

I wanted to thank him, but the words wouldn't come out. Whatever Daniel and I would've had, it wasn't going to happen now. It should've been a relief, but it wasn't. Daniel and Shelby stood close together at the end of the bleachers. I watched his shoulders slump at something she said. She caught me staring at them and grinned, slipping her hand around his waist. I turned away, not wanting or needing to see what happened next. The anger surged in my chest like a tsunami. It didn't matter anymore. Dating wasn't worth all the shit I'd already been through. I was done with guys for the rest of the summer. No more crap from Theo. No more pining over Daniel. I was *done*.

I felt a canyon form in my gut. It was over before it had the chance to start.

BOTTOM OF THE 4TH

The next week went by in a daze. Baseball was the only thing I could concentrate on. Daniel didn't come back to the Habitat house even though his dad did. I wanted to talk to Mr. Cho, but I couldn't bring myself to do it. I didn't want to hear from Daniel's dad what I already knew.

We lost on Tuesday but held on to sole possession of first in our district.

Theo, Andrea, and the rest of my class that went to Europe were scheduled to return late Wednesday night. Andy left me a voicemail that she'd try to get to Thursday's game. The idea of seeing her again made me somewhat happy. And, in a way, I wanted to see Theo to figure out what was going on with our relationship or if we even had one.

But I had a game to play first.

"You a little distracted, Hudson?" Reggie asked from the other end of the dugout.

Adam laughed while Calvin answered for me, "Of course she is. Her boy toy returned last night."

Daniel ran onto the field. Coach shook his head.

"What's his name?" Walter asked. "Theo?"

"Yeah, that's it," Adam said louder than necessary. "It's the only thing she's been talking about this week."

What a bunch of liars. They knew I hadn't said a word about Theo. Just as I knew they only said anything because they were just as pissed at Daniel as I was. This was one of the many reasons I didn't want to get involved with anyone on the team.

Mom hadn't missed a game all week. She brought Grandma with her on Tuesday, but today she brought her friend from the Tea Room, Pepper. Yep, that was her real name. Pepper was part of Mom's inner circle and looked as out of place in jeans as I did in formalwear. Mom and Pepper did everything together from charity bowl-a-thons (without actually bowling), to spa trips to California. Pepper had been a part of our lives for so long that I used to think she was my aunt. They waved from the stands as they sat with Reggie's mom.

Mom didn't come to my games, softball or otherwise. The fact that she was showing up now and bringing her best friend made the universe tilt to the left instead of right.

I couldn't let it distract me though.

Coach hit me eighth. He'd learned to hit Ollie lead off against lefties. I paced the dugout while their pitcher gave up hits to our first five batters. We were up three to nothing. Calvin stepped to the plate and I made my way to the on-deck circle.

"Hey, Victoria," a fairly recognizable voice said behind the fence.

I didn't turn around.

"Leave her alone, dude. She's focusing," Daniel snapped.

I tried to block it out, but I couldn't. Especially with Daniel involved.

"Whatever. Mind your own business, Chinaman," the boy said.

Everything stopped. Our dugout cleared but not onto the field. The umpires called time before I even comprehended what was going on. Then I saw Daniel knocking some guy on his ass behind the fence. Coach took off and I followed.

Reggie and I got in between Daniel and the other guy. I pushed Daniel back, my hands on his chest. His sweat soaked through his shirt, covering my batting gloves. Jayden, Ollie, and Calvin held the other guy.

"Are you okay?" I asked him.

He looked down at me with blazing eyes. "Shouldn't you be asking your boyfriend that?"

"What?" I turned around and saw Theo cuffed by Jayden and Calvin. "Daniel, I'm so sorry. I had no idea."

He pushed my hands off of him. "Forget it, Victoria. It's not like —"

"You ran from me, remember? You ran back to Shelby, so don't blame this all on me." I walked away from him before he could say anything else.

Theo shrugged away from the guys. He smiled as I approached. All I wanted to do was slap that smile off his face. A rock pitted in my stomach. The umpires yelled at Coach to get our team back on the field or forfeit. Calvin grabbed my arm and we hustled back to the game. My mind wasn't anywhere near the field.

Any fight we had left disappeared. We got slaughtered.

"What's your sudden damage, Victoria?" Theo snapped at me in the parking lot after Coach chewed us out for getting our asses handed to us on a platter.

I threw my duffel at his feet. "Me? You want to blame this on me? How is this *my* fault?"

"So he wasn't from China. Big deal."

"Christ, Theo, you get pissed if someone thinks you go to Ladue instead of Xavier." I stepped close enough to see that his pupils were huge. "Holy moley. You're high. When did this start?"

He laughed. "Again, big deal. I smoked a little weed when we got back."

"Go home, Theo. Call me when the real you turns up." I snatched my bag from the ground.

He grabbed my arm. "Oh no, you don't. I've been gone a month and my girlfriend won't even kiss me? Now that's just not right."

"Go home." I yanked my arm away. "What the hell happened to you? And what makes you think we're even still together after you cheated on me?"

My car was on the other side of the parking lot. I walked as fast as I could to get away from Theo. He ran up behind me and grabbed my arm again, turning me around.

"Damn it, Victoria. Why are you acting like this?" He leaned closer to me. "Why are you being such a bitch?"

"Leave her alone, man," Adam said as he strolled up behind Theo. Heather was to his left. Reggie and Calvin were on his right.

Theo didn't turn around. "This is between me and my girlfriend."

"Not anymore." Calvin slapped his hands and rubbed them together. "First you insult Daniel, then you get too aggressive with our third baseman. I think you need to haul ass outta our park, bubba."

"Daniel?" Theo laughed. "That chink was the guy you've been giving 'rides' to all summer? Now it makes sense. Oh, Victoria, when your father finds out, he's going to be so disappointed."

That giant lump that always forms in my throat at the mention of my father appeared. "Leave, Theo," I whispered. I was so incredibly tired. "We can talk about this when you aren't flying in the clouds."

"Yeah, I'll leave." He leaned in to kiss me, but I turned my head and he only got cheek. His lips hovered at my ear long enough to add, "I hope I'm there when your daddy finds out his little girl's humping a Chinaman."

Theo shoved me away and stumbled to his car.

"Should that dude be driving?" Heather asked.

"Probably not." Adam rubbed her arm. He added in a quiet monotone in the general direction of Theo, "No. Wait, stop." Theo revved his engine and sped away. "Nothing we can do about it now."

Reggie watched Theo disappear. "You okay, Vic?"

"Yeah." I shrugged. "I'm sorry, guys. He's not like that normally. He's never been a big drinker and I've never seen him get high like this before. I don't get it."

"Speaking of getting your drink on, there's a party tonight," Calvin said, wiggling his eyebrows up and down. "Come out with us, Vic. It'll be fun."

"I don't drink." *Not after the last time.* I shuddered at the memory.

"Good, then you can drive." Reggie gave Adam a high-five, then added, "Either way, it'll be a rocking good time."

This was the first time they'd asked me to go to a party with them. I glanced back to where Theo disappeared. Daniel and Shelby crossed into my thoughts. A distraction was what I needed from my train wreck of a life. What harm could a party do?

I picked Reggie and Calvin up at eight-thirty. Daniel was the only person I'd spent any time with on the team. Other than that one trip to Hansen's, I really didn't know what most of the guys were like off the field.

Calvin gave me directions from the backseat while Reggie kept messing with the radio. He thought he could sing every hip-hop song he found. He was wrong.

The party wasn't too far from Grandma's house in a nice stretch along Chipenhawk Road. The houses were all brick and looked exactly the same. We had to park two blocks away. Reggie sang the entire way there.

Most of the guys were already inside. I also noticed some of the girls that played on the softball field in our park.

The house was like Daniel's, bigger on the inside than it looked on the outside. The interior was decorated with old-fashioned furniture meant to look authentic. It just looked ancient.

"Hey, you're Vic, right?" a blonde softball girl asked me after I walked into the living room. I'd seen her pitch one day after our game ended. She wasn't bad.

"Yeah."

"I wish you were on our team. We could use a third baseman." She laughed and spilled her beer, just missing her leg. "Why aren't you playing softball anyway?"

A twist to my favorite question. "Because I wanted to play baseball."

"Angel, why are you wasting your time talking to her?" Reggie asked, flinging his arm over the girl's shoulder. "I am *so* much more interesting."

"You're an idiot, Reg," she said, giggling that annoying flirtatious giggle a lot of girls use.

"Come on. Let's get me a beer. That tap set up in the kitchen?" Reggie led her toward the back of the house.

I looked around for Calvin. He was on the couch with two other guys building a beer can pyramid. I shook my head. Boys could be so juvenile. It didn't take Reggie and Calvin any time at all to forget who drove them.

Why did I bother to come here? I don't know anybody.

"Well, well, well. Look who's slumming in the city?"

My entire body turned to ice at the sound of the voice I'd known since kindergarten. *Please tell me I'm in a bad horror movie.*

"Vicky," he continued, "what're you doing here when there is finer meat back home?"

I turned around to face him. Erik Perday had once been my best friend. We did everything together. Then we didn't. Around the beginning of eighth grade, things changed. I don't know why, they just did. Suddenly he was mean to me, calling me names and punching me for no reason. He acted more like a ten year old. At Scott Swisher's birthday blowout our junior year, I got wasted.

And I slept with Erik Perday.

The following Monday, Erik acted like we were some hot new couple. We weren't. When I told him I'd made a mistake and that I regretted what had happened, he told the entire school I was easy and would screw any guy that walked. I countered that Erik had a small dick. Most people didn't care either way. I wasn't popular enough to matter, which was fine by me.

"What do you want, Erik?" I asked.

"Looking to score, Vicky?" He sneered. Erik wasn't ugly. Usually. His surfer boy hair and constantly tan body made some girls swoon. But his bad attitude made them want to throw up. When he sneered, he looked like an evil cartoon villain.

"Shut up." I turned to walk away from him.

His hand landed like an anvil on my shoulder. "Don't you want to get a taste of me instead, Vicky? I recall you enjoyed it more than you'll admit."

I shivered and tried to shrug his hand off my shoulder.

"Is there a problem?" Jayden asked as he walked into view. Calvin stood behind him.

"Who the fuck are you?" Erik asked. Still, his hand didn't move. "You know what, don't answer that. I don't care."

"Let go of her," said the last guy who needed to see this.

I tried to spin out of Erik's death grip unsuccessfully. Daniel stood behind Erik with his fists clenched.

"Go away, loser," Erik snapped. He looked around, realizing he was outnumbered. "This has nothing to do with any of you." He glared down at me. "Where's Theo, anyway? He get tired of your lies already?"

"Man, you need a hearing aid 'cause you sure don't listen," Reggie joined in. He looked over to Jayden who hadn't taken his eyes off Erik. "This boy must have forgotten to clean his ears. I'm pretty sure I heard Daniel tell him to let go."

"Yeah, I heard that too," Jayden said. "Did you hear it, Cal?"

"Yep."

"Daniel, kung fu his ass," Reggie shouted, then added to Erik, "Boy, you better let Vic go. Now."

"Who *are* these losers?" Erik asked me.

"Her friends," Jayden answered. He smiled at Erik and it wasn't friendly.

Erik squeezed my shoulder. It hurt like hell and must have shown on my face. Daniel grabbed Erik and yanked him to the floor, slamming his knuckles into Erik's mouth. Jayden stopped Daniel before his fist could do more damage.

"Get out of here," Jayden said, his voice as calm as the sea before a hurricane. "Or I'll *let* Daniel kung fu your ass. Trust me, you don't want that."

Erik wiped the blood that dripped from the corner of his mouth. Jayden stood over him with Daniel at his back. The room was deadly quiet. Everyone watched as Erik crab-crawled away from Jayden and Daniel. He rose, keeping his eyes on the boys, and backed out of the house. The chatter erupted as soon as the door banged shut.

Daniel took off toward the kitchen without looking at me. I started to follow him until I saw Shelby smiling in the hallway. I hadn't noticed her there. I collapsed on the arm of the nearest chair.

"You okay?" Jayden asked.

I nodded, then took a swig of soda Reggie handed me.

"Then go talk to Daniel."

"Why?" I looked up at Jayden's looming figure.

He crossed his arms. "Just go."

Surely Jayden knew that there was no way I had a chance with Daniel now that Shelby was back. "Shelby's here."

"So."

I stared at him, really taking in his expression. Jayden usually had only one: focus. His muscles and attitude were intimidating, but his dark brown eyes were open and honest. Whatever he thought about me playing baseball, it didn't matter at this moment. He was being a friend.

Shelby laughed in the hallway, her eyes on me. I followed as she headed toward the kitchen. Before I crossed the threshold, I took a deep breath and thought about what I needed to say to Daniel. Then

I overheard what Shelby had to say to him.

"Come on, Danny. Let's get high and really party." Her voice was higher than I'd expected.

"You know I don't do that crap, Shel. And neither should you. Do you want to end up in rehab again? That's where my parents are going to ship you." He sounded tired, not lovey dovey.

She laughed. I suspected she was already high. "They ain't my parents, Danny. They can't commit me."

"I know that, but they are trying to help –"

"Oh, whatever." I could almost see her roll her eyes.

"Don't be like that."

"I don't want their help. I don't need their help. And I don't need your attitude either."

"Then why'd you show up at my house then, huh? It wasn't because that dude beat the snot out of you, was it? You told me you wanted to get clean." Daniel's irritation laced through his words.

"Well, I don't."

"Then leave."

"Fine." She paused, waiting for him to stop her. "Fine, I will."

She pushed by me in the hall. I waited for Daniel to come after her. When he didn't, I went into the kitchen to find him. He leaned against the sink, looking out the window. I watched him as quietly as I could. He smacked the ceramic sink hard with his right hand then spun toward me.

"Oh," he said when he saw me there.

"I just ... um ... I just wanted to thank you. For helping me out back there." God, I felt like a moron.

"You mean with your other boyfriend." He stated it as cold, hard fact.

I threw my hands up. I couldn't take this from him. Not now. "Forget it."

"Wait." He walked up to me and stopped, leaving little room for escape. "I'm sorry. That was ..."

"Mean?"

"Out of line. I don't know who that guy was. Or what he meant to you. I shouldn't have said anything."

"You haven't said anything to me for a while." I leaned closer, tilting my head up toward him.

"I know."

"Are you …" I swallowed the lump in my throat. "Are you and Shelby …"

"No."

"Do you want to …"

He put his hands on my hips. "No."

"Then why have you been treating me like a leper?" I linked my fingers into the belt loops of his jeans.

"Are you still dating Theo?"

"Officially, yes. Unofficially, no."

He pulled back. "What's that supposed to mean?"

I dropped my hands and stared at the floor. "I haven't broken up with him." I glanced up to see if there was any emotion in his eyes and added, "Yet."

He cupped my face in his warm hands. It felt so good, so natural. "Yet?"

All I could do was nod. I put my hands back on his hips. I was breaking my promise to myself to not get involved with Daniel, but the truth was I missed him more that I ever missed Theo.

"Okay." He smiled. "I can deal with that. But, tell me, when's 'yet' going to happen?"

"As soon as I see him again."

"Or talk to him?"

"No. I'm not going to do it over the phone."

He nodded. "Okay." He kissed my forehead. "He's a dick."

"No, he's not. Not usually anyway."

Daniel chuckled. "Don't defend him. Just let me hate him, okay?"

I smiled. "Fair enough."

"What about that douche bag in the living room?"

I pushed away from him. He didn't want to hear it.

"Or do I even want to know?"

The sliding doors opened to the patio and a couple came into the kitchen. No one was outside. I took his hand and led him through the doors. The fresh air gave me the courage I needed. I fell into a chaise lounge. Daniel sat beside me. After a moment, I told him the whole Erik Perday story. Everything. Not leaving out one bit. Well, except for a few minor details.

"What is it with you and assholes?" He slid down next to me, pressing his thighs against mine.

"I have no idea." I turned to my side and put my hand on his

73

stomach.

"I'm not an asshole."

"I know that."

Daniel put his arm around the back of my neck. "So you'll forgive me?"

"For what?"

"Not being very patient?"

Before I could answer him, he pulled me closer and kissed me like it was the first time. Everything a kiss should be. And I didn't want him to stop.

We stayed outside, just talking, until Reggie stumbled upon us. He was wasted and needed a ride home. I reluctantly left Daniel lying there and gathered Calvin, not nearly as drunk as Reggie, to help me drag Reggie to the car. But it was okay.

For once, everything was going to be okay.

TOP OF THE 5TH

Theo refused to return my calls. I tried twice on Friday, then three times on Saturday before heading off to the game. When I got to the field, Daniel and Adam were the only guys there.

"Did you talk to him?" Daniel asked, touching my elbow.

Adam whistled as he strolled through the dugout. What an idiot.

"No, not yet." I slammed my bag onto the bench. "I've been calling him for the last two days. He won't answer and isn't calling me back."

Daniel ran his hand down the length of my spine. My knees quaked. "Maybe he got the hint."

"Doubtful." I leaned into him then remembered we agreed to keep us quiet at the games. Shaking off the need to touch him, I pulled away and started unloading my gear. "I left a message telling him when my game was. Maybe he'll show up. If not, I'll just go to his house this afternoon. I want to get it over with."

"Yeah, me too."

I smiled. Daniel was his old self again. "Come on. Warm me up."

He took one step and pressed his body to mine. "Vic, if you only knew how much I wanted to do just that."

I threw my glove at him and chased him onto the field. Adam waited for us near second base. We started throwing the ball around and talked about the upcoming game. The rest of the team showed up one at a time, looking hungover but no more than usual.

I guess there was another party last night. Coach posted the lineup. Daniel and I were both getting the day off. That was going to make things hard.

Daniel and Adam took off toward the concession stand fifteen minutes before the game was to start. I watched them, okay I watched Daniel, until they turned around the corner of the cinder block building. Calvin was doing some stupid dance to my right, and I started to turn around when Adam waved me over. He looked panicked. I took off in a dead sprint. Why did Adam wave me over and not Daniel? Was Daniel okay?

Adam put his hands on my shoulders before I rushed past him to round the corner.

"Is something wrong?" I asked, straining to look around him.

"Well …" He smiled in a wicked way. "Yes and no. It just depends on how you look at it."

"Adam …" I stopped trying to get around him for a moment. The smile on his face turned into a mixture of amusement and disgust.

"Just don't scream, okay?" He let me go.

As I turned the corner, my stomach was in my heels. I expected to see Shelby holding Daniel in a tight embrace. But Adam wouldn't have found that funny at all. Daniel leaned one shoulder against the cinder block wall and had his arms crossed over his chest. I followed his gaze to a couple making out by the lone shade tree near the softball field. It wasn't hard to tell it was Theo. When he kissed the girl's neck that was when I saw the most heartbreaking thing in the world.

Theo was getting hot and heavy with Andrea. My supposed best friend.

"Sorry, Vic," Adam said over my shoulder. "We thought you'd want to see this yourself."

Anger began in my stomach and escaladed up into my throat. I was either going to blow my top or vomit. I walked over to them, spy quiet. Theo was oblivious, but Andy heard me step on a twig. Her lips were firmly planted on his, but her eyes were on mine. She pushed Theo away.

"Wait, babe, I'm going to tell her after the game," Theo said, pulling Andrea back toward him. He didn't even notice that she wasn't looking at him.

I cleared my throat. "No need. I think I get it."

"Vicky ..." Andrea cried. She took a step toward me, but I held up my hand to stop her. "I didn't mean ... I'm so sorry."

Theo didn't say a word.

"I can't believe you," I snapped, spinning on my heel to get away from her.

Daniel and Adam were still waiting for me. I pushed by them, crying a little. It wasn't that Theo was making out with someone else. That I could deal with. But not if it was Andrea. The one person I could always count on.

Daniel didn't say anything. He didn't try to touch me or make me feel better. He didn't even know who Andy was. He just sat with me. Here I was trying to do the right thing, and what was Theo doing? Making out with my best friend.

We watched the game in silence, side by side on the bench. Neither one of us played. I don't think I could've if I wanted to.

The dugout emptied. Andrea sat in the stands even as they cleared. Mom and Pepper walked with that I'm-better-than-everyone walk, stick up the butt straight and noses in the air. They never came over to talk to me after we won or lost. I glanced around but didn't see Theo.

Against my better judgment, I sat down beside her and said, "So, what's new?"

She squeezed her hands together and stared at her feet. "You weren't supposed to find out like that."

"How exactly was I supposed to find out, Andy?" *And how am I staying so damned calm?*

"Theo was supposed to tell you when we got back. Then he said that your team jumped him for no good reason and –"

"No good reason? Are you kidding me? He called Daniel a 'Chinaman' and he said they attacked him for no good reason?" I shook my head and stood up. "Just forget it."

"Wait, Vicky." She mumbled under her breath. "I'm sorry. We didn't mean for this to happen." The hope in her eyes was too much. "Please forgive me?"

I glanced at my car. Daniel leaned against it, watching every move I made. He had told me to make her suffer, but I couldn't do that. "You're going to have to give me some time to get over this,

Andy. I mean, you're supposed to be my best friend. How could you do that to me?"

"Haven't you ever felt like something was just right? Even if the timing sucked?" she mumbled.

My chest swelled with guilt and I sucked in too much air. "Yeah, I know what you mean."

"You have to believe me," she said, putting her hand on my arm. "I tried to hold him off, but I couldn't. I didn't want to. It only started a few days before we got back."

"He made the first move, didn't he?" I remembered how he'd danced with her at the charity event right before we left. I should've seen it then.

She nodded. "Yeah, on the plane."

"Well, at least he waited until you were almost home." And he'd already cheated on me.

"On the way there." Her words were soft but sounded like a cannon in my ears.

"Jesus Christ, he couldn't even break up with me first? Daniel's right, I do attract assholes." I collapsed back onto the bleachers.

"Theo's not an asshole."

"Ha, shows what you know. He hooked up with someone else on the trip, before you. Did you know that?"

"Yeah, I did," she snapped back. "Him and Stacey, but they were so drunk."

All the air went out of my sails. I wanted to call her a liar, but I couldn't.

"Vicky, please," she begged, closing her eyes. "I really like him."

"You know what, Andrea, you two deserve each other. My best friend and my boyfriend both screw me over. What a great summer."

I walked away, free of the load that had been bothering me but still weighed down by it. It didn't matter that I didn't want to be with Theo anymore. It didn't matter that I'd kissed Daniel. I didn't intentionally go looking for someone else. And I certainly wouldn't have fallen for Daniel if he had been dating Andrea. No, I shook free of my burden and walked to the car with a clear conscience. Theo and Andrea could both kiss my ass.

Daniel's expression didn't change as I got closer. He leaned against my driver's side door, waiting.

"You okay?" he asked when I stopped in front of him.

I didn't answer. I did what I'd been dying to do for the last few weeks. He smiled as I pushed against him and kissed him openly in public. It felt so right. I didn't have to worry about the guilt anymore. He wrapped his arms around me and lifted me off the ground.

"Does that answer your question?" I asked when he sat me back down.

"Yeah, come on. Let's go somewhere to celebrate." He took my keys and waved them in front of me. "And I'm driving."

The regular season was winding down. Each game was more important than the last. The Robins were right behind us in the standings. And our last game was against them. It would come down to the wire.

Tuesday, we played the Bears. We beat them to a pulp the first time. When I got to the field, something felt off. Most of the guys were already there. I was late, but I wasn't *that* late. The game couldn't have started yet. The stands were packed. There were even people lined up in the grass along the fence. Something was definitely up even if I couldn't see it.

The flash blinded me. I fell back onto my ass in the gravel parking lot.

"I'm sorry, Miss Hudson. Forgot to turn the flash off. Don't know why it flashed to begin with." The sun was directly behind him so I couldn't see his face. "Tim Wakefield of the Leader. Can I have a few minutes of your time?"

He stuck a digital voice recorder in my face. I pushed it away and stood up. Wakefield, my mother's favorite society columnist. What was he doing at a sporting event?

"Why are you playing baseball? Is this a feminine protest about sexism in sports? How does your father feel about you playing on an all boys team?" He asked in rapid fire succession.

Oh God. Not now. I brushed the small rocks off my pants and pushed by him.

Wakefield wasn't about to let that stop him. "Are you trying to say that girls can play baseball as well as boys?"

"No comment." Ah, the standard answer. It pissed off most reporters, especially the ones like Wakefield who always got what they wanted.

"Miss Hudson –" he persisted.

"No comment, Mr. Wakefield." I ran into the dugout, knowing he couldn't follow.

Daniel reached out to touch my arm, but I stepped around him with a slight shake of my head. I hoped he noticed. Calvin and Adam opened their mouths.

Reggie didn't give them a chance. He took all the pressure off me. "Come on, boys. Let's warm up. Vic, you better hurry up. They aren't going to delay the game because you don't have your cleats on yet."

The boys jogged onto the field without looking back.

"Thank you," I mouthed to Reggie.

He nodded then started yapping his jaws about hitting a homerun, a feat he had yet to accomplish.

Coach sat beside me as I tied my laces. "What's that all about?"

"Reporter."

"No kiddin', Sherlock," he growled. "What's he want with my third baseman?"

This was too much. I'd managed to go all season without anyone finding out. Why now? "Just a girl playing baseball."

Coach didn't buy my half-truth. "Uh-huh. And?"

"It might be better for the team if I sat out today," I said to change tactic.

"Because of this reporter fellow?"

I nodded. "Yeah, if there isn't a story, maybe he'll go away."

"You sure?"

I wasn't, but I kept up the lie. "Positive. I'd rather be out there but considering the circumstances..."

"Your call, kid. But if it gets tight, I'll send you in." He stood up and yanked his lineup card off the fence. "But you better tell me what this is really all about later."

Freddie got the start at third. I sat on the bench, ignoring most of the talk. Several times, Wakefield tried to get my attention as he stationed himself behind the dugout. Without me in the game, he had no story.

We blew the Bears out of the water again. Coach replaced Daniel with Shane in the seventh. He also subbed Harrison in at second. That left me as the only position player on the bench. Daniel sat too close to me on the bench. I scooted down. The hurt look on his face killed me, but Wakefield would be all over any suspicion of affection between us. He'd been at the charity event when Theo was on my arm and would no doubt remember that. I hoped Daniel would understand.

The taunting began in the eighth.

"Hey, man. Put the girl in."

"What's she on the team for if she ain't gonna play?"

"Come on, Coach. Does she suck or something?"

Then my absolute favorite, "Hey girly, girly, girly."

Coach looked at me for any type of reaction. I shook my head. Not that it helped my cause any. The crowd handed Wakefield his story whether I played or not, but I stood my ground and sat the entire nine innings. The score was twelve to two when it was over. We lined up to shake the other team's hands and I slipped in behind Daniel.

"I'll explain this all to you later. I promise." I whispered to him.

He glanced at me over his shoulder. His expression was blank, but his eyes said it all. He was confused. Who could blame him?

"I'll tell you everything," I said again.

Wakefield stood by the dugout, pen poised. The man was ready for anything.

Coach gathered us around home plate.

"What's going on, Hudson?" Adam asked. He crossed his arms, pissed as the rest of the team.

I took a deep breath. "Look, guys, just do me a favor. If he asks you anything, tell him 'no comment.' Please?"

"Why should we?" Calvin asked.

"I *will* explain everything. I promise. Meet me at Hansen's at six. Don't tell anyone either. Seriously, guys, this is important. You can help me make this all go away."

I looked at each one of the individually. Jayden was the only one that didn't look upset, but his expression only changed from intense to even more intense.

"Yeah, okay," Adam said, answering for the team. "We'll meet you at six. We won't talk to the reporter. Now, let's go. Look happy. We just won."

Everyone put on their best fake smile as we cleared the dugout. Wakefield tried to question each of them as they walked toward the parking lot. I half expected Jayden to break the digital recorder as Wakefield stuck it in his face. He didn't flinch, but there was a slight smile on his face.

I didn't get a chance to see Daniel before the meeting at Hansen's. I had too much to do. First, I had to rent the second-floor party room at the soda shop to assure our privacy. Fortunately, it wasn't already reserved. Then I had to arrange for the menu. The least I could do in this mess was feed them dinner.

Most of the guys were not going to be happy. My father's politics weren't always favorable around here. In fact, most people in the city thought he was a con artist out for his own good. When he was in the state house, he voted to close several schools in the area. He also voted against a state health care plan. Since his election to Congress, he voted in favor of reducing taxes for the rich and for a reduction in EPA standards.

Senator Hudson was not loved in the city, but the rest of the state adored him and that's why he'd gotten elected and re-elected.

After changing into a denim skirt and white tank with a sleeveless plaid button down shirt, I got to Hansen's ten minutes early to oversee everything. And to hopefully see Daniel first. Gina, the owner, set up a buffet per my request. I totally prepared myself for the worst possible reaction from the guys. If they wanted me out, I'd quit.

Daniel showed up two minutes later in khaki shorts and a green polo. This was going to be my hardest sell. I jumped into his arms, inhaling his sandalwood scent.

"I am so sorry." I buried my face into his chest.

"Jesus, Vic. Will you just tell me what's going on?" He pushed me into a chair, then sat across from me. "Are you some kind of Romanian princess or something?"

I smiled half heartedly. "No, nothing quite so glamorous."

"Then what?"

"Okay, it's like this." I reached across to hold his hands, but he slid them onto his lap. "I haven't lied to you. I might have withheld the truth, but I have never lied. Let me get that out of the way. I did move in with my grandmother this summer. And I do go to Xavier."

He nodded.

"Here's the thing ... My father is Senator Hudson."

He didn't react.

"Daniel?" I was teetering on the edge and he could push me over with a single word.

"So, your dad is *The* Senator Hudson? And you never thought to tell me about this?" His voice was cold.

My breath hitched in my throat. "I'm sorry."

"I mean, *The* Senator Hudson that's gearing up to run for President?"

This time I nodded. "Are you mad at me?"

"Why didn't you just tell me?" He leaned back in his chair out of my reach. "My dad hates your dad."

"And you wonder why I didn't tell you." I knew his father wasn't a fan already.

"Why hide it?" he repeated.

"Because I ... It's none of his business. He has no idea that I'm playing baseball. He's been in Washington most of the summer. He really thinks that I'm living with Grandma to help her out." I could tell by the look in his eyes that he needed more of an explanation than that. I poured out my heart, opening a vein I never wanted to share with anyone. "Whenever I do something, he uses it as a platform to say what he wants. When I was twelve, the debate team I was on made it to the state championships. My father sat proudly in the front row as I debated the positive side of oil refineries. After it was over, he stood before the local press with his arm wrapped around me and went on about the value of the American education system. It was one of his platforms for election into the Senate." I sat back in my chair and crossed my arms. The memories wormed their way into my head like poison. "Anyway, that was just one of many moments he stole from me. He used my success for his own gain. Hence the 'trophy daughter' moniker."

"So you just let him do it. You don't say a word." He shook his head and leaned onto the table. "That doesn't really sound like you, Vic."

The truth slammed into my chest like a bullet. He was right in so many ways. Maybe that didn't sound like me now, but it did when my father was around.

"Still, you could've told me." He clasped his hands together.

The throbbing began in my forehead. I rubbed my fingers over it like that would make it stop. "If you would've asked, I would've told you."

"My parents did ask you."

I stood up and pointed my finger at him. "After I sat there and listened to them bash him for voting to strengthen immigration standards."

"They had their reasons for that."

"And I had mine." I pulled the ponytail holder out of my hair, twirling it around my fingers as I paced.

He stood up and blocked my path, his voice growing louder. "You said he was a lawyer."

"He *is* a lawyer." This was not going well. I walked over to the appetizers Gina brought up when Daniel arrived, keeping my back to him. "Put yourself in my shoes for a change. Please."

He wrapped his arms around my waist and rested his chin on my shoulder. "So what do we do now?"

"It's only going to get worse." I turned around to face him. "That reporter is going to show up at every game until he gets what he wants. If we hold him off, it won't turn into anything major that the nationals can pick up. If he gets the story he wants, more will show up."

He nodded and kissed the tip of my nose. "Promise me one thing. That you'll never willingly withhold information like this again."

"That I can do."

Adam, Calvin, and Reggie walked in. Heather trailed behind them. Daniel let go of me and joined them at a table. Heather gave me a little wave before Adam shot her a nasty look. Even though she wasn't supposed to be here, I was glad she was.

One by one, everyone showed except Jayden. They eyed the food as they walked by. Coach Strauss came in last and closed the door behind him.

"Alrigh', Hudson," Coach growled. "You wanna let us in on what's goin' on?"

I nodded and stood in front of the room. It was hard, felt nearly impossible, and I had to fight back the stupid fear tears. I laid it all on the line though. Everything. When I finished, I sat quickly. Daniel put his arm over my shoulder. I didn't look at any of them. I just couldn't.

Adam broke the silence. "Really, Hudson, is that all?"

My head shot up. The guys were looking at me like I'd hit the lotto.

"Come on, Vic. It's not that big of a deal. We won't talk. Hell, we don't have anything to say anyway." Calvin laughed. Then he smacked Reggie. "Expect Reggie of course. We all know that he won't shut up."

"Bite me, Cal." Reggie glared at me. "You know that your dad cost my dad his job when he voted against the government bailout of Energenes?"

Crap, now I had to talk politics. I hated talking politics. "Because the CEO and CFO were planning on giving out thousands of dollars in executive bonuses while laying off hundreds of workers. Even if the company was going under, they were going to get rich. Did you know that? I had to sit there at the kitchen table one night and listen to him on the phone with someone from Delaware." I stood up again, resuming my pacing path. "Look, I don't always agree with my father's political views, but that's not going to stop the media from making more out of this than there is. You guys know me. You know I just want to play baseball. If my father catches wind of this, then he will do whatever he can to make it all about him. We won't matter." I stopped beside Daniel's chair. "None of us."

"What you mean is that you won't matter," Reggie snapped.

Daniel shifted beside me. I put my hand on his shoulder to shut him up.

Adam spoke up before I could. "She matters to us, Reg."

Coach stood beside me. "Don't sweat it, kid. As a team, we all agree to keep our traps shut and not talk to that damned reporter. Right?"

"Yeah," they said in unison.

"Good, I'm guessin' the food's for us?" Coach pointed to the buffet while I nodded. "Let's eat. I'm starvin'."

It was still tense in the room; at least it felt like it to me. Maybe it was my imagination. When I looked around, the guys were chatting like nothing happened. But something did. I became separated. I didn't belong anymore. Even if no one said a word about it, I felt the crevasse open between all of us.

Just another thing my father has taken from me.

BOTTOM OF THE 5TH

The next morning, I ripped the newspaper out of Grandma's hand and rushed down the hall to my room. I tore it apart looking for an article, anything at all that mentioned me. Nothing. I threw the crumpled paper on the bed and checked the Leader's website. Sometimes these things don't make it into print. Nothing there either. I breathed a sigh of relief, albeit a temporary one.

"Are you going to let me in on what's going on?" Grandma asked. I glanced up from my laptop. She leaned on the doorway with coffee in her hand, steam rising from the mug in drifting circles.

I went back to checking other websites and even googling my name. "I've got it under control."

"Apparently not if you're acting like this." She came into the room and sat on the edge of my bed. "Now, tell me what's going on, Vicky."

"It's nothing." None of the other local news websites had anything. The last time I was in the news at all was for the benefit.

"Victoria Christine, I can play this game all day or you can just tell me what's happened." She made a loud slurping sound as she sipped her coffee. "It's up to you."

I closed the laptop and leaned against my pillows. As long as I stared at the ceiling, I could tell Grandma just about anything. "A reporter showed up at the game yesterday."

"Well, you knew this was bound to happen sooner or later."

"No, I didn't." I sat up and looked her in the eye. "I didn't think it would happen at all. I just —"

"Wanted to play baseball. I know, dear, but that doesn't change who you are." Another slurp.

"You know what's going to happen."

"Only if you allow it."

I snorted. "He doesn't listen."

"You don't tell him anything." She sat her mug on the nightstand then leaned in to grab my hands. "Victoria, you've spent your life in the shadow of your father. You've done all that he's asked of you. You've been everything he wanted you to be. You have made him proud. But you need to be your own person. That's one of the reasons I agreed to this charade. You need to tell him about this baseball thing. If one reporter shows up, no matter how much you and your friends keep your mouths shut, the others will come eventually."

I shook my head. For the first time this summer, I felt like I'd made a mistake. "I shouldn't have even tried."

"What are you talking about? Of course you should have. Look at how much fun you've had. The new friends you've made. And you probably wouldn't have met Daniel."

The sinking feeling of impending disaster was enough to make me want to vomit. "Now the Senator's going to ruin it all."

Grandma threw her hands in the air and stood up. She grabbed her mug, spilling some warm coffee on her hand and shaking it off quickly. At the door, she turned around and glared at me. "I give up. You're right. Your father will ruin everything. But only because you let him. It's time you grow up. Or you'll never be able to. It's entirely up to you."

I almost followed her into the kitchen, but I didn't want to fight with Grandma any more than I wanted to deal with my father. An hour later she started slamming her tools around, and I joined her in the hallway and walked with her to the car. We drove in silence to the Habitat house. I tried to think of something to say. Anything to make the argument go away. Once we got to the site, she jumped out of her car and walked toward the watercoolers. Disappointing my father was one thing, but disappointing Grandma felt like the world around me collapsed.

I found Daniel painting in the living room. He handed me a brush and I went to work painting along the windows. The meticulous up and down motion helped numb my mind. It let me forget about what was bound to happen next.

After six hours of painting, nailing, carrying, and doing just about anything else we could find to do, Daniel and I decided to hang out at his house. The hard work at Habitat house wore me out.

"Mom and Dad will leave by six," he said as he cleaned his paintbrush. He glanced around to make sure no one could hear him. "They usually stay out with the Kims until midnight, if not later. Becca's going to be at her friend's house all night. It'll be just us." He smiled and flicked water on my cheek. "Think you can handle being alone with me for that long?"

I bumped my hip against him. "Pretty sure. What about you?"

"Oh, I don't think that'll be a problem." He brushed his lips across mine so fast I thought I imagined it until a couple of the guys wooted. "I'll see you around seven?"

I nodded. He leaned in to kiss me again, but the guys started making more catcalls. Daniel laughed and jogged to catch up with his dad.

"Oh, Vicky, you have that little boy wrapped around your finger," Charles, the foreman and a Grandma favorite, shouted from the other side of the site. He was loud enough that there was no way Daniel didn't hear him.

"Now, leave her alone, boys," Grandma chided. "She's got enough on her plate. She doesn't need your crap."

"You're a little sassy, missy," Charles said. He took three long steps over to where she held her ground and lifted her over his shoulder. "You need to promise to make me some more of your brownies if you want me to get over that bossy little comment."

Grandma laughed as her face turned flaming red. All the blood was rushing to her cheeks. "Charles, I make you brownies once a week."

Which explained why I always smelled them but never saw them. I crossed my arms and waited, amused by my grandmother's playfulness.

"What if I make you some cookies instead?" she asked between bursts of laughter. "Liven up your diet."

He sat her back on her feet. "That sounds good. Chocolate chip?"

"Oatmeal." She grabbed a cup from a nearby sawhorse and dumped it over Charles' hard hat before he had time to react.

Grandma took off running with Charles on her heels. She laughed like she was a little girl again. Some of the other guys stood around, watching Charles chase Grandma down. I couldn't stop myself from smiling at the two of them.

"They're something together, aren't they?" Wanda said. She was Grandma's right hand. When Grandma wasn't around, Wanda took charge.

"What do you mean?"

"Her and Charles." She nodded to where Charles had just caught my grandmother around the waist. "I can't believe you haven't noticed it before."

I took a hard look at both of them. If Wanda said anything else, I didn't hear it. Charles was older than I thought. His square face, sharp chin, and bright blue eyes made him appear young. Beyond all that, there were wrinkles, crow's feet, and a head full of gray hair. I turned to ask Wanda how old Charles was, but she was gone.

I twisted back to take in my grandmother in the same manner and noticed how much younger she appeared when she was around Charles. She didn't seem tired or old-lady-ish. She looked happy.

My father wasn't going to like this.

That made me smile even more.

Daniel opened the door while I was still knocking. He grabbed my hands and pulled me inside toward the kitchen. It was small with no room for a table and chairs. The room smelled of tomato sauce, oregano, pepperoni, and burnt cheese.

He pulled two oven mitts over his hands and opened the oven. "I timed this perfectly. I made two pizzas. Grab the soda out of the fridge and we'll go upstairs."

"What kind of pizza?" I found a two liter on the top shelf and showed it to him. "This one?"

"Um, yeah," he said, glancing over his shoulder. He sat the pizzas on the stove. "One pepperoni and one sausage. That okay?"

I nodded and waited while he sliced the pizzas. They were the frozen kind, but Daniel had added more meat and cheese. My stomach growled.

We went up to the attic and settled onto the couch. Daniel turned on a movie that I didn't pay attention to. We ate in silence as the movie began.

"You look beautiful tonight," he whispered in my ear.

"Thanks." I glanced down at my white tank and khaki shorts. Simple, yet sexy. Low key, yet carefully selected.

He ran the back of his fingers up my bare arm. Goose bumps trailed behind. A shiver crept up my spine. The pizzas sat on the coffee table, forgotten. I leaned my head on his shoulder, pretending to watch the movie. His fingers continued their path, barely touching my skin. He rested his head on mine. I knew he wasn't watching the movie either.

"This is nice," I said to break the silence.

"Understatement."

I turned my head to see him. We'd been waiting for this moment for what felt like forever. It was the first time we'd been alone since the thing with Theo. Since Shelby. Since the party.

A frown crossed his face for a second, but it was enough to disturb me.

"What's wrong?" I tucked my knees underneath me and faced him.

He took both of my hands, more goose bumps, and grazed his lips across my palms. More shivers. "Nothing."

He pulled me down on top of him and slid his hands around my waist. It was slow at first, gentle. Then it started to get too fast and too much. I jerked back but didn't move away from him.

"Daniel ..."

"Victoria ..."

The way he said my name, it was like it was meant for his lips only. I bent back over him and kissed his neck, inhaling the musk he'd dabbed over his throat. He tightened his arms around my waist, letting a tiny moan escape. He slipped his fingers under my shirt and ran his fingers up and down my spine. His hands were warm and slightly damp from sweat. He didn't grab or grope,

91

which made him that much hotter. I lifted his shirt and touched his chest.

"Oh God, Vic." He put a hand on my neck and pulled me back to his lips.

My heart ricocheted around my ribs. Instinct took over. My fingers were tugging at his shirt to free him of that cotton burden when the doorbell rang. We both froze in mid-unshirt.

"You just got saved by the bell," Daniel said. He sat up and tucked his shirt into his jeans, but his eyes never left mine. "You're beautiful."

Daniel kissed me one last time before rushing down the stairs as the doorbell rang again. I fell back onto the couch, wondering how far I would've let it go and if I would've been able to stop. The movie continued to play as a couple declared their undying love for one another. He'd made sure it was a cheesy chick flick. I laughed at his movie choice, even though I knew he did it for me. After about five minutes, I started to wonder what was going on downstairs.

I tiptoed down each flight, hoping not to hit the one squeaky stair all houses have, even Chez Hudson. The voices were loud enough to be heard on the second floor, but I couldn't understand what they were saying. Daniel's bedroom door stood open and the room was spotless. I could even see his blue plaid comforter spread across the bed.

The voices grew louder, almost to a yell. The newcomer sounded familiar, but I couldn't figure out who it was. I crept down the last flight and could hear them clearer. I stopped midway down to listen.

"I'm not doing this again. Don't you get that?" Daniel snapped.

"Don't be such a wuss. It's not a big deal," the girl whined. Her voice was nasally and creeping me out.

"What part of 'no' don't you understand?"

It hit me like a wall of the Habitat house falling over me. I knew who the other voice belonged to and hurried down the rest of the stairs not caring whether they heard me or not. They stood in the parlor.

"Get over yourself, Danny." Shelby threw her hands in the air. "You're so damn righteous."

"Leave. Now." Daniel was expressionless.

"Maybe I don't want to," she purred and rubbed her hand up his arm. "Maybe I have something else in mind."

Daniel took a step back, pressing his back against the doorframe to the dining room. "Leave, Shelby."

She pushed her chest into his. My blood boiled, but I waited.

"And I said I don't want to leave, Danny." She stood on her tippy toes and tried to kiss him. He moved his head to the right and his eyes caught mine just as she planted one on his cheek. "What's —"

"Daniel told you to leave." I remained calm only because my nails were digging into my palms.

Shelby turned around. Her face went from mock innocence to angry bitch as soon as she saw me. "Go away," she said. "He's spoken for, loser."

"You got it right that he's spoken for, but I'm not the loser." I stormed into the room and grabbed her hair. She squealed when I yanked her away from Daniel and used her nails to scratch the back of my hand.

Daniel moved in between us before I could beat her ass. He grabbed my hands and wrapped my arms around his waist as he faced Shelby. "Do I need to tell you again?"

I stretched to see around him. Shelby glared at Daniel then walked out the door. Personally, the satisfaction that I'd won was amazing. After the door closed, Daniel turned and looked at me like I'd just escaped the mental ward.

"What?" I asked.

"That was hot."

I pulled away from him, laughing. "You're such a jerk."

"Nope, I'm a guy and two chicks fighting over me? That is hot."

I shook my head. "Dork."

He pulled me back against him. "Yep."

I led the way back upstairs, stopping outside his bedroom door. He kissed me with such caution, such patience; I knew we weren't going to finish the movie.

I woke up the next morning feeling more alive than ever. Then I remembered I had a game. For the first time all summer, I didn't look forward to getting to the field.

The park was as packed as it was Tuesday. Wakefield waited for me in the parking lot. When I pulled in, he started toward me. Adam, Calvin, and Reggie became my entourage and escorted me to the dugout.

"Nice. I have my own posse," I joked as I tied my cleats.

"Like being a celeb, Vic?" Calvin asked. He smiled so I knew he was kidding. "We can take you out clubbing so you can look scandalous. Maybe even get you into a tabloid or two."

"No, thanks."

He leaned down so only I could hear. "Then don't get used to the posse."

I took a swing at him, but he leapt out of the way and ran onto the field. He told Reggie something. They looked at me and started laughing.

"Glad I'm here to amuse you," I mumbled to myself. It was nice though. My team never took themselves too seriously.

Daniel and I didn't want to flaunt our relationship in front of Wakefield. Plus, we agreed to be "just teammates" on the field. It wasn't easy after last night. He was looking especially nice in his baseball pants.

Just before we took the field, Daniel surprised me by whispering, "Vic, you may be able to ask us to keep quiet, but there are lots of other people Wakefield can talk to."

He nodded toward the stands. Shane's parents were engaged in a lively conversation with the reporter.

"I can't worry about that now." I smiled. "We've got a game to win, Cho. Get your ass out there."

"Yes, ma'am." He put on his mask, then blew me a kiss.

"Alrigh', team," Coach bellowed. "Take the field, boys." He smiled as I glared at him. "And girl."

There was no way that damned reporter was going to ruin the rest of my season. Jayden smirked as he tossed a few grounders my way. It bugged me, but I didn't know why. Maybe because he never smirks, or smiles, or anything.

The first half of the inning went fast. Walter threw three pitches and the other team, the Ravens, hit three grounders to short. At least T.C. had a little fun. I was set to lead off our half of the inning. Wakefield stood at the backstop, waiting for me with his new photographer at his side. The guy snapped away like he was a paparazzo while I swung the bat to warm up.

"Batter up," the umpire yelled.

I dug my heels in and waited. Their pitcher called time and I stepped out of the box.

What's he playing at?

The Ravens coach jogged out then motioned for the umpire to the mound. I glanced toward our dugout and Coach joined me in the on-deck circle.

"What's up, Blue?" Coach asked as the umpire headed back behind home plate.

"Just a problem in the stands, Bernie. I got it under control." The ump walked to the backstop and told Wakefield to sit down or leave, before telling the photographer to stay out of the line of sight of the pitcher or he'd get booted from the park. Both of them protested with the standard First Amendment argument but eventually moved. There isn't a story if you can't see it.

But they were crafty. They'd find a way.

I nodded to their pitcher and he responded the same.

Then he threw me a nasty curveball for strike one.

Oh, game on, baby.

Another curveball outside for a ball and a fastball up and out for ball two.

Inside. I adjusted my back leg just an inch.

He threw an off-speed pitch that wasn't supposed to hang in the middle of the plate. But it did. And right where I liked them. I turned on it, pulling it down the left field line and just over the third baseman's head. They weren't playing me to pull. The left fielder had to race to get to the ball before I could get to third.

I won.

Ollie knocked me in to make it one to nothing in the bottom of the first. Jayden came up next and made it two to nothing by hitting Ollie in on a double into right.

In the second, the Ravens realized that they could hit the ball to other positions and left T.C. alone. Reggie and Calvin got a couple of pop outs, but not before Walter gave up a double then a single. Two outs with runners at first and second. Walter threw a very good fastball. Their third baseman turned on it and hit a hot line drive my way. There wasn't time to think, only react as the ball came whizzing at my head.

My feet slid forward and my butt headed for the dirt. I stuck my glove up. The ball slammed into it, almost knocking the glove off my hand. I rolled into a backward somersault, raising my glove to show I caught the ball. The ump called the out and I tossed the ball to the mound. My hand started throbbing the minute I took the glove off.

"WooHoo, Hudson," Adam shouted.

We jogged into the dugout. All the guys slapped my arm or head, but Daniel smacked me in the butt with his glove. I didn't think twice about it. Ball players do that stuff all the time.

"Nice catch, kid," Coach added.

I walked my next at bat but didn't score. Then I struck out and flied out. Other than a couple of soft grounders, nothing else came my way in the field. We ended up losing by one run after Walter broke down in the fifth. It was a tough loss.

"Miss Hudson, can I have a word?" Wakefield asked as we left the dugout. My teammates circled around me like vultures and led me to the parking lot.

"No, bubba, you can't," Ollie said.

"Sure he can, Ol." T.C. turned to face Wakefield, walking backward. "Here's your word, 'no comment.'"

Wakefield fell back from the group before anyone else could tell him where to shove it. That was suspicious.

"What's he up to?" I asked no one in particular.

"He's probing, Vic. Don't worry about it." Adam opened my door for me. He leaned in the window after I got in. "We won't talk."

"I know. Thanks though." I smiled at Adam as he backed away from the car.

Daniel jumped in the passenger door and slid beneath the windows. He put his hand over mine on the gear shift. "Can I drive?"

"Not like that."

He squeezed my hand and laughed. "Then let me drive once we're out of the park."

I started the car and backed out. "Why?"

"What fun is that? Can't a guy surprise his girlfriend?"

My phone rang before I could answer.

"Ah, saved by the crappy ringtone," Daniel said, sitting up straight.

"We'll discuss that comment later." Before answering, I checked the caller ID. "Hi, Mom."

"Oh, Vicky, there you are. I haven't seen you in over a week. Come home for dinner tonight," Mom said without taking a single breath.

"I ... uh ... kinda got plans," I stuttered. It's not like she hadn't come to some of my games. Daniel raised his eyebrows at me and I pulled the car over on a side street.

"So bring this new boyfriend of yours. Your grandmother told me all about him already." She sighed that my-daughter-doesn't-love-me-anymore sigh. "Although I wished you would have shared this."

"Um ..." I tried to think up an excuse, any excuse, but my mind was as clean as a chalkboard on the first day of school.

"I won't take no for an answer. Dinner is at seven. You can bring him by around five. The pool has barely been used all summer. To think we are throwing our money away on that useless pool boy."

"Marcus isn't useless, Mom. He's –"

"I'll see you around five." She dropped the handset as she tried to hang up the ancient rotary phone that she kept more for style than use.

I bit my lip. "So, guess what?"

He slid back down in his seat.

"We're going to dinner at my mom's."

"No choice in the matter, huh?"

I dropped my phone in my lap and started driving toward Daniel's house. "Nope. We're expected at five. Dinner will be served at seven. And you must bring swim trunks. She mentioned the pool."

He looked out the window.

I tried to lighten the mood. "You going to tell me where you wanted to take me?"

"Nope." He didn't turn around. His shoulders were tense.

"What?" I should've known he wouldn't want to go.

"Nothing."

"You don't want to go?"

"It's not that …"

My voice cracked. "Then what?"

He sat up and motioned to the side of the street. We were a block from his house. "Pull over."

"Why?"

"Just do it, Vic."

The street was packed, but I managed to squeeze into a spot. He stared out the windshield, expression unreadable.

"What?" I asked for what felt like the millionth time. "Just tell me, for God's sake."

He turned to face me. "This is going to be awkward, isn't it?"

"What? Dinner? It's just my mom, not the Spanish Inquisition."

He didn't say anything.

"My father won't be there." *I hope.*

He took my right hand. "You didn't tell her about us?"

God, please tell me he couldn't hear her big mouth. "No."

"Why?" He brushed his thumb over mine.

"I haven't talked to her." It was the truth. I hadn't really talked to her all summer. With work on the Habitat house and baseball, it felt like I never had time for anything else.

"She'll hate me." He dropped my hand.

"Shut up. She won't hate you." I jabbed my finger in his side to make him laugh. It didn't work.

"I'm not from your world –"

"Get over yourself, Daniel. She doesn't care about where you're from. She already knows who you are."

"She does?" He looked doubtful.

"Yeah, Grandma told her about us." I slapped his legs a couple of times. "It's not that big of a deal."

He smiled and it reached his eyes. "So she knows you're dating a Korean?"

I sighed. "No. I can't say that."

His face dropped. "See, there might be an issue."

"She knows you're Asian, but I doubt she knows exactly what the country of origin is. Just relax."

"Have you dated Asian guys before?" he asked.

I stared at him for a second to see if he was serious or not. I couldn't tell, so I deadpanned, "No, but the Korean maid we had last year was like family."

He waited for me to smile. "Seriously, Vic." He glanced away from me for a moment. When he turned back, his eyes were too intense. "Look, when I was a freshman, I asked Amanda Nell to the homecoming dance. Dad drove me to her house to pick her up. I stood on the front steps sweating like a pig in an oven, holding a single rose in my hand. As soon as the door opened, I knew I was in trouble. Her dad smiled until he looked at me." Daniel paused, and I sat frozen. "He told me there was no way his daughter was going out with a chink and slammed the door in my face."

His pained expression tore me up, but there wasn't anything I could do about the past. "Look, I'm sorry that her father was a prejudiced jerk, but not every person out there is like that. Regardless of what you might think about my father's politics, he isn't a racist. Neither is my mother. If they were, he'd never gotten elected to anything."

He nodded.

"It'll be fine, Daniel. I promise."

He opened the door to get out. "You were kidding, right? About the maid?"

I rolled my eyes, such a girly thing to do. "Yes. Lilly's worked for us forever. She used to be my nanny. And she *is* like family."

That finally made him smile. He brushed his lips across my cheek.

He sprinted the final block to his house. I drove home, but Grandma wasn't there. I dropped my equipment bag in my room and took a shower. I stood under the almost scalding hot water, thinking about what my mother was up to. Maybe she did miss me, but that didn't make a whole lot of sense when she was never home anyway. Maybe this was a surprise visit from the Senator. In that case, Daniel and I were equally screwed. I hopped out when the water started to cool.

Ten minutes later, I heard the front door open and Grandma yelling, "Vicky?"

"Yeah?" I yelled back. I walked down the short hall knowing that "come here" would be her next words.

She had four reusable shopping bags in her hands and looked like she was going to fall over. I took three of them and led her into the kitchen.

"Oh, thank you. I thought my arm was going to snap for a moment." She noticed my perfect ponytail, bikini top, and shorts. "Going somewhere?"

"I've been summoned to Chez Hudson." I took the bananas and apples out of the bag. "Mom said she wanted to meet Daniel. How'd she know about him?"

Grandma laughed. "Maybe because I told her. That's probably why she called me earlier." She scuffed her feet over to the phone, and then touched my arm sending a jolt of electricity through me. "I better call her back."

"Not funny, Grandma." I looked at the shag rug that lay between the hall and kitchen. How she got enough static electricity off of that was a mystery.

I finished unpacking the groceries while she talked to Mom in the other room. I didn't hear any bit of conversation, but I didn't think I needed to. When I shoved the broccoli into the crisper, Grandma came back into the kitchen. She didn't look so great.

"What's wrong?" I asked, succeeding in forcing the nasty green veggie into the overstuffed drawer.

"Vicky, sit down." Once I did, she started pacing the room. "Did you mother tell you this would be a dinner party?"

I shook my head no.

"Apparently, she learned about your falling out with Andrea –"

"No –"

"And she invited Andrea over –"

This was turning into a showdown. "No –"

"And her parents –"

I stood up. "No –"

"And the Perdays –"

"Oh God, no –"

"And the Tudors –"

"What?" I started shaking.

She sighed. "And the Fords."

"I'm not going." I fell back into the chair and hid my face in my hands. This was a disaster.

"Honey –" Grandma knelt before me.

"Don't 'honey' me, Grandma." I stared at her so she would know I was serious. "I. Am. Not. Going."

"You have to. You already agreed."

"I don't have to do anything." I pushed her away from me gently. This wasn't her fault after all.

She sat back on her heels. "What if the Tudors were uninvited?"

"First, Mom would never do that. Second, she also needs to uninvite Andrea and the Perdays too." *God, not Erik Freaking Perday.* I hid my face in my hands again.

"She thinks you might miss your friends."

"She doesn't even know why I broke up with Theo."

"No, she doesn't. She just knows that you're dating a boy on your baseball team."

"Wait." My head shot up. "I thought you told her I was with Daniel."

Grandma pushed herself up and shoved my hand away when I tried to steady her. "No. I just let her know you were seeing a boy from the team."

"Oh shit." I put my hand over my mouth. Grandma didn't like me to cuss. She glared at me. "She doesn't know it's Daniel?"

"Does it matter?"

"To him it does. He's afraid she'll freak out because he's Korean." I stood up and started to pace Grandma's usual path. "And he thinks Mom knows it's him because I assumed you told her."

"Never assume anything," she muttered. She walked to the sink and began cleaning the lettuce she'd left there.

I ignored her. "And why even invite Theo?"

"I don't know, Vicky. She probably thinks that you guys just aren't dating anymore. Plenty of people stop dating but remain friends."

"I'm not going."

"Look, I know this will be uncomfortable. I know it will be hard for you, but you already agreed to go. She's acting like this will be a big surprise party for you." She waved a dishtowel in a circle. "I'm not telling you any of this. It just didn't seem right for you to go in and get ambushed by your mother."

My shoulders sunk. I was defeated. "Who else?"

"The Gallaghers, the Marshalls, the Mosbys, the Trones, the Walkers, the Smithtons, and ten of your friends."

"They aren't my friends." It felt weird to admit that, but once I said it, I knew it was true. None of them knew the real me.

"They were."

"Is this a formal dinner party? Do I need to call Daniel and tell him to bring a suit?"

"No. Just nice pants and a polo."

The whole situation reeked of failure. "Great. Just fu –"

"Watch your language, young lady."

"Sorry, Grandma, this is crap." I hated myself for falling into a stupid trap.

"Yes, it is. And I will be there to help you." She raised her eyebrows. "But watch your language."

The light bulb went off in my head with the most brilliant scheme. "Grandma, you just gave me the best idea."

"What?"

I didn't answer. I kissed her cheek and ran to my room to make the call.

TOP OF THE 6TH

Daniel waited outside for me as I parked in front of his house. He tossed a duffel over his shoulder and strolled to the car.

"I have some bad news and some good news," I said as soon as he opened the door. "Bad news first?"

He settled in the seat and tugged at his seatbelt. "Shoot."

"We're getting ambushed."

His head shot up just as the seatbelt locked in place with a loud click. "Excuse me?"

"This whole dinner with my mother thing is actually a 'surprise' party." I hadn't bothered to put the car into drive yet. He could've backed out and I would've totally let him.

"And?" he asked.

"My mother invited Andrea." *Maybe I'll wait on the Theo and Erik thing until we're almost there.*

"Nice." He leaned across the console and kissed my cheek. "Guessing she doesn't know that Andrea's with Theo now."

I did a quick shoulder check and pulled onto the street. "Nope, she just heard we had a falling out."

"So much for the gossip in Hillside." He switched the radio off. "Who else?"

Crap. I stayed focused on the road and told him the partial truth. "And she invited Erik."

"The jackass from the party?" His hands clenched into fists on his lap.

"The very same."

He smashed his head back into the headrest. "This can't get worse."

"Oh, wait," I said, deciding to just tell him and get it over with. "She also invited Theo."

"Are you kidding me?"

I shook my head.

He put his hand on the door and unbuckled his seatbelt. "Let me out. I'm not going."

I kept driving, hoping he was joking. "You'd leave me alone with those people? And their parents?"

"They *are* your 'friends'."

I took a deep breath to stay calm. "Which brings me to the good news."

"How can there be good news?" His hand was still on the door.

"We're going to pick up Adam and Heather."

He let go. "Really? Why?"

"Yes really. I figured they'd make a good buffer. We can hang with them and ignore the other crap. If all else fails, we also have some back up if Erik or Theo try to start anything."

"I don't like this, Vic." He put his seatbelt back on.

"Neither do I." I reached across the console and squeezed his knee. "Just be glad Grandma warned me after she talked to my mom."

"Your grandma's cool. Is she going to be there?"

"Yeah." I smiled knowing that Grandma would be another buffer. We might be safe after all.

He smirked. "Is Charles coming?"

"Not that I know of." The thought of Grandma bringing Charles to Chez Hudson almost made me laugh. "Is it that obvious that they're into each other?"

He laughed. It was good to hear since I expected I'd get gloomy Daniel all night. "About as obvious as we were."

Heather and Adam waited for us outside Hansen's. Each had their own bag with a change of clothes. Adam wasn't too keen on coming along until I explained the whole Theo-Andrea thing in full. Then he had no problem with it.

Adam and Daniel argued about some local band I'd never heard of on the way to my mother's. Heather shifted in the backseat and stared out the window. I felt bad for putting her on the spot.

When I drove through the gates, Adam shut up. I pulled around the back of the house and parked by the garage. We were twenty-five minutes late, but I really didn't care. No one else had parked back there, but they normally don't. Whenever we have any kind of dinner party, it's like a show of who has more money. Guests rarely drive themselves. A tiny speck of hope sprung up in my chest.

Then I heard a splash in the pool and a murmur of voices.

There went that speck.

I led the way into the kitchen. Lilly smiled at me. Her eyes widened when Heather squeezed in beside me on my left. Daniel tried to push between us, but Heather wasn't about to budge so he was left in the background. When Adam came in and slipped in beside me on my right, Lilly's smile brightened the room once again.

Uh-oh. Smiling at Adam could only mean one thing. It didn't help that Adam had to stand sideways and his chest was pressed against my arm. Lilly's expression was enough to convince me that she thought Adam was my boyfriend. I hoped Mom didn't make the same assumption. This wasn't good.

"Your mother is in the sitting room," Lilly squeaked. Then she went back to basting a turkey.

"Thanks, Lilly."

The sitting room was on the other side of the house with a view of the pool. I led my friends through the ridiculous hallway and oversized staircase. It felt wrong to be here.

Heather muttered a "wow", and I felt ashamed. This house was too much for anyone with less than twenty kids. We didn't need all the room. We didn't need all the crap either. I stretched back and grabbed Daniel's hand, pulling him up beside me. Just outside the doorway, we all stopped.

"Ready?" I asked, hating the quiver in my voice.

Nobody said anything, so I led us into the lion's den.

Mom held court from the wingback chair facing the door. Everyone Grandma had listed was already here. The Marshalls wore matching tennis outfits, which is a fashion faux pas no matter where you live. Erik's dad was refreshing two drinks when we walked in while his wife sat with Mr. Smithton at the piano. They chatted away, unaware that we'd even entered the room.

I squeezed Daniel's hand for good measure.

I feigned surprise and asked, "What's going on, Mom?"

"Oh, Victoria, I'm so glad you're finally here. You remember everyone." She motioned around the room as she walked over toward us. Her eyes dropped to where my hand was intertwined with Daniel's. Like a pro, she showed no reaction. "I have a special surprise for you. All of your friends are out by the pool." She noticed Adam and Heather. "I'm so sorry. We haven't met."

That woman never missed a beat.

"Mom, this is Adam and his girlfriend Heather. And you remember Daniel." I equaled her tone and charm. Two could play this game. And I learned from the best.

"It's so nice to meet you." She held out her hand to Adam and Heather but not Daniel.

I smiled as fake happy as I could. "So, who's out by the pool?"

"All of your friends." She put extra emphasis on the word. "Andrea, Theo, Erik, Logan, Rachel, Eva, Shanna, and Millie. They're going to be so happy to see you, dear." She swept her hand to the hallway. It was permission to leave the room. "Now go out there and have a good time. I'll have Lilly call you in for dinner at six-thirty so you can change." She noticed our bags. "Oh, and leave those at the bottom of the stairs. Lilly can take them up."

"I'm sure Lilly has enough to do, Mom. We'll take them up first."

She gave me a tight smile. "That would be nice."

Just to piss her off further, I took the steps two at a time. When we got to the second floor, I almost started laughing. Part one of hell day was over. Part two, the pool, was going to be far worse. We may not even make it to part three. Dinner.

Lilly may have had a lot going on, but I had an ulterior motive for bringing the bags up myself. Call it a stall tactic. Daniel snickered at my girly room covered with baseball posters. Heather drooled. It must have been a Barbie dream room to her. Adam looked like he was unimpressed. It was one of the reasons I liked him.

We managed to goof around for fifteen minutes before Lilly found us under Mom's direction. Five minutes after that, we made our way out to the pool.

Andrea bolted up from her cushy chaise lounge when we walked out the patio doors. Rachel pulled herself to her elbows and ogled

Adam. The guys were nowhere to be seen. Out of the corner of my eye, I noticed Heather pull Adam closer.

"Vicky," Eva shouted, "get over here. Tell us about this baseball thingy you're doing."

"And introduce us to your new friends," Rachel added as she stared at Adam over her too expensive sunglasses.

We skirted the pool and it took all my strength not to push Daniel in just for the fun of it. Under my breath, I said, "It's all good."

Daniel put his hand on my lower back. Tremors exploded up my spine.

"Hey, Eva." I nodded to Rachel and Shanna. "This is my friend Heather and her boyfriend Adam." Heather smiled at me. "And this is Daniel."

The girls smiled and introduced themselves. Andrea and Millie argued a few seats over. I strained to hear them, but they kept their voices too low. Andrea stood up and I expected her to storm out like a diva. She didn't.

"Vicky, can we talk? Please?" she whispered.

I wanted to say "no" but didn't.

She nodded toward the other end of the pool and we walked over in silence. Daniel's eyes never left me while he sat down with Heather and Adam at one of the tables. The girls went back to their sunbathing and gossip.

"I'm so sorry, Vicky," Andrea began. She wrung her hands together. "Can we please move on from this?"

"Why should I? It's not like you didn't know –"

"He told me you guys had broken up already. When you found out about Stacey." She was almost desperate enough for me to believe her. "After what happened at the benefit –"

"What happened at the benefit?" I snapped. The night replayed in my mind. There wasn't anything out of the ordinary. Other than Theo getting invited.

"He said you were mean. He said you told him to shut up." Now she just looked confused. "He said you blamed it on your dad, but he thought it came from you. That's why he hit on me on the plane. He thought you guys were already through."

The anger started in my toes and vibrated up my legs, through my torso, and into my head. By the time it got to my mouth, I exploded.

"What. The. ...," I said, surprisingly calm for as pissed as I was. "And you believed him?"

She shrugged. "I guess I just wanted to believe him. When he said all that, I stopped thinking of him as your boyfriend. He was charming and romantic. I assumed you wouldn't care since you guys weren't together anymore. Does that make any sense?"

Unfortunately, it did.

"And it's not like you were pining away for Theo." She glanced at Daniel. He laughed at something Adam said. I loved how the corners of his eyes crinkled when he smiled. It made me melt. "I mean you guys were hooking up before Theo cheated, right?"

"What?" The more lies he told her, the more I hated him. "No. We weren't."

"Theo was so sure you were."

"Well, I wasn't. I couldn't even if I wanted to. Ask Daniel. He'll tell you that too." I glared at Andrea and felt I owed her the truth, no matter how hard it was to admit. "I knew it was over between me and Theo, but I felt I owed it to him to at least break up in person. I was going to do that the day I saw you guys at the park. You can tell Theo that if you want."

Her face dropped. "No, I can't. We aren't together."

"That was quick."

"I know. The whole thing felt wrong, especially after we got back. Just wasn't the same as it was in Paris." She shrugged, and I knew that bastard had dumped her.

"Is he really here?" I asked, hoping that he wouldn't have the balls.

"Oh, yeah. He's in the pool house with Erik and Logan. They're playing video games." She looked toward the building. "He's up to something."

"Why do you say that?"

She turned back to face me. "If I tell you, promise you won't get mad."

"No." I wasn't going to lie. I was tired of all the damn lies.

She closed her eyes. "He told me the only reason he went out with you was so he could meet your dad." She paused and her eyes popped open. She stared at me for a moment before adding, "Don't you remember when he asked if you'd help him get an internship?"

"Why are you telling me this now?"

"Because he's here for the same reason. He wants to get in good with the Senator." She reached for my arm, but I stepped away from her. "Theo is only out for Theo. Vicky, you know it's true."

"Why should I believe you?" I asked, even though I did.

A splash interrupted our conversation. Rachel had jumped into the deep end. Shanna and Eva followed. The water did look inviting, especially since it was a typical St. Louis summer day: eighty-five with enough humidity to curl the straightest hair. A quick glance at Daniel told me I needed to get back to him. He looked uncomfortable and so did Adam and Heather. It was time to play hostess.

"We'll talk more later," I told Andy and went back to my friends.

"What'd she want?" Daniel asked as soon as I sat down. When I told him what Andrea said, he nodded. "Yeah, I can see that."

I stood, slithered out of my shorts, and pulled off my tee. "Come on."

He smiled and took his shirt off too. His smooth chest took my breath away. Daniel was perfect, thin but not too thin. He had some clear definition but not too sculpted. It took everything in my power not to reach out and run my hand down his skin.

Adam and Heather followed us into the pool. We stayed at the shallow end, talking about the team. Rachel came over, eyeing Daniel. Shanna joined us along with Andrea and Eva. They started asking the guys about how good or bad I was. Soon the girls were telling Daniel stories about me, some I wasn't sure he needed to know.

The boys didn't bother to come out of the pool house. For that I was grateful. Once Theo, Erik, and Daniel saw one another, hell might very well break loose. Lilly called us in to get ready for dinner. Daniel and Adam were the only guys that needed to change. Lilly led us up the stairs, ushering Daniel and Adam into a guest room. The girls were directed into my room. Lilly stood in the hallway until I closed my door. And as soon as it did, I was bombarded with twenty questions.

"Vicky, Daniel is h-o-t hot. Are there any more like him on the team?" Rachel asked as she stripped off her bikini top. Shanna and Eva chimed in to agree. "And I bet he could even teach me a thing of two." She looked at me with her vixen smile. "He *is* good, isn't he?"

No way I was fessing up to that. At least verbally, my cheeks felt warm with a blush. "I wouldn't know. We haven't been together long enough."

Shanna laughed. "What? But he's so into you. I can't believe you haven't done it yet."

I shook my head. Andy held back a grin as she combed out her hair. She knew me too well. I slipped into my closet to get away from the conversation and pulled on a cotton halter dress in pale orange. My shoes that Andrea had taken with her on the trip were back in my closet. They were perfect for this dress.

"Thanks, Andy," I said as I came back out.

She smiled. Her sundress was white with pink flowers. She wore her blonde hair cascading over one shoulder. Shanna had put on a black skirt, her favorite color, and a lime green sleeveless top. Eva, in a powder blue dress with gladiator sandals, and Rachel, in a vampy yet still summery red spaghetti strapped dress, looked their usual elegant selves. The epitome of class and wealth all in one room.

Lilly knocked on the door, the two-minute warning. I glanced at Heather as she sat at the vanity in a brown floral baby doll dress and black flats. She hadn't said a single word since we came upstairs. I pulled her hair up into a low ponytail and ditched the claw clip she was so fond of. Heather wasn't a conventional beauty, but she wasn't ugly either. I combed some gel through with my fingers to tame her thick blonde strays. Lilly knocked again.

Andrea opened the door. "We'll be down in a minute, Lilly. Thanks."

It didn't feel right so I braided the ponytail and Andy jumped in to touch up Heather's makeup. It took all of five minutes, but the results were striking. Heather smiled at us in the mirror then we headed downstairs.

Daniel and Adam stood on one side of the hallway. The other three guys leaned against the opposite wall. It looked like an 80s movie standoff.

Adam grinned when he noticed Heather. He hurried over and whispered, "You look great, babe."

I felt horrible about overhearing that but incredibly satisfied. Fingertips brushed against my back, sending that familiar shiver snaking up to my neck. I smiled over my shoulder at Daniel. He looked pretty good. I didn't know what to expect since I'd only seen him in shorts or his baseball uniform. He wore a pair of pressed khakis and a black polo. Gel tamed his shaggy hair.

He ran his fingers down my arm and linked them into my hand, giving a reassuring squeeze. Together we took a deep breath and crossed the hall toward the dining room. Adam and Heather fell in behind us. The only two left in the hallway were Erik and Theo.

I did not like this one bit.

We walked by them. Daniel tensed beside me. We kept our eyes toward the dining room, not once looking at Theo or Erik. They didn't say anything that I heard, but Daniel heard something.

Adam jumped in between them before Daniel could do anything stupid. Erik and Theo pretended to be innocent. Daniel and Theo glared at one another in a show of male posturing. Nobody said a word as the tension rose in the hall. Adam pushed us into the deathly quiet dining room.

We took our seats, but Mom motioned for me to join her in the hallway before my cushion could get warm. A faint murmur began as people started talking. Daniel and Adam had their heads bent together.

Mom waited for me, quietly tapping her five-hundred-dollar pumps on the marble floor. "What was that all about?"

"I don't know, Mom." I echoed her stance: arms crossed, right hip jutted out, and too much attitude in the way we both drummed our fingers against our forearms. "It might have something to do with the fact that you invited my ex-boyfriend and my current boyfriend to the same dinner party. God, what were you thinking?"

"But I didn't realize that you were –"

"Seeing Daniel? You said Grandma told you." I threw my hands in the air. I'd seen her do this a million times when she was mad about something blatantly obvious to her.

"She told me you were dating a boy from the team," she snapped. "I didn't think that meant exclusively. I didn't know you and Theo had –"

"Split up?"

She pooh-poohed that. "I thought you might still be friends. Children your age are rarely serious –"

I tossed my hand in her face to stop her. "He cheated on me, Mother. With my best friend. Why would you think we'd still be friends?"

"How was I supposed to know that? You don't tell me anything anymore."

I closed my eyes and sighed. "Can we finish this discussion later, please?"

She glanced into the dining room. "Yes, we will. But you are spending tonight here, young lady."

I shook my head. "No, I can't. I have an early day tomorrow and I have to drive everyone home."

"You can drive back." She smoothed her shirt then her hair for no real reason other than to comfort herself. "Now, let's get back in there."

The soft click of heels came from the kitchen and down the hall. "Ah, Meredith, Victoria." Grandma smiled and clasped her hands together. "Sorry for being so late. I got held up." She glanced between us, not missing a thing. "Shall we go in?"

Mom walked in with her fake smile beaming across the room.

"Do you want to tell me what that was all about?" Grandma whispered as she sat beside me.

"Later."

Daniel and Adam still had their heads down in whatever deep conversation they were having opposite me. As casually as I could, I kicked Daniel under the table. He cringed when my foot connected with his shin harder than I had intended. *Oops.* Heather let out a loud laugh before covering her mouth.

Dinner went without further incidents. Lilly prepared gazpacho, a five-herb salad with dill vinaigrette, and grilled salmon with mango salsa. It was delicious. I hadn't eaten this well since I moved in with Grandma. Dessert was fruit compote with homemade vanilla ice cream.

After dinner, everyone congregated in the music room. Mom and her friends talked, ignoring the rest of us. Andrea, Rachel, Shanna, and Eva headed back to the pool with Eva hiding a bottle of wine behind her back. Theo, Erik, and Logan followed them.

Daniel leaned down and asked, "We aren't going back out there, are we?"

"Oh, hell no." I grabbed his hand and tugged him into the hallway. Heather and Adam followed. "Come on."

We went through the kitchen and up the back stairs to the second floor. Adam and Heather stopped at the guest room to grab the guys' bags. Daniel followed me into my room.

"This place is unreal," he said as he fingered the canopy lace above my bed.

"Not what you expected?" I took a couple of dresses from the closet and shoved them into a bag.

"The baseball posters, yes. The frilly girl crap, no." He sat on the bed while I threw more clothes into a different bag. "What're you doing?"

"Oh, I'm just getting some stuff. Why?" I looked at a light pink silk shirt before deciding against it and throwing it back into my closet.

"Looks like you're moving out." He bounced on the bed. "Soft."

I shoved my jewelry box and three pairs of shoes into a third bag.

"What did your mom say, Vic?" He stared at the floor.

"She's just mad at me. Nothing major." I put the bags with Heather's by the door. "What'd Theo say to you before dinner?"

He shook his head. I walked over to my bed and stood in front of him. When he looked up at me, the rage in his eyes told me it was as bad as I thought it was.

"Tell me. Please?"

"It doesn't matter."

I ran the tip of my finger over his bottom lip.

"You're driving me up the wall. You know that, right?" He put his hands on my hips.

"How so?" I stepped closer, forcing him to strain his neck.

"That dress for starters." His traced the seam of my dress and stood up. "The bikini earlier."

He dipped his head and brushed his lips against mine so fast there wasn't time to react.

"Tease," I said just as someone knocked on the door.

He laughed.

Adam opened the door. "We aren't interrupting anything, are we?"

"Not that it would stop us," Heather added as she walked in.

Daniel's arms dropped, and he went to grab the bags.

"No, let's get out of here," I said.

I took us back down the servant's stairs. Lilly stood in the kitchen, staring out the back window. The smell of coffee brewing filled the kitchen. Mom preferred French Roast which was stronger and smelled like a coffee shop. I rushed up to Lilly and kissed her on the cheek.

"Thanks, Lil. It was great as always." Adam, Heather, and Daniel were already out the door when I turned to add, "Don't tell Mom I left."

After dropping off Heather and Adam outside her duplex, I drove us to the Habitat house. I didn't know where else to go. Grandma could be home at any time. Daniel's parents were home. There was no way we were going back to Mom's. We sat in the car.

"What're we doing here?" Daniel asked after a few moments of silence.

"Is there anywhere else you'd like to go?" I put my hand on his knee.

"Actually, yes. Move." He reached for the door handle.

I pushed the driver's seat back and climbed into the passenger side. Daniel occupied it so I sat on his lap and leaned back against him.

"Hi," I said. His hands found their way around my waist. "I thought you wanted to drive."

"Oh, yeah." He kissed my neck. "I do."

I reached down the side along the passenger door and pulled the handle that reclined the seat. Daniel fell back and I turned to face him. My lips found his and my fingers curled into the fabric of his shirt.

Then he pulled away. "Wait. You know I could do this all night, but we have to stop."

I responded by kissing him harder.

"Vic…" he pleaded. "You have to be the one to stop. I don't think I can," he said as my teeth tugged on his ear.

"Why?" I whispered.

"I don't have anything with me."

I froze and stared down at him. "That just sucks."

"You have no idea."

I climbed back into the driver's seat and put my hands on the wheel. Daniel tucked his shirt back in, but he didn't set the seat upright. It took all my will power, which wasn't much at that point, from climbing back into his lap. He opened the door and came around the front of the car.

"Let me drive, please," he said opening the driver's door.

Once we had switched sides, Daniel started the car and drove off.

"Where are we going?" I asked. Disappointment crowded out any enthusiasm in my voice.

"I told you, it's a surprise."

He drove in silence. I didn't push it. Something was on his mind and I knew Daniel well enough that he'd tell me when he was ready. He made so many twists and turns that we ended up leaving the city without getting on a highway. I was totally lost.

My phone rang in the cubby between the seats. I ignored it.

Thirty minutes from the time we left the Habitat house, Daniel turned down a dirt path. The trees kept out the light of the moon. It was the middle of summer and the smell of pine floated through my cracked window. The headlights bounced off the bumpy road for ten minutes. We drove into an open area along a river. It ended before a small cabin that sat completely dark. Daniel parked the car and we sat there.

The cabin was a simple log home. There was a concrete patio covered by a short tin roof over the front door.

"Where are we?" I asked.

Daniel smiled and his eyes took on that daydreamy quality. He shook it off. "This is my parents'. Dad bought the land when we were kids and built this house. We used to come to the river almost every weekend in the summers. Not so much anymore."

We got out of the car and crossed the gravel driveway to the front door. Daniel unlocked the cabin, and I stepped into the single room. There was a full-sized bed along one wall with two cots folded beside it. Opposite the bed was a small kitchenette with a round wooden table and four chairs. Daniel lit a lamp that sat in the middle of the table.

"No electricity?" I asked.

He shook his head. "No. Dad likes to 'rough' it. He thought that this would build character."

I stood in the middle of the room. The sound of the river was clear through the thick log walls. Daniel watched me as I walked over to the kitchenette and turned on the water. Running water but no electric. I guess Mr. Cho didn't mind a few conveniences. The window above the sink looked toward the river.

Daniel stood behind me. He rested his chin on my shoulder. "I love you, Victoria."

No one had ever said that to me before. I tensed and he noticed. Daniel disappeared and the warmth he left behind grew cold. I stared out the window a moment longer, wondering if that had been real or my imagination.

"Vic —"

"Really?" I turned to face him. "Do you really mean that?"

He leaned against the bed post and nodded. "Just so you know, I've never brought anybody here before either." He paused then said the one thing I needed to hear. "Not even Shelby."

"Not once?" I asked, taking a cautious step toward him.

He did the same. "Never."

We stood in front of each other. Everything had just changed. Daniel had said he loved me. Better yet, he meant it. The world felt right.

BOTTOM OF THE 6TH

"Daniel," I began. He looked up at me, thoroughly exhausted. "I love you, too."

"You're just saying that because I rocked your world." He kissed my nose.

"No." He looked shocked so I added, "I mean, that's totally true, but I've never had these kinds of feelings for a guy before." He sat up on his elbow as I continued, "I think about you. All the time. Everything I wear, even if I'm not going to see you, I wonder what you'd think. I wonder where you are when we aren't together. And the thought of you having an ex-girlfriend kills me with jealousy. And, when you touch me, even just holding my hand, I feel like exploding. I just –"

He put his hand over my mouth. "Point made."

I licked his fingers.

"Stop," he laughed. He grabbed my hands and pinned them to my sides when I tried to tickle him.

"When do you have to get back?" I asked. My phone glared on the floor next to the empty condom wrapper. I was glad he'd lied about not having anything with him. This place was perfect for our first time together.

"Midnight curfew. You?" He settled back into one of the fluffy pillows.

"Grandma and I never discussed it, but we need to get out of here. It's almost midnight." The time blinked on my cell.

"Oh, that's awesome," he said, throwing off the sheet and leaping out of the bed. "We've got to go."

"You know," I said as I stood up, "if you were a good girl like me, that wouldn't be an issue."

He smiled. "If you're parents only knew what you had been doing up here …" He let the sentence hang.

That was enough to creep me out. "I'd prefer they didn't."

"Yeah, me too."

I ran my fingers up his still bare chest.

He kissed me, biting my lower lip. "We need to go. Like five minutes ago."

We left a few minutes later, but it was still too late. Daniel was going to miss his unforgiving curfew. He called to let his parents know about a mythical flat tire. By the sound of his dad's voice on the other end, he didn't really believe Daniel.

"That went well," Daniel said when he hit end on my cell. He handed it back to me. "I bet this will cost me two weeks."

"Two weeks?"

"Yep, grounded. Dad and Mom usually ground in two-week increments. Although, Becca did get a month once." He glanced over at me. "She called one of her friends a bitch in front of Mom."

"Two weeks?" How could I go two weeks without seeing him outside of baseball and the Habitat house?

"Don't sweat it, Vic." He put his hand on my knee. "There are ways out of these things. Plus, I wouldn't change any of this if I could."

"Me neither."

Daniel drove at arrestable speeds to get back to his house, hoping this would stop his parents from grounding him. It was only twelve twenty-five when I got home.

"Where did you go after you snuck out of your mother's house?" Grandma asked from the dark living room. She was waiting like a vulture circling prey. She clicked on a light. I felt like I was suddenly in some 50s detective movie. "And then you don't answer your phone."

I stood in the hallway, smelling of guilt.

"Your mother's freaking out." She stood up and walked by me into the kitchen. I followed her. "Fortunately for you, I convinced her you were just upset by the entire situation."

She pointed to a chair and I sat down. The tea kettle whistled.

"She expected you to return after dropping off your friends." Grandma sounded way too calm and slammed two mugs onto the counter. "And she thinks they're a bad influence on you. Including Daniel."

I leapt from my chair, ready for a fight. "She doesn't even know Daniel!"

"Calm down. I told her that." She put the mugs, along with tea bags, on the table. "She's basing that opinion on Daniel's reaction to Theo and on your hasty exit. Naturally, she thinks you are completely innocent. But we both know better, don't we?"

I felt the blood rushing to my cheeks. "What do you mean?"

"I wasn't born yesterday, dear. You and Daniel are head-over-heels for each other. And I know that you are probably the one who made the decision to sneak out of your mother's. Daniel would've stayed. For you."

Guilt weighed down and my anger weakened. "What was she thinking?"

"Honestly, I have no idea." The tea kettle whistled. Grandma stood to get it. "But I think she feels so far outside your life these last few weeks that she wanted to get you back somehow. She reacted without thinking things through." She turned off the stove and added, "And it's my fault in a way."

"Why do you say that?" I asked as she walked back to the table.

She poured water over the tea bags and put the kettle on a hot pad. "Because I mentioned that you were dating a boy on the team." She paused and stared at me. "You used to tell your mother everything, Vicky. She heard about this from a third party and freaked out. She didn't even know you and Theo had broken up." She took a sip of tea. "She knows Theo and his family. She doesn't know Daniel."

I only had more questions now. "So why invite Theo if she knew we had broken up? And why invite Andrea?"

"She didn't know why you and Theo broke up. I think she believes that it's Daniel's fault. Which it was —"

I started to protest, but she held up her hand.

"To a degree. You fell for him pretty quickly. But your mother didn't know about Theo's ... extra activities. And she didn't know that he started dating Andrea."

The tea scalded my tongue. I sat the mug back on the table with a thud. "I didn't cheat on Theo."

"I know, but you were going to break up with him regardless of the situation with Andrea." She looked at the clock on the wall and yawned. "You should at least remember that the next time you see her."

I nodded and stirred some fake sugar in the tea, watching white swirls form.

"And, as for Theo, he's an idiot. You're better off."

I glanced up at her and smiled.

"Now, I know you've had the sex talk with your mother."

The horror must have shown on my face. How in the world could she bring that up now? My embarrassment was twofold. The truth was that Mom and I never had any sex talk. I learned everything I needed to know in biology, plus what my friends and I discovered online, not that I was going to tell Grandma that.

She smiled in an effort to reassure me. "Just promise me that you'll be careful. I know that you and Daniel are headed that way if you haven't been there already."

My eyes grew as wide as saucers.

She reached over and patted my arm. Her calm bugged me more than any anger would have. She gathered our mugs and walked over to the sink. As she flipped on the light, she said, "That's what I thought."

My entire body fell limp at the table. I stared at the yellow and white weaved placemat as Grandma rinsed out the mugs. I heard her put the mugs in the dishwasher. When she started to walk by me, I blurted, "I love him."

She stopped and put her hand on my shoulder. "Yes, I believe you do. Just be careful. Love can sometimes be fleeting. Or it can last a lifetime."

"Are you dating Charles?" The words flew out of my mouth before I even thought about saying them.

"Yes," she said, squeezing my shoulder. "Is that okay?"

I stood up and hugged her, glad that the spotlight was off me and glad that she didn't lie. "Yeah."

Grandma laughed, relief clear in her tone. "Good. Now your father will be a challenge."

"Isn't he always?"

"No. He's a good man, Vicky. I wish you'd see that. But he'll be upset about Charles. Your father thinks I should live as a hermit. And Charles is a different kind of man than your grandfather."

"Probably true." I sat down in the chair with a thud. "He's not going to like Daniel, is he?"

"I don't know." She sat back down at the table.

My head dropped to the table. "He won't."

"You can't say that for certain."

"I know it though." I glanced up at her concerned face. "Just like you know he won't like Charles."

"Honey, I'm not saying he won't like Charles. He will have a hard time accepting him."

"Same diff." I sat up with an idea so brilliant that I couldn't believe I hadn't thought of it before. It would solve all my problems. "Grandma, do I have to move back?"

She was caught off guard. "What?"

"Can't I stay here?" I bounced a little in my seat. This was totally the right thing to do. "He could use this to his advantage in the media that I'm helping my poor, elderly grandmother or something. There'd be no political downfalls from that."

She didn't answer. Her eyes were focused on the floor and she smacked her lips with little sound. Grandma did that when she was thinking. "Why?" she asked.

I shrugged, not ready to admit she didn't like the idea and not saying what I felt. *Because this feels more like home.*

"I don't think your parents will allow it," she said, drawing out each word like I was five and didn't understand anything. She stood up again. "But we can discuss it after your season is over, okay?"

I jumped up and hugged her again.

"I'm not saying yes."

"I know." *But you aren't saying no.*

"Okay then. Now we need to fix this situation with your mother." She walked over to her calendar and pointed to the upcoming Saturday. "You will invite Daniel and his parents to your mother's for dinner that night."

I crossed my arms. "Come on, Grandma. You know that's not a

good idea."

"No ifs, ands, or buts. If you want your mother to even consider letting you live with me, which I'm not sure is a good idea, then you need to let her meet Daniel properly. And that includes his parents."

"Fine, but he has a little sister too," I pouted. Like Becca was going to get me out of this mess.

"Just invite the family, Vicky."

"One condition," I said like I was in a position to make demands. "You have to be there."

"Of course, I will." She started to walk to the hallway, yawning.

I dropped the bomb. "So does Charles."

"Oh, now that's not necessary." She stumbled, catching the wall to keep from losing her balance.

"Yep, that's the deal breaker. Mr. Cho knows Charles. That'll make him more comfortable." I leaned closer so she would know I was serious. "If I'm going down, I'm taking you with me."

She laughed. It was both a nervous and funny laugh. "Fine. You win. I won't throw you to the wolves alone. Now get to bed. We have an early morning tomorrow."

I kissed her cheek and skipped to my room. The dinner with my mother couldn't be that bad.

TOP OF THE 7TH

Grandma let me see a different side to her charity work the next morning. Once a month, she went to the battered women's shelter to deliver food and clothing she'd collected. This time she invited me to tag along. A lot of it actually came from my mother's friends. The designer tags stood out as I helped her take everything out of each bag while we worked in silence in the shelter basement.

Jacqueline, the director of the facility, eyed me with suspicion when I showed up with Grandma. I waited by the back of the truck as they talked about whether bringing me was a good idea. Whatever Grandma said, it worked. I was allowed inside. Not that we saw anything or anyone. Jacqueline let us in with the clothes and pointed us to the basement. I heard voices behind me but didn't turn to see who it was.

"Why all the secrecy?" I asked after sorting my second bag of clothes into sizes.

"These women are basically in hiding." Grandma looked at a white silk shirt that had a coffee stain on the front and tossed it into the trash.

"I'm not going to tell anyone," I said, shocked at having to defend myself.

She didn't stop sorting. "Not intentionally."

"What's that supposed to mean?" The fact that my trustworthiness was in question bothered me. A lot. I was Senator Hudson's daughter for crying out loud.

123

"You could give directions to someone who might turn around and give them to someone else who's looking for a resident." She handed me another bag. "These women live in a certain amount of fear. The mere thought of their husbands or parents or boyfriends coming after them might send them into a panic. They could simply disappear without getting the help they need for themselves or their kids."

"Kids?" I opened the bag. Inside were baby clothes. On top of the tiny t-shirts was a stuffed rabbit.

"Of course, where did you think the children go?"

I pulled out a pink onesie with "Princess" in silver sparkles across the chest. "I never thought about it I guess."

"Most people don't." She tossed a pair of dress pants toward the washing machine. "They think it's easy for a woman to leave abusive situations and just start over. They don't stop to think that these women are victims and not just too lazy to leave."

"Why don't they? Leave, I mean."

"It could be just about anything really. Financial reasons for one. They can't afford to leave, especially with children involved. Or they don't know how to live in a world where men don't beat on them. There may be mental issues or it could be plain old fear."

"Fear?" I held up a toddler's t-shirt that read "Rock Star."

"It's the biggest reason most people do things or don't do things in their life. Think of the one thing you fear most in the world. What do you do to remedy the situation? Is it really as easy as someone else might believe?"

I folded the last two bags in silence. The tiny clothes bothered me more than what Grandma said. How could any kid live like this? I thought of my mother's house with the pool, the designer dresses I never wore, the top tier gaming systems in the pool house, and the flat screen TVs.

The biggest problem in my life was my controlling father. But he never hit me, and I knew he never would.

I didn't see Daniel Friday night. His aunt arrived from Chicago for her annual visit. I hoped that this inconvenience would put off Saturday's dinner. I was wrong. Mom loved the idea of Daniel's aunt joining us. At least, she pretended she did. She had everything planned with Grandma by the time I fell asleep Friday night. And what an appalling night's sleep it was. I couldn't get it out of my head that something horrible was going to happen when the Cho family showed up at Chez Hudson.

Saturday morning, I woke up with that same feeling of dread in my chest. It didn't take long to find out why. On the front page of the local news section, there was a picture of me at the plate. It was huge. I sat down at the kitchen table and thought I'd be sick. I skimmed the article and turned the page to finish it. There was another picture of me looking up at Daniel as we walked to the dugout. It looked like his glove was on my ass. And I only felt worse after I finished the story.

> Victoria Hudson, daughter of U.S. Senator Warren Hudson, fights sex discrimination in the city's summer baseball program. Hudson, 17, will be a senior at Xavier Preparatory School for the upcoming school year. This summer, in an effort to admonish sexual discrimination in local athletics, Hudson joined a local baseball team.
>
> Hudson reportedly found a loop hole in the district's registration packet that allowed a female to participate in the program. This particular district's rules do not stipulate that players must be male to participate. In fact, the application does not ask for gender. Hudson's application did not, however, list her complete name. Instead, she wrote "Vic" in an effort to mislead officials. The district initially intended to remove her from the team based on this omission but found no legal means to do so. The team's coach, Bernie Strauss, pointed out to district officials that two other male members of

his team would also be forced out if the district removed Hudson for such a reason. The two teammates in question are Troy "T.C." Notts, the shortstop, and Oliver "Ollie" Venter, the second baseman. Strauss also argued that all other districts would be forced to remove players that used nicknames on applications as well.

Hudson, who refused to be interviewed for this story, plays third base for Coach Strauss' Wolverines.

"She plays well, but she's making a joke out of baseball," a teammate who asked to remain anonymous stated. "No one takes us seriously."

It would also appear that her presence on the team is a distraction for at least one player.

"Yeah, some of the guys forget what's going on when she's on the field. Now that she's dating one of them, it's even worse," our source added.

The teammate Hudson is dating appears to be Daniel Cho, son of local architect Ray Cho. According to our source, Cho's playing ability diminished considerably from last summer. Cho, and several other team members, refused multiple requests for interviews.

"She's a completely different person," classmate Theo Tudor told us. Tudor, who dated Hudson for six months, also stated, "This person playing baseball isn't the Victoria I know. I've been to some of the games and she's a raving lunatic on the field."

It is hard to say what motivated Hudson to morph from the girl next door to a mad

woman on the baseball field. Known as a
nice respectable young lady, Hudson's
actions have been noticed by a lot of
people.
One thing is certain; the district is
already revising the rules for next
summer so that this type of situation
does not arise again.
"The boys aren't trying to play
softball," District Athletic Chairman
Joel Wasson stated. "Why should the girls
force themselves onto a boys' baseball
team?"
As for Senator Hudson's thoughts on his
daughter's baseball interests, his
office refused to comment.
It is widely speculated that the Senator
will make a run at his party's nomination
in the next Presidential campaign.
Hudson's next game is this afternoon at
3:00 pm at Jackson Memorial Park.

I'm not ashamed to admit it. I cried. Out of anger.

Grandma waited for me to say something. She stood in her usual spot at the kitchen sink, staring at me.

"Who talked?" I asked.

"I don't know, baby."

"Why would someone do this to me?" The phone rang on the wall behind me. Without thinking, I reached over my head and answered, "Hello?"

"You aren't answering your cell," Daniel said with a hint of panic. "Did you see the paper?"

"Who talked?"

"Whoever it was is going to get their ass kicked. Adam and Ollie called me. I know it wasn't them. But I can't say about anyone else for sure."

"Delvin?"

"I don't know," he grumbled. "I doubt it though. He likes you. We all like you."

"Except Jayden." I slammed my hand down on the table like the maniac Wakefield made me out to be. "Damn it, Daniel. It had to be Jayden. That's the only person that makes any sense. He didn't come to Hansen's, remember? He hates that I'm on the team. He told everyone that I'm making fun of the game. And that's the quote in the paper."

"We're going to have to come right out and ask him."

"Coach is going to be pissed."

"No kidding. We should get a call from him before long."

I took a sip of the coffee Grandma put in front of me. Sweetened perfectly. "Daniel, I'm so sorry."

"For what?"

"They named you in the article."

"So."

"And that picture."

"It looks like two teammates."

"It looks like your hand is on my butt."

"Well, it was for a second." He snorted. "Don't worry about it, Vic. I'm not."

"Still, I am sorry for all of this, Daniel."

"You know Aunt Rita is really looking forward to meeting you now," he said with extra cheer in his voice.

I slapped my forehead. "God, I totally forgot about that."

"It'll be fine, Vic. Trust me."

"I hope you're right," I whispered. He had no idea how much I meant that.

"Always am. I'll call you later, okay?"

As soon as I hung up the phone, it rang again.

"Victoria," Mom screeched. Her voice took on inhuman octaves when she was crying. "Your father just called me about the story in the paper. That reporter never even called his office." She sobbed. "I'm so sorry, Vicky."

I knew she wasn't sorry that he found out. There was more behind her words. "For what? What's he going to do?"

She sniffled. "He'll be home tonight."

"Great. Just great." I made no attempt to hide the sarcasm. "I'll call Daniel and cancel dinner."

"Why?" Any sound of tears in her voice disappeared. "Your relationship with this boy –"

"His name is Daniel."

" – is one of the things he wants to discuss." She cleared her throat. "He wants to talk about this baseball obsession too."

This was not a good idea. "It isn't an obsession. There isn't anything to talk about."

"But that photo –"

"The one of me and Daniel? What about it, Mom?" My voice started rising and I didn't fight to keep it down. "It looks like two teammates after a game. If I were a guy, it wouldn't be a big deal."

"If you were a boy, it wouldn't be newsworthy," she snapped. "You never think, Victoria. You never once think about how this might affect your father."

"Just like he never thinks how this is going to affect me." I slammed the phone down. Then I picked up the receiver and slammed it down again and again until Grandma pried it from my fingers.

"Are you okay?" Grandma asked. The room was so quiet it felt like being underwater. When I didn't answer, she added, "This isn't that big of a deal."

"Which part? The newspaper article or the Senator coming home because of it?"

It was her turn to not answer.

"I just …" The words stuck in my throat, holding back the sobs that wanted to follow.

"Tell me."

I looked at her. Grandma really wanted to know. She cared. Whenever my mother said "tell me," she looked like a lioness on the hunt.

"Vicky..."

"For once, I felt like my own person," I blurted. "I felt like me and not Senator Hudson's daughter. I wasn't a campaign promise or a piece of the perfect family. I was just me." The tears came like rapids on the Colorado. "Does that make any sense?"

She rushed over to me and wrapped me in her arms. "More than you know."

The phone rang again. I had a sinking feeling that it wasn't going to stop any time soon.

"Hello?" Grandma answered in her perfect political mother voice. Then she handed the phone to me.

As soon as I put the receiver to my ear, Coach Strauss bellowed, "Hudson, get your ass over to my house at one o'clock. We're havin' a team meetin'."

He rattled off the address and disconnected. The phone rang again as soon as I hung it back on the wall.

Grandma answered. I heard her say "no comment" as I walked down the hall to my room. It was only eight in the morning. I had five hours to kill before I needed to be at Coach's house. The only thing I wanted to do was hide.

BOTTOM OF THE 7TH

Mrs. Strauss was not what I expected. For some stupid reason, I thought she'd be a shrively old lady in a housecoat and slippers. When I rang the doorbell at quarter to one, an athletic woman answered. She had crow's feet and a few gray hairs, but she was in better shape than most of the girls in my class.

She directed me through the modern living room to a set of stairs that led to the basement. I arrived early to talk to Coach alone and was glad I did.

When I stepped off the stairs, I knew this was hallowed ground. I'd entered Bernie Strauss' man cave. Military paraphernalia lined the walls. Then I saw a photo of Mrs. Strauss holding an M16 in full camis. This wasn't a man cave so much as a room filled with memories. When I first met him, I assumed he was a Marine. I loved being right. The far wall was covered with photos of graduating Marines and Coach Strauss stood with them as their drill instructor.

Above the television was a picture of Coach in his dress blues with his arm around his wife in her Navy whites on their wedding day. The bouquet gave it away. Beside that was a picture of a young man with Coach's nose and his wife's eyes, also wearing dress blues.

"Hudson, you're early," Coach growled from a recliner that had seen better days.

"Yes, sir." I felt the need to salute.

"Well, sit down," he motioned to a couch of faded brown leather.

131

I sank into it and never wanted to get up. "What's on your mind?"

I looked at the floor. "I'm sorry."

"For what?"

I shrugged and looked up. "For the newspaper article this morning. For even thinking I should be playing baseball. For dragging everyone down."

He shook his head. "I never pegged you to be stupid, Hudson."

"What?"

"You heard me. You can't stop what people write about you. And you ain't a bad ball player. And, as for draggin' us down, that ain't happened."

"But –"

He didn't let me finish. "No buts, kid." Then he stood up and walked through a door and came back with a couple of sodas. "Now, you know who talked. Whaddya wanna do about it?"

I caught the soda as he threw it at me. "I just want to know why he did it."

He huffed and sat in his chair. "You ain't figured that out yet?"

"Then you tell me why Jayden would do this." I sat the can on the coffee table and leaned forward.

"Hudson, don't you see? You're givin' him a golden opportunity here. We've only got a few games left. We're poised to make a run at the city championship. Scouts go to those. And with the media all over you, they'll be at all our games. Make sense now?"

Unfortunately, it did. "He's using me."

"Pretty much."

"Still doesn't make it right."

"Nah, it don't. But can you really be mad at the kid? He ain't goin' get the shots that the rest of you get. And he can play college ball. The rest of the guys ain't gonna. They might try and get on the team, but Jay's got a chance to really get on the field. Other than Delvin and Ollie, the other guys will be goin' off to college or the military."

"Why not Delvin and Ollie?"

"Prolly headed for construction jobs. Don't get me wrong, kid. They're good boys, but college ain't for them. They know it." He chugged his soda. "Let me ask you something. Do you even know what most of these boys wanna do after high school?"

"Daniel wants to be a doctor. Adam wants to work with

computers. Calvin and Reggie both talked about going into the Army."

He grunted. "Army."

"T.C. mentioned that he wanted to draw comics once."

"But you don't really know much about them, do you?"

He was right. Other than Daniel and Adam, I didn't know them. They were just guys I played ball with. I shook my head no.

"These boys live in a different world than you." He held up his hand to stop me from interrupting. "I'm not sayin' that you're slummin' or nothin'. Like I said, these kids aroun' here ain't bad. They ain't all super poor. Hell, most of 'em ain't slightly poor. Jay's the only one who ain't got much. His momma works two jobs just so he can live in a better neighborhood and go to a better school. But don't you go and feel sorry for him either. He won't have any of it."

"He still didn't have to talk," I said without much conviction.

"Nah, but he did and now we have to move past that." He looked toward the stairs as someone clumped down them. "That's what this is all about. Get it all out. Get past it. If we don't, this team's as good as cooked."

Ian, Reid, and Gil came down first. They didn't say much except to point out that they didn't talk to Wakefield. Daniel and Adam came down a moment later. They were up to something but didn't share. The rest of the team showed one right after the other, with Jayden walking in last. He reeked of guilt and had a look of defiance on his face like whenever he faced a pitcher that had gotten him out before.

"Alrigh', now that you'll are here, let's get it out in the open." Coach leaned against the wall, giving his recliner up to Jayden. "This ain't gonna be a free for all, got it? We're gonna do it like you'll are in school. So if you got sumthin' to say, raise your hand."

They guys looked at one another, except Jayden. I stared at him. Ollie raised his hand and Coach nodded at him.

"I didn't say anything, Vic," Ollie said. "Just so you know."

"I know, Ollie. It's okay."

"No, it isn't," Adam snapped without raising his hand. "We agreed not to talk. Vic asked us not to and one of us did anyway. That is not okay."

"Yes, it is –" I began.

"Whoever talked is a coward," Daniel jumped in. He glared at

Jayden.

"Whoa, whoa, whoa. Now we ain't gonna name call," Coach barked.

"It's true, Coach," T.C. defended. "He needs to come clean and own up to it. Or he is a coward."

I stood up and said as loud as I could without yelling, "It doesn't matter, guys."

They started talking at once. Except for Jayden, who glared at me.

Coach let out an ear-piercing whistle and the guys shut up.

"Just listen to me, okay?" I begged. "It doesn't matter who talked." Coach nodded as I took on a role I hated: politician. "We need to move on. Can you guys do that without calling him out?"

Adam stood up. "No. Sorry, Vic. This isn't just about you. He let us down. All of us. He needs to apologize like a man."

"No, I don't," Jayden roared. He got in Adam's face. "I didn't do a damn thing wrong."

"How in the hell can you say that?" Daniel yelled, getting in between them. Adam gripped Daniel's arms and held him back.

"I didn't tell Vic I wouldn't talk to Wakefield. I didn't go to that little get together where she confessed that she's just a poor rich girl who isn't understood at home." He changed his voice to sound like a toddler as he said that. Then he grew somber, "Wakefield asked me what I thought of her on the team. So, yeah, I told him. And there's no way I'm apologizing for it."

Daniel tried to break free from Adam's grip.

"Stop it. All of you!" Coach shouted and growled at the same time. The guys stopped moving like his voice froze them in place. Coach nodded to me. "Vic, speak your peace."

I nodded and looked at Jayden. "You're right. You didn't make any promises, but I did ask the team as a whole. That included you. Everyone agreed. Majority rules." I sat back down. "I don't know why you did it. I don't care either. It doesn't matter now. The damage is done."

"What damage, Vic? How in the hell did this hurt you? It'll only help your daddy in the polls." Jayden jabbed his finger toward me.

I shook my head and tried not to become overly emotional. I closed my eyes to calm down and let it seep into my voice. "Look Jayden, you don't know anything about me. You've never bothered to learn. You prefer to think I'm some joke. You think I'm a mockery to everything you hold on a pedestal. But you don't get it." The room was silent except for the ticking clock on the wall. "Go play softball then. Try. See how it feels when they tell you that you can't. Try out for volleyball next year. Or join the girls' track team. Oh, but you can't because you're a boy. Because you're the 'superior sex'.

"I've told you guys that I'm not playing baseball because of some grand scheme to prove girls are as good as boys. I'm not trying to make a point. I could've played softball. I could've gone to Europe. But I *wanted* to play baseball. It's a different game and you all know it. And I love it.

"After this summer, I'll never get another chance to play competitively. So, Jayden, I'm sorry if you think my motives aren't pure. Tough. I just wanted to play ball and be a normal person for once in my life. *You've* taken that away from me." I looked around at the team. "Now you guys are going to have to deal with what it's like to be Victoria Hudson. Welcome to my hell."

Coach put his hand on Jayden's shoulder. I could tell I hadn't gotten through to him. He didn't care.

"There may not be other reporters at the game today," I continued. "If it hits the national wire, and it probably will, the chances of more reporters showing up are pretty good. So, talk. Don't talk. I don't really care anymore. You think I'm some privileged princess. Fine, live in my world then. But I have to warn you, this will be way worse than anything I've had to deal with in the past."

"What do you mean worse?" Calvin asked.

"My father's going to announce his candidacy for President. The press has been speculating this and it's true. The media eats this stuff up. It'll get political. Heck, you may even have to deal with tabloids." I looked at Daniel. "They'll go after you and your family first. I'm sorry."

Daniel nodded. Saying it out loud made it real.

"And, guys, the Senator is coming home. Tonight."

Even the clock went silent.

"He was going to write the story anyway," Jayden mumbled.

"Yeah, but you fuelled the fire," Coach said. He stepped into the center of the room. "So here's what we're gonna do. First, no one talks to the media. I ain't kiddin'. You talk and you're benched. Got it?"

Everyone nodded once in unison.

"Second, we meet here before every game the rest of the season. We go as a team. We leave as a team." He looked around at each one of us. "It's almost two now. Y'all got your gear?"

A chorus of "yeps" and "yeahs" echoed in the suddenly smaller basement.

"Third, y'all are gonna get over this thing with Jay. We can't change it. We need to move forward. As a team." He ran his hand through his hair. "Look, kids, you'll probably gonna make the tourney. Hell, you got a damned good chance to win it. Don't let some stupid crap blow that outta the water."

We grouped into cars. Daniel climbed into the passenger side of my car while Adam and Reggie jumped in the back. Daniel used my cell since his was dead to call his parents and warn them what to expect. With Aunt Rita in town, they were coming to the game.

"Oh, this is not happening," I blurted out after he hung up.

"What?" Daniel asked. "What else could possibly go wrong today?"

"Remember when I said my father was coming home tonight?"

Daniel nodded. I could feel Adam's eyes boring a hole in my head from the back seat.

"He'll be home in time for dinner." I glanced at Daniel in time to see his face fall.

"Okay, the freak-out was warranted." Daniel called his father again and relayed the information. They started arguing in Korean.

Adam distracted me by asking, "How big will this media circus be?"

I shrugged. "Today, I'd say mostly the local news. It may only be Wakefield though. In about a week," *or less*, "it could explode."

"Why a week?" Reggie asked as Daniel hit the end button on my phone for a second time.

I cringed at the thought. "Because, if things go as they usually go, my father will play this up to his full advantage."

The parking lot was full. I squeezed into a newly formed space on the grass. As a team, we walked to our dugout with me in the center. The stands were crowded and lawn chairs lined the fences again. I spied Mom in the bleachers in a deep conversation with

Pepper. They didn't even bother to try to blend in now. Wakefield was easy to spot. He lingered near our dugout. Then I saw someone totally unexpected talking to him. Or rather at him. Robert Belton, my father's campaign manager. He nodded toward me but didn't crack a smile.

It was our second meeting with the Panthers. The first one did not end in our favor. We knew it would be tough going in. We huddled in the dugout before warming up.

"Well, I'll say one thing about all this attention, Hudson," Reggie said, smiling into the stands. "I'm going to get a few phone numbers out of it."

I followed his gaze to a couple of girls. He waved at them and nodded. I jammed my elbow in his side, making him double over.

Daniel and I walked onto the field when Daniel touched my back. Barely. But it was enough to hear Wakefield say, "Thata boy."

My head dropped.

"Sorry," Daniel whispered as he pushed by me.

The guys joked around like it was any other game. After we stretched and warmed up, we gathered in the dugout for Coach's pep talk. Daniel stood on the opposite side of the circle and didn't even look at me. This was going to be harder than I thought.

The Panthers started swinging their bats. I felt their eyes on me as we ran onto the field and the cheers erupted. I did my best to ignore it but couldn't stop my face from burning. Jayden tossed some grounders and T.C. moved closer to me.

"Hey, Vic." He smiled. "How's it feel to be a celebrity?"

I ran up on a grounder and threw it as hard as I could at Jayden's head. Then I turned to T.C. and snapped, "It feels like everyone is watching my every move. It feels like I'm under a microscope. And it sucks."

"Bet it does." He leaned over so only I could hear him. "But thanks."

Jayden looked bored as he tossed another grounder my way. "For what?" I asked as I threw the ball.

"I wanna play college ball. The scouts that usually show aren't going to look at me twice with Jayden around. Maybe now there'll be someone that will." He reached down to touch his toes. "I mean, if some new ones show. People will come to see you and I'll be right beside you. Maybe I might get a shot."

I smiled. "Yeah, I hope they do."

After my chat with T.C., I relaxed a little. Maybe some good could come of this mess. I focused on the task in front of me: the Panthers. We had one advantage over them. Me.

I was benched when we first played them but not today. I put on my game face and ignored the crowd, even as they chanted my name when I stepped into the batter's box to lead off the bottom of the first.

Their pitcher walked me on four straight pitches. None of them even came close to the plate. Ollie hit into a double play. Jayden hammered the ball into deep right center, but they played him to go deep and had no problem making the out.

And that's how the game went. Back and forth, no one scoring. Adam pitched more like Nolan Ryan than a seventeen-year-old boy. By the sixth, he was still working on a no hitter.

I was set to lead off our half of the seventh. The Panthers' pitcher hadn't walked anyone since he walked me in the first. He was almost as unhittable as Adam. T.C. and Reggie had the only hits of the game, but they never made it past first base.

In the sixth, I found a pattern he'd settled into after he struck out Adam looking.

I nabbed Ollie as we started back into the dugout. "He's pitched fastball, fastball, curve then breaker."

"What?"

"You heard me. Just watch the catcher from the corner of your eye to know where he's throwing, but that's *what* he's thrown the last two innings."

Ollie nodded. I relayed the pattern to Jayden. He snorted. But if I got on and Ollie got on, I knew Jayden would listen. I couldn't believe that the catcher let the pitcher settle into such a pattern. Or that we hadn't noticed it before.

I dug my left foot into the box. As much as I didn't want to, I had to take the first pitch. The catcher shifted inside.

He threw the fastball at my ankles. Too low. Ball one.

Same set up. Again, I planned on taking the pitch. Right at my knees, but it caught the corner of the plate. Strike one.

The next pitch was the one I wanted. His curveball had been left hanging in the middle of the plate one too many times. No one had been able to take advantage of it. I knew it was coming and I knew

I could rock it.

He wound up and threw the pitch, right down the middle.

The bat cracked as it connected. I took off as the ball went sailing into a gap in left center. I rounded first. When I touched the bag at second, their left fielder picked up the ball. But he was near the fence and I knew I could make it. My legs burned as I hustled. Coach was screaming at me, forgetting about signals. I don't know what he said. All I could hear was my ragged breath and my feet pounding against the infield dirt. Then he threw his hands down like he was pushing the air out of his way. Momentum was on my side. I had to dive in head first. My hand slid under the third baseman's leg, hitting the bag before his glove smashed into my back.

"Safe," the ump shouted. "Safe."

I called time.

The ump nodded, granting. The third baseman took his glove off my back and walked to the mound.

"Not your prettiest slide, kid," Coach growled as he knelt beside me.

My thighs burned from scrapping along the loose rocks. "Yeah, but I made it." I dusted off the dirt as I stood with my right foot on the bag. Blood started to seep through the thick white fabric of my pants on my left knee. That's when I felt a burning sensation eating through my leg. *Great.* "Get me home, Coach."

Ollie followed my lead. He took the first two pitches then hit the same hanging curveball over the second baseman's head. I trotted home with little effort. My knee hurt, but I ignored it. I stood in the dugout, cheering as loud as I could as Jayden smashed the second fastball over the fence to make it three nothing.

That was still the score as Adam almost lost his no-hitter in the top of the eighth. The batter smacked a line drive to my left. I dove for it. The ball bounced off my glove and into T.C.'s. I fell hard on my left side. My knee burned and I felt the skin tear. When I looked down, the spot of blood had grown into a patch.

"You okay, Hudson?" T.C. asked.

"Yeah, thanks for the save." I got to my feet and dusted my pants for a second time even though it was pointless.

"Just doing my job."

A new pitcher held us to our three runs, but that was all we needed. Adam was lights out. He struck out the side in the eight.

There was a scare in the top of the ninth when their left fielder hit a long fly ball into right center. Reggie ran it down, making a diving stop. It was a thing of beauty, especially since Reggie wasn't the guy anyone expected to dive for a ball. The crowd, thankfully, recognized the effort. An easy grounder to T.C. ended the game.

We jumped on Adam, knocking him to the ground in a dog pile. After a few playful punches, we let Adam up and headed toward the dugout. I limped along. My knee started throbbing at some point, but I didn't notice it until the game was over. When I looked down at the patch of blood, I saw a field. I sat on the bench with my leg straight out. Daniel sat beside me, beaming like the rest of the team.

Then he saw the blood on my pants.

"Ah man, Vic, when did that happen?" He lifted my leg and put it over his lap.

"When I slid into third." I winced as he tried to pull my pant leg up to my knee. "Ow."

Coach handed Daniel the first aid kit that we hadn't needed all year. Why was I the only one getting hurt on this team?

"Vic, I need to cut the pants," Daniel said as he slipped the scissors under the elastic.

Coach stood over us. Daniel cut along the seam on the outside of the leg and stopped just above the knee. He tugged the fabric away from the cut. I almost fainted when I saw how much blood hadn't soaked through my pants. Then he poured rubbing alcohol over it.

Every cuss word in the book flew out of my mouth.

"What's wrong?" my mother shouted as she pushed her way through the guys that circled me. She saw my knee and screeched, "You're going to the hospital. Now."

I clenched my jaw. "I'm fine, Mom." Daniel poured more alcohol over it and I bit my lip to keep my mouth shut. "It's not that big a deal."

"But —"

"Trust me." I saw her through the gathering tears in my eyes. To say that my knee hurt was an understatement. I wanted to scream at Daniel to cut the damned thing off. I gritted my teeth and suffered the burning sensation that spread to my toes.

It stopped bleeding and burning after the alcohol bath. Mom sat behind me, letting me lean against her while Daniel doctored me. That huge amount of blood came from one small cut in the center of one huge rug burn. Daniel put ointment on it and covered the entire thing with gauze and tape.

"Come on, Vicky," Mom said as she stood up. "Let's get you home."

"I'm okay, Mom." I jumped up and held back any hint of pain when I landed. "I'll see you tonight, okay?"

She glanced around and saw somebody in the crowd. Without looking back at me, she said, "I'll see you at six."

My mother started to walk away, and I reached out and hugged her for a moment. When I let go, I said, "Daniel and I will be there at six."

She nodded and disappeared into the crowd. I teetered a bit, but Daniel steadied me.

"Oh, I like this," he said, grinning like a raccoon.

"You like that I'm in pain?"

"No, never." He put his arm around my waist and leaned in. "But I like that you have to let me drive." I wanted to smack him as he laughed. "Don't put any pressure on it yet. Hey, Adam, can you get the other side?"

"What're you going to do? Carry me?" This was getting ridiculous.

"You know, that is not a bad idea." He lifted me an inch off the ground.

"Stop, please," I said as I laughed. If Wakefield hadn't been there, I would've enjoyed the idea.

Daniel nodded to Adam and they put their arms around me. Reggie walked behind us carrying our equipment. We barely made it out of the dugout before Wakefield descended.

"Miss Hudson, are you okay?" he asked, walking alongside Adam with a digital recorder stuck in my face.

I ignored him.

"Any comments on the game then?" he pushed.

"Actually, yeah." Daniel and Adam tensed. They stared at me with mouths open. I smirked and leaned closer to Wakefield's recorder so he wouldn't miss a word. "That was one of the best pitching performances I've ever seen. Adam Marshall's no-hitter should definitely be reported in your paper. I hope you do it justice."

"Thanks, Vic." Adam beamed.

"What happened to your leg?" Wakefield was drooling now. I'd given him a bone.

"No comment," I said, smiling my best good-little-girl smile. "Come on, guys."

"How did your mother react when she saw Mr. Cho's hands all over you?" he pressed.

Daniel started to turn toward Wakefield.

"Don't," I said with too much bite. I leaned forward and said as sugar as possible, "Mr. Wakefield, you have my comment on the game. Any other questions will receive my standard 'no comment.' Have a nice day."

Daniel's body felt like a rock. Well, more so than usual. Wakefield, always the professional, stayed with us until we were almost to the car. Then he asked, "How does your father feel about your relationship?"

"Keep going," Adam whispered as he picked up the pace. "Ignore him, Daniel. He's just trying to get a rise out of you."

Reggie stepped in between Wakefield and Adam. He started asking Wakefield where he got his suits and a bunch of other crap that Reggie really didn't want to know.

"I'd really like to smack the daylights out of that guy," Daniel muttered.

"And that's what he wants. You'd feed right into his hands." My right foot bumped the ground, sending a jolt of hurt into my knee. "Just get me home, please."

Daniel took Adam to Hansen's first. The guys planned an impromptu party in his honor. I felt horrible for missing it, so did Daniel. He knew the situation and was okay with it. We only had an hour and a half before Daniel and I were expected at Chez Hudson. He was quiet as he stopped in front of his house. I waited while he ran inside to grab his stuff.

We were a block from Grandma's when he finally said something. "Does your dad know I'm half Korean?"

"Not this again," I murmured. "I'm sure he does. I'm also fairly certain he knows your entire family history." I reached over and squeezed his knee. "I'm sorry I got you into this mess."

"No, you aren't." He smiled for a brief second.

"Why do you say that?"

He put his hand over mine. "Because I'm not sorry. Neither should you be." He pulled into the driveway behind Charles' truck.

142

That made me raise my eyebrows. He stared at the faded bumper sticker on the truck's tailgate. "Vic, before we go inside ..."

I poked him in the side. "What?"

He took both of my hands and kissed the backs of them. "I just don't want this to fall apart. For any reason."

"This? As in us?"

He nodded.

I leaned over and kissed him. Then I lied. "It'll be fine. Don't worry."

TOP OF THE 8TH

I knew that it wasn't going to be fine and that thought ate at me as I showered. Nothing was ever fine when my father was involved. He would try to ruin my relationship with Daniel just as he tried to control every aspect of my life. I couldn't let that happen.

Grandma rebandaged my knee while Daniel showered. It was easier that he got ready at my house. Then I didn't need to drive back and get him after I'd dropped him off.

The scrape-slash-cut throbbed, but the pain was minimal. Grandma used a home remedy, which was basically aloe mixed with something that smelled rather pretty, instead of over the counter ointment.

I let Daniel drive again. Grandma and Charles were asked to show up at seven, but, knowing my grandmother, she was planning on getting there at six-thirty. Charles looked relieved that their relationship was out in the open.

This time, Daniel knew to park in the back. Lilly wasn't in the kitchen when we walked in. Daniel followed me as I led us into the hallway and toward the sound of light conversation in the sitting room. Mom and Lilly sat on the couch, staring at some binder resting on my mother's lap. The early evening sun bounced off the pool.

"Um, hi, Mom," I said.

She looked up then glanced at her watch. "Oh, it's already six." She handed Lilly the binder. "Here, Lil. You're right, of course."

Lilly smiled as she hurried out of the room. I knew what just happened. Mom didn't want something Lilly had already made. Lilly let my mother look at the menu and Mom would concede that Lilly made the right choice. Same old story.

"Please, have a seat," Mom said like we were international dignitaries.

"Where's Joba?" I asked since my dog didn't come running up to knock me over. I missed him.

Mom waved her hand like it wasn't a big deal. "He's at the kennel spa for his monthly grooming." She regained her formal posture.

"Are you okay, Mom?" I asked as Daniel and I sat on the cushy loveseat.

Mom smoothed her skirt and moved into a wingback chair. "Yes, I'm fine. How's your knee?"

I didn't like this stiff, formal tone she'd adopted toward me. "Much better," I said with an abnormal amount of perk. "Grandma put some special ointment on it."

"Ah, I see." She recrossed her legs. It was like her back had an invisible wall behind it. It was only making me, and Daniel, more uncomfortable. "So, Daniel, where do you go to school?"

"Lincoln High." He stared at her, ready for the challenge.

"And when will you be graduating?"

Daniel smirked. "I'll be a senior this year."

"I see." She fake smiled. "What about after graduation? Do you have any plans?"

"Yes."

She stared at him, waiting for more to the answer. Daniel didn't say anything. He was playing her game. As a politician's wife, my mother knew better than to give away more than what was asked. Granted, she did pull this off with a lot more grace than Daniel, but at least he was trying to go toe to toe with her.

"What do you intend to study?" she asked through gritted teeth.

"Medicine." Daniel tilted his head as if to say "and what do you think about that." It was sexy the way he challenged her. I hoped he could do the same against the Senator.

Mom's resolved weakened and she smiled naturally at him. "That's a wonderful career. Have you narrowed your focus, or do you plan on waiting until med school to determine that?"

Please don't say gynecologist. Please don't say gynecologist, I repeated, hoping he could telepathically hear me.

"Probably pediatrics."

Really? I wonder if that's true or just a rouse.

They continued chatting about Daniel's future when I realized that this was the first time I'd heard it in this much detail. He really had it all planned out. He even had contingency plans if anything failed. Maybe we didn't know each other that well.

"Vicky will be attending Mizzou, of course," Mom stated. She lifted her chest with alumni pride.

"Really?" He flicked his eyes at me.

I told him that. Didn't I?

"She'll major in law of course." Now she just looked smug.

"You, a lawyer?" Daniel's stance weakened. She had caught him off guard.

"Oh, you didn't know?" Mom mocked surprise. Maybe there was a hint of real surprise, but I doubted it.

"We've only been dating for a few weeks, Mom," I said.

"Really?" Now she really was faking her shock. "I thought it had been much longer."

My mother looked ugly to me. Absolutely hideous. I hit her where it would hurt. "Nope, guess your intel was wrong there. And I don't know if law is what I want to do. Maybe social work."

My mother's cool façade disappeared. Championship roses could wilt under the glare she gave me. Daniel squirmed, and I crossed my fingers in hopes that reinforcements would soon arrive. He cleared his throat and a light bulb went off above my mother's head. Her face resumed the normal elegant trophy wife perfection.

"Oh, forgive me. Would you like something to drink? Some lemonade perhaps?" She didn't wait for an answer as she stood and walked out of the room.

"Do you feel like you just got ran over by a Mack truck?" Daniel asked.

"I didn't know you wanted to be a kid's doctor. And I didn't know you were going for a cross country scholarship –"

"I didn't know you wanted to be a social worker."

"Well, yeah. I've always wanted to help people, but even more now after working on the Habitat house. My parents want me to follow the family business and be a lawyer. I'm starting to think that's not for me." I took his sweaty hand. "Do you really want to be a pediatrician?"

"Yeah, why?"

"I think that's pretty cool."

He relaxed and grinned. "So does your mom."

Lilly walked in behind Mom with a tray of lemonade. Fresh lemon slices floated around the ice.

"Your father should be here any minute," Mom stated as if I asked the question. "He stopped by the office to get some papers."

More like to get a dossier on Daniel's family.

"Daniel, I'm really looking forward to meeting your parents. I'm surprised that I haven't run into them at any of your games." Mom was back in politician wife mode. Whatever points Daniel scored in the opening round, they no longer counted. "Tell me a little about them."

I'd never thought about why Daniel's Mom and Dad hadn't come to a lot of games, but it was like that for most of the guys. Reggie's mom was the only parent that showed up to every single one.

"Mom takes Becca, my little sister, to her soccer games on Saturdays. They almost always end up starting around the same time the ball games. Dad works on the Habitat house on the weekends."

Mom looked at our hands. "What does your father do?"

"He's an architect at Crabtree, Blaine, and Ubeck." Daniel squeezed my fingers.

"Really? Would I know anything that he's worked on?" Mom smiled wider now like a mouse that got the cheese from the trap.

Daniel said, smiling back at her. "He doesn't talk about work much."

"And your mother. What does she do?"

Poor Daniel. The more points he scored, the more he got grilled.

"Mom works at Becca's school as a teacher's aide."

"A teacher's aide?" Mom looked utterly baffled with a hint of disgust. A million thoughts could be growing through her head at the moment and none of them good.

Daniel needed a break from the interrogation. "Mom, when did you say –"

"Your father should be pulling up any minute now," she interrupted. "Now, Daniel, I'm not certain you were given a proper tour of the house the last time you were here –"

"Mom –"

"I know you saw the guest room and Vicky's room –"

"Mom –" I raised my voice.

"And I believe you were here one other time and saw the pool –
"

"Mother –" I snapped.

"What is it, Vicky?" she said, sounding exasperated.

"Just stop." It was a simple request. Well, a command really, but it didn't get through to her.

"Stop what?"

I stood up. "Daniel, will you excuse us for a moment?" Then I grabbed my mother's hand and yanked her into the hallway. It wasn't pretty, but it was effective.

"Victoria Christine, what are you doing?" Mom tried to sound confused and pissed. I knew better.

I didn't answer as I dragged her into the dining room where Lilly was setting the table. I didn't want Daniel to overhear any part of my impending argument with my mother. Lilly saw us, finished the last place setting, and then shuffled out of the room.

"I'm not going to ask you again –"

I didn't let her finish. "What are *you* doing?"

"I don't know what you mean," she said. This was not my mother but Senator Hudson's wife. She was so fake, so conniving that I didn't recognize her. Nor did I want to know her.

"Mom, I really like Daniel and you're torturing him like he's a servant that was caught stealing." I'd seen it happen. When I was five, the cook sent my father to the hospital by making a peanut sauce. He was allergic. When I was seven, the gardener had a pair of shears in his back pocket when he left. He didn't bring them back the next day. Mom accused him of trying to steal them. She put him through her version of the Spanish Inquisition.

"Don't be ridiculous…" She put her hand on her forehead and started pacing. "I don't know why you've started acting like this."

"Like what?" I controlled my voice even though I just wanted to scream to the skies.

"Since you moved in with your grandmother, you've been acting like a complete stranger." She stopped in front of me and crossed her arms. "When I see you, I barely know who you are. That's *if* I even see you. You used to tell me everything, Vicky. We used to talk. I knew this whole baseball thing was a bad idea. You should've gone to Europe. You should still be dating that nice boy Theo –"

"Oh. My. God. Mom, Theo cheated on me. And he was all over Andy before they left American airspace. And you think he's nice?"

"He comes from a good family –"

"So does Daniel," I interrupted. Okay, I screamed.

Mom's smug face smiled. She patted my arm as she walked by me toward the hall. "I'm sure he does."

"But what, Mom?"

She stopped, and her shoulders dropped like giving me her opinion was weighing down on her. "I just don't think he's good for you."

I hurried around to get in front of her. "Excuse me? You don't even know him."

"I know enough." There it was. That glint in her eye that told me she knew something that was too important for her daughter to know.

"I don't understand." I searched her face for the answer.

"Really, Vicky, just look at the boy."

I don't know what fell faster, my stomach or my jaw. I knew what she meant. I just didn't want it to be true. "You mean because he's Korean?"

She didn't answer. She didn't need too.

"You are unbelievable, Mother," I whispered.

I stormed through the hallway, almost knocking over Lilly as she stood with my father's briefcase by the front door. The sight of the brown leather with the monogrammed lock sent me into a sprint. When I entered the sitting room, Daniel and the Senator were in a stare down.

"What's going on?" I asked through gritted teeth. I needed to calm down and not think about my mother. The Senator relaxed in the wingback across from Daniel. I kissed him on the cheek, inhaling the stale airplane scent on his suit.

He stood up and hugged me. "It's so good to see you, Vicky."

I sat next to Daniel, weaving my fingers through his with a reassuring squeeze. My father stared at us for a moment with a blank expression. He was calculating.

"Tell me, Daniel." He leaned forward and rested his elbows on his knees. Standard understanding father-slash-lawyer move. "Is my daughter any good?"

A million thoughts went through my perverted mind.

Thankfully, Daniel knew better. "She's not bad, sir."

I elbowed his side.

"I mean, she plays very well." He smirked then added, "For a girl."

I should've smacked him.

"Vicky, why didn't you tell me about this?" His eyebrows furrowed. I couldn't tell if he was hurt, curious, or both. "Is this why you moved in with your grandmother?"

"Yeah, Grandma lives in the only district that didn't specify gender," I answered with as much confidence as I could. Well, answered the second question anyway.

"Then why keep it a secret?" he asked.

I glanced at Daniel and muttered, "I don't know."

Grandma and Charles walked into the room, saving me from further explanation. I couldn't tell him the truth. This wasn't the time for a full out brawl.

I focused on his reaction to Charles. My father cocked an eyebrow and nothing more. Grandma looked her usual elegant self with her silver hair pulled into a bun. Charles appeared uncomfortable in a dress shirt and tie. I bet Grandma had to tie it for him.

"Hello, everyone," Grandma said. Her voice shook a little. Only someone who lived with her could've heard it. "Charles, this is my son Warren."

My father stood immediately and shook Charles' hand. It was clear the Senator was caught off guard. Only someone who lived with *him* would've seen it.

After the mandatory how-do-you-dos, Grandma led Charles to the love seat as my father dropped back into the wingback chair. Mom snuck in and leaned against the chair. She smiled at my father but didn't glimpse my way.

The room was tense and quiet. My father kept glancing at Charles out of the corner of his eye. I felt like I needed to say something, anything, to break the tension. Charles didn't deserve the tenth degree anymore than Daniel had.

"Anything exciting going on in Washington?" I asked. It wasn't much, but it was enough to distract him. "I mean, how's work?"

My father's smile could dim the lights on Broadway. He loved Washington and everything about it. "Things have been very busy.

I'm sponsoring legislation to tighten education standards." He launched into a speech, no doubt prepared, on how the education in this country has declined since he was a boy. "Even Xavier could use some higher standards, Victoria." He shook his finger at me. "You get one of the best educations in the country, but it still could be better. This bill has been a lot of work, but I think I'll get it passed."

"That's wonderful, Warren," Grandma said.

"Thank you, Mother." He noticed Charles fidgeting next to Grandma. "So, Charles, what do you do?"

Charles stared my father straight in the eye, ready for a challenge. "I own a construction company."

"Really?" Mom asked, sounding fake-impressed. "Which one?"

"Whitelodge."

So, maybe I was wrong about Charles all along. He wasn't fidgeting from nerves, but probably because of the tie.

My parents looked at one another, clearly impressed by this. Daniel seemed as puzzled as I was. Whatever Whitelodge was, it made my parents much happier.

The doorbell gonged throughout the house. Lilly rushed by us in a blur of black and white. She led Daniel's parents, his aunt Rita, and his little sister Becca into the room. I made the necessary introduction and watched for reactions from my parents. As usual, they were polite and blank faced. I tried to take comfort in the fact that they wouldn't embarrass me.

"Can I see your room?" Becca whispered. She bounced in her patent leather red flats as she stood wide-eyed in the middle of the ugly Persian rug that Mom loved.

Mrs. Cho hugged Daniel and said something in his ear that only he could hear. He closed his eyes and nodded once.

"It isn't anything exciting," I whispered back. *What's going on now?* To my mother, I said, "I'm going to show Becca around."

She nodded. Her eyes were cold. Whether it was for me or for the situation, I didn't know, but I was willing to bet she was still pissed at me.

"Come on, Daniel." No way I was leaving him with the wolves.

When we got into the hallway, Daniel took my hand and gave it a hard squeeze. Becca rattled on about the house. She sounded more like a six-year-old than a twelve-year-old. I led the way to my room and opened the door. It felt wrong, like I'd stepped into someone else's life. It didn't feel like mine anymore.

Becca snatched up my Xavier yearbooks and decided that I had to look at them with her right then and there. Daniel stared out the window while I explained the rules of the Russian club as we looked at my junior yearbook.

Lilly knocked on the door and instructed us to come downstairs for dinner.

"I hope I get into Xavier," Becca told me as she walked down the main stairs beside me. "It would be so awesome."

Daniel snorted behind us. His hands were deep in his pockets and his shoulder slouched. Something was bothering him. Other than the obvious.

"What?" I asked.

"What's so awesome about it?" he grumbled.

"For one, academics. Most of my classmates will be able to pick and choose whatever college they want."

"Yeah, Danny," Becca matched my tone and crossed her arms as we continued to the dining room.

"Yeah, I know, but you don't get to do any fun stuff."

I rolled my eyes.

"Like what?" Becca asked.

"No baseball team." He shrugged. "And no softball. No cross country. No show choir. No marching band."

I held up my hand to stop him. "Okay, I get your point."

He reached for my hand, but I moved out of the way. Becca went into the dining room ahead of us and Daniel stopped me from following her.

"Why're you so down on Xavier?" I asked, allowing the hurt to seep into my voice.

"Because you're acting all high and mighty about it." He waved his hands above his head and mocked my voice. "'Oh, the Russian club is so much fun, Becca. We only speak Russian during our meetings and hold a Russian festival at the end of the year.'"

He pushed by me and I held back the urge to drag his ass back into the hallway to finish this. Maybe I didn't know Daniel at all. He had never said anything like that about Xavier. Or me. Or anybody. Something else was going on.

Putting on my own fake smile, I followed him into the dining room. Dad and Mr. Cho sat at the head seats. Mom had Lilly arrange the seating. Naturally, that meant Daniel was at the other end of the table from me. For the moment, I was fine with that.

The appetizers were met with conversations about the weather. It wore on my nerves. I kept sneaking glances at Daniel and stared until my mother cleared her throat. I couldn't have cared less, but it wasn't proper etiquette to stare at someone during dinner. Even Becca knew that.

The soup and salad were served next. The soup tasted like watered down beef broth and the salad looked wilted under the runny dressing. Lilly's food usually appealed to me, but nothing looked good so far.

Dinner was quiet. They ran out of things to say about the weather. It's hot. It's humid. It's a typical St. Louis summer. What more was there to say?

"Are you okay, Vicky?" my father asked in a hushed tone.

I gave him a half smile and nodded. He squeezed my hand under the table then asked Mr. Cho about golf.

Becca said something to me. I remember nodding in agreement as I tried once again to get Daniel's attention. I don't know what she asked, but my answer was enough to get her to hug me. I felt my mother's disapproval across the table.

"That's a great idea, Rebecca," my father boomed, shaking me out of my reverie. "I'm sure Dr. Tennant would love for Vicky to show you the campus."

Crap. My head swam in the midst of misinformation. I glanced toward Daniel and caught his glare before he turned away. *This is getting ridiculous. Just because Daniel doesn't like Xavier, doesn't mean Becca can't see it.*

The senseless talk continued as my parents rattled on about how great Xavier's been for me. Then I noticed the heartbroken expression on Mrs. Cho's face.

The main meal arrived. The chicken was dry. The potatoes were lumpy and the green beans limp. I stayed quiet and watched Daniel. He was stiff, and it annoyed the crap out of me.

Manners be damned, I needed to fix this.

Now.

I slammed my fork down just as Lilly served desert.

"Victoria," my mother scolded.

"Sorry, Mom." I put on that fake smile again; one that I hoped to never use in the presence of my boyfriend and here I'd used it twice on him in one night. "Will you all excuse us for a moment? Daniel?"

He threw his napkin on the table and followed me outside. I led us around the pool, fighting the urge to turn around and push him in. I flipped on the light switch as soon as I stepped into the pool house and turned on him. He'd only gotten one foot in the door when I started.

"I am not going to feel like a zombie all night because of you."

"What?"

"Xavier is a great school. Becca's smart enough to get in. There are scholarships available if there are any financial issues. Payments can be made. So don't make me feel like it's my fault because you don't like the idea of your sister going there." The words came out so fast that it sounded like one long word. I took a breath and waited.

"You think this is about money?" he asked as he stared at his feet.

I sat on the couch. "I don't know. You were too busy snapping at me –"

"She didn't get in." He looked up at me. "Mom and Dad found out today. They haven't told her yet." He collapsed beside me. "It's not always about the money, Vic."

I didn't know what to say. I'd assumed ... I felt like an ass.

"Every day since she applied, since she found out about Xavier, it's the only thing she's talked about." He crossed his arms and closed his eyes. "It's gotten worse since she met you. She's excited that she'll know a senior as a seventh grader since the middle school is so close to the high school. She thinks you will be her best friend." He opened his eyes and stared at me. "This is going to crush her."

"I'm sorry, Daniel. I had no idea."

"I know. I was going to tell you, but I just ... I couldn't."

"Maybe the Senator –"

"No, I couldn't ask you and my parents would freak out if he said anything to Dr. Tennant." He put his hand on my knee as we slouched together. "I'm sorry I snapped at you."

I leaned my head on his shoulder, wishing I could fix this for Becca. "What're they going to tell her?"

"It won't be the truth. I think Dad's going to tell her he can't afford it. Then it will be his fault and not her's."

I nodded. That was stupid, but how would I have reacted?

"Are you still mad at me?" He pushed his shoulder into me. I pushed back.

"No. I mean, you were just trying to soften the blow for her, right? Big brothers are required to do that."

"Uh-huh." He cupped my face in his hands and kissed me like it would be the last time. "We need to get back inside, Vic. The elders will think we've abandoned them."

"Screw them." I tried to pull him closer, but he resisted. I used the only Russian curse word I knew and let him lead me back to the house.

I felt the hostility before we walked back into the dining room. Daniel felt it too. His body went rigid. It was deadly quiet as we went back to our assigned seats.

"Is everything okay?" I whispered to my father.

"Mr. Cho and I were just discussing the immigration legislation that was voted on during the winter session," he responded so everyone could hear.

Uh-oh. That's what Daniel's parents were discussing when I had dinner with them. When I failed to mention who exactly my father was.

"Yes," Mr. Cho began in his rich baritone, "I was explaining to your father that my grandparents would not have been allowed in this country the way things are now. A relaxation in standards would provide the opportunity for thousands of people looking for a better way of life than what they know."

"But times are different now, Mr. Cho," my mother crowed. "Surely you agree."

"That does not make the situation any less dire for those who wish to immigrate," Mr. Cho replied.

I was impressed. No one ever spoke to my mother or father like that. It was awesome.

"Mr. Cho, your viewpoint is duly noted," my father said with such a fake amount of joviality that he could've been a Mall Santa. "Now, I want to hear more about this baseball team our children play for." He looked at Daniel with raised eyebrows. "Robert tells me that you will make the playoffs."

I'm sure he's told you so much more than that.

"It's possible," Mrs. Cho said in her soft voice.

"That's fantastic. Now, Victoria, I understand you play third base?"

"Yes, sir."

"Have you gotten many hits?" My father knew so little about baseball that I'm surprised he knew what a hit was. Football was his game. If I tried to play football, he would've been happier. Not that I would've told him.

"She hit a triple today," Mom blurted. Her knowledge of the sport used to be worse than my father's. I suspected Reggie's mom had something to do with this newfound interest in scoring. "And tore up her knee."

I threw Mom a thanks-a-lot glare.

"But it isn't that bad, Warren," Grandma jumped in as my father's face faded to red.

Grandma got a thanks-for-the-save smile.

"She might have needed stitches," Mom countered.

"But she didn't. Daniel patched her up after the game." Grandma's face was tight, like she had just gotten a face lift. "You were right there, Meredith."

"She should have seen a doctor," Mom argued.

"Cut it out, Mother. It wasn't that bad." I smiled with a wicked idea forming in my head. "I was hurt much worse after our first game." Out of the corner of my eye, Daniel's head dropped. "Some idiot pitcher beaned me in the back. I had a bruise the size of a dinner platter for about a week. Coach forced me to sit out an extra game after I served my suspension."

"Suspension?" Mom gasped. I'd never been suspended from anything, so this was quite a shock.

Daniel coughed to get me to stop, but I kept going.

"Yes, I was suspended for going after the guy that hit me. It was intentional."

The room was so quiet you could've heard a bug scurry across the floor, if any bug dare entered Chez Hudson.

"You never told me that you were suspended," Mom said with more venom than a snake could handle.

"It wasn't a big deal. It was only one game. And I wouldn't have been able to play anyway with that monster bruise on my back."

"You still should've told your mother," my father snapped.

Suddenly I felt like I was five all over again. I wanted to stomp my feet and pout. It would've been nice if I got an "atta girl" for standing up for myself. Nope, I got nothing but guilt. So I caved.

"Sorry, Mother," I said with a hint of sarcasm. *Why did I even open my mouth?*

Silence filled the room, mixing with open hostility. Charles tried, and failed, to start any type of conversation. Grandma spoke with Mr. Cho. My father bristled in his seat. Aunt Rita, who hadn't said a damn word all evening, stirred her tea and chatted with her silverware. I think she was certifiable. Becca bounced in her seat while Mrs. Cho hushed her. Daniel and I stared at each other, and Mom stared at me.

Quite the dinner party.

"Daniel," my father boomed, "my wife tells me you're interested in a career in pediatric medicine."

"Yes, sir," Daniel said as evenly as possible.

"Quite a noble profession."

"Thank you."

Lilly stepped into the room to save the day. "Coffee is ready in the music room, ma'am."

"Great. Thank you, Lilly," Mom said. The relief was clear in her voice. It was as if she thought a change of location would help change everyone's attitudes. She stood and motioned to the hallway. "Shall we?"

Becca wanted to see the pool. Mom and Mrs. Cho walked outside and talked about rose gardens. Grandma, Charles, and Mr. Cho went into the music room to enjoy Lilly's French Roast coffee. The Senator excused himself to make a phone call. More than likely to call Robert.

Daniel and I sat at the piano. He pretended he could play but only used one finger to pluck at the keys. Becca joined us when she was finished with the pool. She quizzed me about Xavier and I said any tiny little thing I could think of that would make it look less magical to her.

Finally, it was time for the Chos to leave.

As we said our goodbyes, Mom pulled me aside.

"Your father and I would like to talk to you." She looked around to see if anyone overheard her. "Alone."

"About what?" I asked, feigning innocence. It never occurred to me until that moment how much we faked in this house.

"We will discuss this after your guests leave." She lifted her chin high and glared at me down her nose. Usually, she reserved that look for Joba.

"I'm leaving too, Mother."

"No, you aren't. Daniel can go home with his parents. You're staying here."

"But –"

"No buts, Victoria." She put on her fake smile and strode back into the hallway, directly toward Daniel.

He looked over her shoulder as she spoke at him and nodded. I stood in the door, defeated. He went to his dad first and then walked over to me. I backed into the sitting room where this all began.

"Don't leave," I pleaded.

"What am I supposed to do? Tell your mother no?"

"Yes, that's exactly what you're supposed to do." I choked back tears. "I don't want to stay here."

Daniel stepped closer, closing the widening gap. "So don't. Leave with me. Come over to my house."

I shook my head. There was no getting out of this. I couldn't walk out the front door without making a scene. "You know I can't."

"Sneak out later." He cupped my elbows and drew me closer. "We can hang out for a while. You know my parents like you."

It was a knife in an already damaging wound. "Is it that obvious?"

"That your parents hate me? Oh, yeah." He smirked. "And it doesn't matter."

"I just don't want to hear about it."

"Then don't."

I shook my head. He'd never get it.

"Vic, you're seventeen. Stand up to them." He lifted my chin so I couldn't look anywhere other than in his eyes. "For once in your life, tell them how you feel."

He leaned closer and I tilted my head higher.

"Victoria, could you please come back in here," my mother demanded with no hint of the anger seething inside her.

"In a minute," I responded, not holding back any ounce of hostility. But Daniel had already let go and stepped away from me. I dropped my arms to my sides. "Okay, fine."

I didn't try to hide my frustrations as Daniel and his family left. Grandma and Charles were still there, so at least I had some allies. Anything to delay the inevitable was welcome. No way would this battle begin with Charles here. Grandma took down all the white flags when she sent Charles on a tour of the house and grounds with Lilly.

"Okay, Warren, get it off your chest," Grandma said as soon as she was certain Charles was out of earshot. She sat on the couch and smoothed her long skirt.

My father sighed and fell back into his usual wingback. "What do you mean, Mother?"

"About Charles. About Daniel. About the Chos. Just lay it all out in the open."

"Charles seems like a nice man." He looked up at my mother as she handed him a scotch on the rocks. "Thank you, Meredith."

"And Daniel?" I asked, dropping my head to deflect any blow his words might cause.

He adjusted in the chair and took a sip of his scotch. "Daniel ... he's very different from the boys you normally date."

"Because he's Korean?" I asked.

Grandma let out a little gasp of air. Whether that was directed at me or my father, I couldn't be sure.

"No." My father sat his drink down and got out his chair. He knelt in front of me, putting his heavy hands on my shoulders. "That has nothing to do with it, Victoria. He's just not good enough for you."

I searched his face for any hint that would tell me what he was thinking. As usual, there wasn't anything there.

"No boy will ever be good enough for my daughter." He kissed my forehead then went back to his seat. "Now is that all, Mother?"

"And the Chos?" Grandma asked. She was not about to let one detail slide.

"They seem like a respectable family. I'll know more about them later."

"My God, Warren, you didn't have Robert create a file on them, did you?" Grandma shrieked.

"Mother, you know what my future looks like. I need to be careful about who my family associates with. I need to make sure there aren't ulterior motives –"

"Daniel is not dating me because of some political cause!" I jumped up and shouted.

"Calm down." My father put one hand in the air as if that would repel my attack. "I'm not saying that is the case. But someone in his family could be poised to exploit the situation. I need to be cautious. Not just for the safety of my political career, but for the safety of this country."

"Don't pull this crap with me, *Senator*," I snapped. "They didn't even know who I was until the damned reporter showed up."

"Victoria, watch your mouth," Grandma said. "Warren, you're being unreasonable. Victoria's personal life and your political goals are two separate things."

"But they will always be intertwined. Surely you can see that, Mary," my mother interceded.

"We'll deal with this after I read what Robert compiled." He raised his hands to stop the argument and leaned forward in the chair. Mom perched on the arm of the wingback. "Now we need to talk about this baseball thing."

"I'm not quitting," I said as I plopped on the couch.

"I'm not asking you to. But we need to be prepared for people to jump on this story. Once it gets out, reporters will swarm the fields." He looked at Grandma then at me. "How are we going to handle this?"

I didn't say a word.

"They are going to ask a lot of questions. We need to give them an answer," he pushed.

"No, we don't." I glared at him with determination I usually only had on the field. "We don't have to say anything."

"Yes, we do," Mom said. "You aren't just some girl playing baseball. You're the potential First Daughter. That alone requires a statement of some kind."

"No, it doesn't." I'd said this before but not with the passion I felt now. They needed to understand. "There is nothing other than the fact that I wanted to play competitive baseball one last time."

"Well, that's all fine and dandy," Mom said after a brief pause in the conversation. "But your father's goals are bigger than you."

"Don't even talk to me, Mother." I felt the steam coming out of my ears.

"Victoria," Grandma said, sounding both shocked and impressed.

I turned to her. "You have no idea what she said to me about Daniel."

"Whatever it was, you should still treat your mother with respect," my father said. "And I will hold a press conference about your baseball games. I will tell them what you just told me. I'll have Robert arrange for a security detail. Okay?"

"No! No press conferences. No reporters. No campaign managers. And absolutely no security." My hands shook. "This is my life, not some campaign strategy."

"Honey," he said as if I was still in diapers, "if I don't say anything, then this will get blown out of proportion."

This was too much. It didn't matter if I begged, he was going to the press. He was going to do it all over again. "Whatever."

Grandma stood when she heard Charles and Lilly in the foyer. "Let's go, Vicky. You can ride with us."

I stood, and Grandma put her arm around me.

"No, she can spend the night here," Mom said. She looked at me then Grandma. "Where she belongs."

"I'm going home," I replied.

"You are home," my father said.

"No." I looked up at Grandma. "No, I'm not."

BOTTOM OF THE 8TH

Exhaustion kicked in when I parked in front of Daniel's house. I sat in my car and stared at the steering wheel. It was still early, only ten in the evening. Daniel rapped on the passenger window. Mindlessly, I unlocked the door to let him in. As soon as he shut the door, I collapsed into his arms in tears. He let me cry and held me close.

After a few minutes, he broke the silence. "Tell me. What happened?"

"Everything I told you would happen," I spit out between sobs.

"So let it."

I whipped my head up. "What?"

"Just let them have it their way. It's not worth it, Vic." He ran his finger down the length of my jaw.

I stared at him then blurted, "My mother's a racist."

That caught him off guard. "Your mother?"

"She doesn't like you because you're Korean."

He shrugged. "I don't care what your mom thinks. Or your dad. As long as you like me, it doesn't matter what anyone else thinks."

"I hate this," I said as I buried my face in his chest. His heart held a steady rhythm that tried to lull me to sleep.

"I know. Me too. You know, I asked my mom if she had to deal with any of that kind of stuff. She didn't talk to her parents for three years after she married Dad. They only reconciled after I was born." He kissed the back of my head. "Vic, I can't change who I am anymore than you can. They'll just have to accept me as is."

"I can go three years without talking to my parents."

Daniel laughed. "No, you can't. And you wouldn't want to even try, no matter how mad you are at them right now." He stroked my hair and I felt myself drifting again. "You going to be okay?"

I nodded and wiggled to get closer.

"Come on. Let's go inside."

I called Grandma and left her a message so she wouldn't worry. Daniel's parents were polite even though they had every reason to be cold. I couldn't have hoped for much more. Becca hid in her room. She'd found the rejection from Xavier when they got home. Apparently, it wasn't pretty.

Daniel and I headed up to the attic room. As we walked by Becca's room, I heard her sobbing. I put my hand on the door, but Daniel pulled me away with a shake of his head. I wouldn't have known what to say anyway.

I collapsed onto the couch as Daniel put on a movie. I fell asleep in his arms, listening to his heart grow faster as mine slowed into sleep.

It was the final stretch of the regular season. I hadn't seen or heard from my parents since Saturday night. We arrived at the field as a team after meeting at Coach's house. I felt more at ease than I had in weeks. The cat was out of the bag, so to speak, and I didn't have to hide anymore. Everyone knew.

The game was a blowout. Coach heard a few choice words from the stands when he sat me after the third inning. Wakefield clucked and bristled while scribbling into his notepad.

We needed one more win to take the district. And we had one more game left. If we lost, we were through.

Wednesday's paper had a brief article and a shot of me playing third. And a picture of Daniel beside me in my car. I had no clue why Wakefield thought my boyfriend was a story. I didn't bother to read it as I readied myself for a day at the local homeless shelter. At first, I hated going there, but I didn't tell Grandma that. Volunteering was a condition of living with her.

And my big mouth mentioned this to Adam, who told Heather,

who decided she wanted to come with. I couldn't say no.

The shelter was in an old church that had sat vacant for almost a decade before becoming useful again. The residents were basically kicked out every morning at seven to do whatever they wanted. Off site, the charity that ran this shelter provided employment counseling, health evaluations, and some job training.

Heather and I were in the laundry room sorting and folding donated clothes. Grandma left us for the kitchen after making sure we knew what to do. Like it was so hard.

"Can I tell you something?" Heather asked after we made it through the first bag. It amazed me that so many people threw away good clothes. It also amazed me that they never washed them before donating.

I pulled out a long wool coat. "Sure, what?"

"Well, I didn't know Daniel last summer, but Adam said he's a totally different guy now." She rolled her eyes. "I just thought you'd wanna know."

"I wonder what he was like before," I said as I tossed the coat in the trash pile. It had a hole in the back that wasn't fixable. I'd seen people wear stuff like that before, but it didn't seem like they should. "I mean, I know they said he was pretty miserable after the whole Shelby thing, but no one told me what he was like when he was with her."

"Adam said he was a real jerk. Daniel and Shelby were always fighting and she walked all over him." She held up a white dress shirt with a stain on the front then tossed it into the trash pile. "Shelby's a big dope head. I've heard she's into meth more now."

I nodded as I folded a thick gray sweatshirt that looked almost new. That info wasn't anything new.

Heather held up two shirts that were stuck together then threw them toward the washer. "Gross. Anyway, I've smoked a joint here and there, but Shelby did it like every day. Then she'd beg Daniel for cash and tell him that it was for milk or whatever."

"I'm surprised Daniel got taken in by her."

"Sex will do that to you."

"That is something I did *not* need to hear." The smell coming from the trash bag in front of me made me cringe almost as much as Heather's comment did.

"Sorry," she said. "I just mean that it's like a drug, you know?

You guys have hooked up, right?"

I didn't answer. I liked Heather and all, but we weren't that close. I hoped we could become good friends later. After the media frenzy died down. Right now, I couldn't trust anybody.

"You don't have to tell me if you don't want to." She stopped smiling. "I mean, Daniel told Adam you guys had, but guys talk big like that all the time."

"What?" I didn't like the thought of Daniel sharing any of our intimate details with anyone, even Adam.

"God, Vic, Daniel is so gaga over you. I think he just needed to talk to someone, you know?" She sighed. "Adam's great. I mean, my last boyfriend just didn't get that sex is about more than him. Adam likes to take it slow."

"Why are you telling this?" Honestly, I didn't want to hear about her sex life.

She smiled, and if I didn't know her at all, I would've thought there was malice there. "Just girl talk."

The "just girl talk" ended up in the newspaper on Thursday. I had never felt more humiliated in my life.

An anonymous source informed this reporter that Senator Warren Hudson's only daughter, Victoria Hudson, is involved in a sexual relationship with her teammate Daniel Cho. Senator Hudson's office issued the following statement when contacted about this scandal:
Victoria Hudson is an intelligent young woman. The allegations from this anonymous source are outrageous. How can Miss Hudson defend herself from a coward that refuses to be named? Unless Miss Hudson or Mr. Cho state to the media that they are involved in an intimate relationship, any anonymous information must be considered libelous and without merit.
Victoria Hudson and Daniel Cho could not be reached for comment.

"I'm not going," I said to Grandma. We sat at the table together, coffee in hand. "How can I show my face there?"

"You have to go, Vicky. If you don't, then they will know that it's true. If you show up, there will be doubts." She reached across the table and put her hand over mine. "It is, isn't it?"

I couldn't hold back the tears. My most intimate relationship, my *only* intimate relationship, was in the newspaper.

She sighed. "You need to be the bigger person here. You need to stand tall and not let it get to you. You need to be your father."

I snorted. Not the person that needed to be mentioned at that moment.

"Who do you think called Wakefield?"

"Who else?" I said through my waning tears. "That rat Heather."

"Why do you think it was her?"

"Yesterday, she kept asking me questions about it. She said Daniel told Adam, who told her." I felt so stupid. "She wanted to hear it from me, but I didn't say anything about it."

"Then you still have deniability." She patted my hand. "Do you think Daniel will say anything?"

I shook my head. "I don't think so." Sobbing harder, I buried my face in my hands. "Grandma, what am I going to do?"

"Oh, baby," she said, pulling me into a bear hug. "Everything will turn out okay. You're going to do what any good politician does: deny, deny, deny. And you'll do it with the same finesse as your father. Just take a page from his book, and you'll be fine."

"I just wanted to do one thing. Just one little thing. That's all." I wiped my eyes with the sleeve of my t-shirt and drew away from her. "Why can't they leave me alone?"

We sat in the kitchen for at least twenty minutes until I cried myself out. Then I felt like an even bigger ass for letting it bother me so much. Grandma was right, I had the upper hand. Wakefield wouldn't expose his "source", aka Heather the Rat, without exposing her to my father's lawyers.

I hid in my room until it was time to leave for the game.

The first blow came at Daniel's house. He wasn't there. In fact, no one answered the door when I knocked. When I got to Coach's house, Reggie and Calvin stood outside. They didn't say anything right away, but I could tell by the look on their faces that something was wrong.

"What's going on?" I asked as I stopped in front of them.

"Daniel's parents came over here," Reggie said with a grimace. "They want him to quit."

"Yeah, Coach talked them out of it. They took him to the field and the rest of the guys left too." Calvin glanced at Reggie. "We couldn't leave you hanging so we waited."

"This is freaking ridiculous." I leaned against the car for support. "They want him to quit because of some stupid article in some stupid paper? They don't even know if it's true or not."

"It doesn't matter if it's true or not. You know that." Reggie shook his head. "They don't like the media poking into their lives. They don't like your parents. They don't like the politics."

"Politics?" I looked back and forth between them. "What does my father have to do with any of this?"

"Everything," Calvin snapped. "He's the only reason you weren't honest with us to begin with."

Reggie smacked Calvin on the back of the head. "They don't want Daniel's life dragged through the mud, Vic. Most of us, we don't care about the reporters. No one else has met your dad. My mom thinks your mom's alright. But your dad's a different deal. A lot of people in our neighborhood don't like him."

I fought back another round of tears. "This is such bull."

Reggie leaned on the car to my right. "Yeah, it is. But you knew this could happen, didn't you?"

"Yeah, Vic," Calvin said, sitting on my left. "You had to know this was gonna happen."

"No, I didn't," I said just as the tears escaped. "I'm gonna quit. I have no choice. You guys can win without me. It'll be easier without the damned reporters."

"You aren't quitting," Calvin said, smacking me on the shoulder.

"Why not? I've brought nothing but misery −"

Reggie stood up and glared at me. "Man, if you want a pity party, I don't want an invite. You started this, you're gonna finish it. Stop being such a girl."

I laughed without meaning to. Calvin tossed his and Reggie's bags into the trunk. They got into the car without asking if I was driving or not. I didn't have a choice. I drove to the park, still believing that my only option was to quit the team.

I had to park on the street that went into the ball fields. Reggie, Calvin, and I trudged up the short hill, joking about getting warmed up this way. When we got to the parking lot, a guy in a dark suit approached.

"Miss Hudson," he said with a nod, pushing between me and Reggie.

I glanced up and saw an earpiece and wire. "Don't tell me, Secret Service?"

No expression as he continued to lead me toward the dugout. "Former. I'm your security detail."

Adam ran out to greet us from the concession stand. The former Fed held up his hand to stop Adam a few feet away.

"Daniel's not going to quit," he blurted as he skidded to a stop. "Hey, Vic. What's up with the suit?"

"He's not?" I ignored the question about Supercop. We started toward the dugout and Adam fell in step beside me.

"No, he's not." He reached out and touched my elbow. Supercop stiffened. "Vic, I'm sorry. If I knew –"

"That your girlfriend was such a bitch –"

"God, you're so self-righteous, you know that? Do you even know why she talked to Wakefield?"

"Do I care?"

He put his hand up and started to back away. "You know, Vic, not everyone lives in a fucking mansion."

"So that gives them the right to talk about those of us that do?" I threw my bag on the ground and pointed at his chest. "I didn't ask to live there, Adam. I didn't ask for a father who happened to be a senator."

I grabbed my bag and took off at a jog to get away from him. The rent-a-cop kept up with me easily. Reggie and Calvin jogged to catch us. I could hear Adam's footsteps a few feet back.

Just outside the dugout, I ran into the Chos. Becca glared at me. Her parents stared. I wanted to say something. To deny everything. Every word in the English language stuck in my throat. They pushed past me without looking back.

"Come on, Vic," Adam said as he guided me by the elbow to the bench.

I searched for Daniel, but he was already on the field in his gear. He didn't look toward me once. My newly appointed protection detail stood behind the dugout with his back to the field. I glanced around and spotted three more throughout the park. My hell's grown bigger.

"Have you talked to him?" I asked Adam as we put on our cleats. He shook his head. "He's not talking to anyone." He put his hand on my shoulder. "I really am sorry about Heather."

"How did you know it was her? Did she tell you?" I tugged on a batting glove and avoided looking at him.

He stood up and slapped his glove against his thigh. "Some things you just know, Vic."

Adam ran out to warm up. Calvin and Reggie jogged after him, passing Daniel as he made his way back to the dugout. I watched him for a moment then took off into the field, staying a good ten feet away from Daniel. If his parents didn't want me anywhere near him, no reason to push it.

It drove me nuts for the first half of the game. Their pitcher walked me, and I scored off Jayden's double in the first. Daniel didn't give me a high five. He sat at the end of the bench, alone.

The game was tight. Delvin's pitches all looked like fastballs down the middle no matter what Daniel called. Coach gave Delvin until the fifth to straighten out but finally pulled him. Gil took over and shut the other team down. They held us scoreless in the sixth.

I was set to hit second in the seventh with the game tied six to six. Gil got on with a blooper up the middle. Then I walked again on four straight pitches. Their pitcher was tired. I could see the exhaustion in his eyes. After he walked me, he got pulled in a double switch.

Ollie struck out looking. Then Gil was picked off at second. Two outs.

Jayden dug in and gave the pitcher his "evil eye." It was pretty creepy. Coach gave me the sign I wanted. I felt the sweat drip in slow motion down my face. This pitcher had a slow wind up. I could make it.

I took a huge lead off first. He tried to pick me off, but I was well on my way to second. I slid head first, never a good idea, and looked toward Coach with my hand on the bag. He waved at me frantically to get to third. I hustled, almost tripping as I stretched my legs and pushed them to the limit. I went down again, sliding feet first this time. My left foot hit the bag a split second before the tag slapped my thigh.

"Safe," the ump shouted. "Safe."

Thanks to a bad throw by the first baseman, I had a chance to score.

Coach patted me on the back as I called time and dusted my legs. The blood started seeping through my pants again. I felt no pain as I took a short lead off third.

The pitcher didn't even look me back. Probably a good idea considering who was at the plate.

Jayden hit a soft liner into right field. I ran hard in case of a throw, but the right fielder was too far back to field it in time. The guys shouted "atta girl's" and "way to go's" as they swarmed me in the dugout. They kept it up even after it became just plain embarrassing. After all, Jayden hit me in. All I had to do was run.

The moment of happiness disappeared when I saw Daniel sitting alone at the end of the bench with his head in his hands.

TOP OF THE 9TH

We ended up winning by that one run and clinched our district. For those few hours while I played, the world melted away. It rushed back as soon as I stepped off the field. Wakefield waited along with two other reporters I'd never seen before. The blood rushed to my cheeks and I was glad that my face was already flushed from the game.

My new security detail flanked me and led me to an SUV that no doubt had bulletproof glass.

"I can drive," I snapped at lead rent-a-cop.

His head tilted down, and I could only assume he stared at me like a petulant child. It was hard to tell beneath the aviators. "Wilson will take your car back to your house. You will ride with Jones. I will drive." He put his hand to his ear and nodded once. He nodded to the other suits who opened up enough space to let Daniel through.

I threw my arms around his neck and inhaled his sweaty sandalwood scent. He stiffened, not lifting his arms.

"What's wrong?" I asked as I stepped back, pressing into the rear passenger door.

His voice hitched. "I can't do this, Vic."

No, no, no, no, no.

My body turned ice cold. I knew what he meant, but I had to hear his say it. "Do what?" I asked.

He closed his eyes and clenched his jaw. He didn't bother to open them when he finally answered. "It was one thing when ... Do you

171

have any idea how much it hurt my family to read that in the paper this morning? How much it hurt me?" He paused but still didn't open his eyes. "I can't do this, Vic. I can't wake up every morning and wonder what bullshit will be in the papers. I ... I can't spend every day wondering if someone's watching my house, waiting for me to screw up so they can report it." His eyes flew open and the rage burned through. "There were five fucking reporters outside my front door this morning. They practically attacked Becca. I can't let that happen."

I opened my mouth to say something, *anything*, but there wasn't anything I could say. He shook his head and back out of the human shield that saved me from being publicly humiliated.

The stony-faced guards turned around. I threw my keys at Wilson and climbed inside without another word. Once the door was closed, I broke down in tears.

Being Victoria Hudson sucked worse than ever.

I went to see Andrea the next day without calling. Part of me hoped she wouldn't be home, but she answered the door and acted like nothing had ever come between us. We sat by the pool while I replayed everything that had happened with Heather.

"Why would anyone do that?" she asked after I told her about Heather.

"I guess he paid her for it." I rolled onto my stomach to get sun on my back. It had felt like an eternity since I'd last lounged by a pool.

"Money's money." She coated her leg with sunscreen that smelled like a coconut breeze. "It not like you can't get it somewhere else."

"Says a girl whose parents are loaded."

"You know what I mean, Vicky." She looked at me over the sunglasses that probably cost more than Wakefield paid Heather.

"Adam said she was pretty poor though, so maybe she couldn't." Why was I defending Heather?

Andrea stood up and shook off her towel. "That's not an excuse to sell out a friend."

"Yeah, that's what I thought at first."

We didn't talk as we soaked up the sun. The quiet was nice. It gave me time to think about everything that had happened this past summer. It had gone by so fast. I felt like a new person because of it all. I wanted to tell her about Daniel, but it hurt so much that it was easier to bury it inside.

"Vicky, will you ever forgive me for the whole Theo thing?" Andy asked.

I stared at her for a minute. Her eyes were hidden under the oversized, too-dark shades. "Yeah. I think so."

She paused and then asked, "Will you ever forgive Theo?"

"Not in a million years."

She laughed and snorted at the same time. "Me either. Bastard."

"I guess the only thing I'll wonder is why he did it."

"Theo's a user. I can't believe neither one of us saw it before." She sat up and stretched. "You know, he has this competitive thing with Erik. They bet on everything, even grades." She took a deep breath and I waited for the bomb. "You were one of the bets."

I bolted up. "What?"

"God, Vicky, I swear I only found this out a few weeks ago. So don't be mad, okay? I mean at me, don't be mad at me." I nodded, and she continued. "Erik told Theo that you had ... you know. Anyway, that's why Theo was so intent on you guys hooking up in Europe. He bet Erik that you'd do it with him too, but you'd remember it this time."

I fell back onto the chaise lounge. "God, I make one freaking mistake and it's going to haunt me forever."

"They're both dicks." She leaned forward and straightened out her towel. "One more thing."

"Can I handle it?" I dropped my arm over my forehead.

"In honor of total disclosure or whatever, I found out – again after the fact – that Theo was hooking up with Stacey before we even left for the trip. He thinks her dad's an 'up and comer' on the county board." She leaned over me so I would hear her. "I'm sorry, Vicky. You know how Theo's always into the political stuff. He saw you and Stacey as an opportunity."

"Great. Just great." It sucked to hear all of this, but getting it out there was something that needed to be done. Forgiving Andy was one thing, trusting her was another. "He probably talked to Wakefield to get even with me. I'm surprised Erik hasn't talked yet."

"Oh, I think Erik's got other plans. He wants your team to get to the championship game to face his team. He wants to play against you."

That made sense. Erik was a pitcher. Sometimes that's a fun match up. Sometimes it can be dangerous when two people hate each other. Plus, he never liked the fact that I was a better player than he'd ever be.

"Vicky, thanks for coming over. I've missed you so much."

I hugged her. "I've missed you too." The alarm on my cell went off. "Crap, I need to go."

I slipped my shorts over my bikini bottoms and grabbed my purse. We walked to the house chatting about nothing.

"Can I ask you something?" Andrea asked.

"Yeah, go ahead. I don't have anything to hide."

"Is that newspaper article true? About you and Daniel?"

The sound of his name made me want to curl up into a ball and cry.

"What's wrong?" she asked.

I shook my head and slid onto the marble floor of the foyer. Grief took over no matter how much I tried to keep it down. Finally, I managed to admit what I'd hoped had been a bad dream. "It's over. He ..."

Sobs prevented me from telling her why. It didn't matter to Andrea. She sat beside me, wrapping her arms around me until I couldn't cry.

"He's an idiot, Vicky," she whispered. "This won't last forever."

I nodded. As I drove toward Grandma's, I wondered if she was wrong about that.

BOTTOM OF THE 9TH

The first playoff game was Friday afternoon on neutral ground in Forest Park. The tourney was single elimination. There were eight teams that had won their districts, so it only took two wins to get to the championship game. But they'd be hard fought.

The field at Forest Park had more room for fans. People that ran on the bike path could stop and watch for a moment before continuing on. It was a nice change of pace from our own park, which felt more and more cramped with each passing game.

The stands were crowded, but something felt off. Then I saw the microphones standing near the backstop. The media was there and this time it was national. Robert rushed toward us and the bodyguards closed ranks around me.

"I need her. Now," Robert demanded.

"What's going on?" I asked with more attitude than he probably deserved. The guys stood behind me, and I could feel the tension rolling off them.

"Press conference," Robert said, pointing to the staging area. "Your father would like you by his side as he makes his announcement."

My whole body went numb. Not here. Not now.

Robert ushered me to a secure spot away from the reporters. My father stood there in his best suit and rosy cheeks. Mom fixed his tie. She had on a pale-yellow suit jacket with a matching knee length skirt. She looked like a reincarnated Jackie O.

When the Senator saw me, he beamed from ear to ear. "Vicky, sweetheart, come over here." He looked me up and down. "Don't you look fetching in your uniform."

Mom stood beside him, pale-faced and expressionless. There were a few advisors running around under Robert's direction. My security detail lined up around the dugout, keeping the reporters from my teammates. I ignored them and focused on my father.

"Today's a big day, Vicky. Big day." He slapped my shoulders and bounced on his heels. I hadn't seen him this happy in a long time. "We are going to make headlines today. Me and you."

"I don't want to make headlines." The words sounded stronger in my head than when I said them.

He actually laughed. "This is a day to remember, Victoria. A day for the history books."

This time the words came out louder than intended. "Not today. Damn it, don't do this today."

"Victoria, watch your language," Mom snapped. "Haven't you shamed this family enough –"

"Shamed this family?" I turned and let all the walls crumble. Everything I'd been holding back for seventeen years came out. "You're so crazed about your reputation. You're so concerned with how the world fits into your perfect box. Get over it, Mother. I'm not a doll to be dressed up and shown off." I turned to face off with my father. "Why are you doing this to me? Why do you have to take anything that's mine and make it about you?"

He looked like I had smacked him across the face. "What are you talking about?"

"When did you announce your bid for councilman? At my kindergarten graduation. When did you announce your bid for the state house?" The tears rolled down my cheeks, falling onto my uniform. "Three years later after my dance recital. When did you announce your bid for the U.S. Senate? When I won a statewide debate competition." I grabbed my hair and screamed into my pursed lips. "And now you're going to announce that you want to be President. Here." I waved my hand around the field.

I stared at him for a moment. He didn't even flinch.

My heart tore into a million irreparable pieces. "Why can't you leave me alone?"

Mom took a step behind my father and put her hands on his arms.

She scowled at me over his shoulder. I waited for something, anything to come from him. For the first time, he was speechless. I turned on my heel and marched toward the dugout. The team needed me to be on today. The guys needed me to play. All I wanted to do was run and hide and be totally forgotten.

I put on my game face as I sat on the bench and pulled on my cleats.

"You alrigh', kid?" Coach asked as he sat beside me.

"Fine."

"No, you ain't."

"It doesn't matter, Coach. Right now, all that matters is that we've got a game to win." I looked at him and wished my father would give me the same look Bernie Strauss was giving me. One that said it would be okay and that he cared. "Ignore the crap behind the fence, Coach. Tell the guys too. The Senator is announcing he wants to be President." I tugged my cap down over my eyes and slapped my glove on my thigh. "No matter who it hurts."

I ran onto the field and started throwing with Calvin and T.C. They watched me, but they didn't ask. Everybody watched me, even the other team, but those few minutes of silence were enough to let me focus, even as my father smiled for the cameras behind home plate. I moved as far to the left as I could so that I wouldn't be in the frame with him.

He stepped away from the microphones and the questions five minutes before the game was scheduled to start. The reporters swarmed him, clamoring for more. Robert shooed them away and the ump yelled at them to get their equipment out of the way.

"Hudson, you hear me?" Coach bellowed.

I shook my head as I came out of my reverie. My father had distracted me enough for the day. Even as he made his way to the bleachers to watch me play. It would've been bad if he had left. After all, he wanted to be seen as a family man.

We were the home team. I took the field and felt the cameras on me.

"Shake it off, Vic," T.C. said as he jogged by me.

I nodded and stretched, tossing soft lops to Jayden as he sent grounders my way. Delvin wound up for the first pitch and the game was on. I forgot about the reporters. I forgot about my father. The game was all that mattered.

The third batter hit a hard line drive to my left. I dove and caught it to end the inning. My first at bat came moments later and I hit a soft grounder back to the pitcher for the first out.

Ollie smacked a hot fastball down the right field line for a double. The pitcher walked Jayden intentionally. Smart move, but Daniel brought Ollie home with a sacrifice fly.

The rest of the game went like that. Ollie owned their pitching. Jayden was walked at almost every bat. The rest of the guys brought the win home. My bat was quiet, and my swing was off. It didn't matter. We won five to nothing and were in the semis.

My parents came over to congratulate us. The reporters followed them like sharks looking for a snack. I could've helped my father out here. If I wanted. His advisors kept the media away as he approached me. Mom smiled behind him, but it was all fake. I wondered, not for the first time that summer, if she was ever sincere.

"Victoria, we need to talk," he whispered through a gritted grin. "The way you acted –"

I hugged him, faking a smile of my own. "The way I acted? You can't let anything be mine, can you?"

"I really think we need to talk about this." He pushed me away and held me at arm's length. "And about your relationship with that boy," he said, beaming at me like I'd just won MVP at the World Series.

"Leave Daniel alone," I said. "You can add him to the list of things you've taken from me."

Reggie came up beside me with his hand in the air. I high-fived him and turned to fade into the team.

TOP OF THE 10TH

When the security detail dropped me off at Grandma's, there was an Escalade in the driveway. I almost asked them to take me to Chez Hudson instead. I almost called Daniel. Of course, that would've been a bad idea. I almost called Andrea to come get me. There were so many things I thought about almost doing that I didn't see Grandma before she grabbed my arm and pulled me into her one car garage.

Then I almost peed my pants.

"Why are they here?" I asked.

"I think you know why. The question is, what are you going to do about it?" She put her hand on my shoulder and turned me to face her. "Vicky, you need to tell them everything and you need to do it calmly. Your father's confused. Your mother's upset. They seem to think this is stuff Daniel's put in your head."

I opened my mouth to protest, but she clamped her hand over it. I muttered, "Not fair."

"Listen to me. You have held this inside for so long that they don't see that there *is* a problem." She held up her finger to stop me from protesting again. "Make them see it, Vicky. Don't yell. Don't scream. Just talk to them."

I looked at the street and kicked the loose rocks. She was right. I started this on the field. Now I had to finish it. "Fine."

The walk into the house took a lifetime. When I got inside, I felt thirty years older. My parents waited for me in the living room. I peeked in and then continued to the kitchen. Grandma and I had all our in-depth heart-to-heart conversations in there. It seemed like the perfect place for this one too.

The coffee pot was full of Mom's French Roast and the aroma gave me strength. I poured a mug. When I turned around, my parents were sitting at the table while Grandma leaned against the doorway.

"We need to discuss your outburst today," my father said. He was in a gray golf shirt. I don't remember the last time I had seen him in anything other than a tie.

"Fine." I sipped the coffee, burning my tongue and not caring.

"Victoria, your father and I –"

"I have nothing to say to you, Mother," I said, forcing the calm into my voice. "You're a liar."

They stared at me. Mom felt behind her for a chair and sat down. I never talked back. Never. Even when I wanted to, one look from my father would shut me down. Neither one of them knew what to think.

"And you're a racist." I shook my head and took another sip of coffee, wishing I'd added sugar and creamer. The cup shook as I sat it down.

"How dare –" she whispered.

"Me? How dare me?" I pointed at her emphasizing each word. "'Just look at him,' you said. What were you talking about? Was his hair too long? His nose a little off center? Nope, you were talking about the fact that he's Korean!"

Neither one of them said a word. The Senator stared at my mother for a moment. And it hit me. He was looking to her for her guidance.

"How did Wakefield know about the team?" I crossed my arms and leaned against the counter.

Mom's face went ashen. She didn't answer.

"He's not a sports reporter. He doesn't write about politics." I smacked my palm on my forehead. "God, I'm such an idiot. Wakefield is a society columnist. You called him, Mother. *You* did this to me." I'd never seen it before this night. My life wasn't screwed up because of him. It was all her.

"I –"

"Just admit it, Mom," I said, cross-examining her with the skill of my father.

"Did you call him?" the Senator asked with a disdain I'd only seen from him after eating bad shrimp.

She glanced between us, panic on her face.

"Why did you ..." I choked on the words. The tears welled up behind my eyes, blurring the vision of my father. It was time to put everything on the table. "Why do you keep using me for your campaigns?"

His head snapped around. "Using you? I've never used you, Vicky."

"Yes, you have. Did you forget everything I said earlier? What you called my outburst? How can you not ..." I sobbed, choking on the tears as I tried to stop them from falling.

He stood and walked over to me, wrapping his arms around me. "Vicky, I never meant to hurt you. If I did...."

I felt like I was five again, crying over the hamster that died. He held me, let me get it all out. He never told me to stop or get over it. Everything I thought I knew about my father, I learned from my mother. I felt more defeated than ever.

Mom sat alone at the table. After I cried myself out, he leaned against the counter beside me. We waited for Mom to say something. She wrung her hands together and stared at the floor.

"Meredith, did you call –" the Senator began with a tone he usually reserved for Capitol Hill.

"Yes," she murmured. She cleared her throat and straightened her back. "Yes, I called Tim Wakefield. This was the perfect opportunity, Warren. You're always concerned about young mothers and swing votes that I thought this was the chance to show them who you really are. A father that supports his daughter as she plays baseball ... Warren, can't you see –"

"No, I can't." He shook his head.

"It was always you, wasn't it?" I asked her. She didn't need to answer. I knew that it had been her all along. She used me to further my father's career by planting the seeds in his head.

"Why would you do this to me?" I blubbered.

Mom started bawling. I mean full on bawling. "It was for you, Warren."

"Me?" He walked over and knelt in front of her. "What do you mean?"

"All of it. I knew you could go far. I wanted to help. Then Victoria kept presenting these … opportunities to put you front and center." She buried her head in her hands. Dad rubbed her arms. "Vicky, I didn't … I never …"

Everything I ever believed had changed in ten minutes. I didn't know what to think about either one of them. Exhaustion overtook me. All I wanted was to curl up in my room and sleep until September.

I rolled my eyes at Mom's overdramatic tears. "We are so done here."

"Not yet," the Senator said over his shoulder. "Meredith, we'll discuss this later." He patted Mom on the knee and stood to face me. "Will you be bothered if we come to your games? I enjoyed watching you play."

"Really? No cameras? No press?" I was totally ready for more fighting. This caught me off guard. I wasn't sure about this idea, so I shrugged.

"I can't …" he began.

Grandma cleared her throat. She hadn't moved from the doorway. I waited for her to say something, but she didn't.

"Yes, Mother," he said as helped Mom to her feet.

"Victoria has … expressed an interest in staying here longer than her baseball season." She stared my father down, challenging him to object. "Given the circumstances, it would be a good idea."

"How so?" Mom asked. She sounded more bitter than curious.

"Well, you'll need to get on the official campaign trail sooner rather than later. Vicky's absence can be explained by her caring for her old decrepit grandmother. Here, she will be supervised." She glanced at me then added, "And she likes it here."

My parents looked at one another, but my father answered, "We'll think about it."

We said our goodbyes and Grandma ushered them out of the house. I sat at the table and waited for the analysis to start. Grandma joined me right after she closed the front door and turned the lock.

"Are you okay?" she asked.

I continued swirling the mug of cold coffee around. "I guess." I spun the mug away from me and looked at her. "Just shell shocked. All this time I blamed him."

"Warren isn't entirely innocent. He didn't have to listen to Meredith."

"Yeah, I know." I shrugged and shook it off as it settled in my heart. "It doesn't matter now."

She took my mug and stood up. "Get some sleep, Vicky. We can talk more in the morning."

I knew she was right. I couldn't focus on anything anyway. But it was over.

After a hot shower, I collapsed into bed. As I waited for sleep to come, I thought about my father. He'd heard me. He'd understood why I was upset. Finally, it really was over.

BOTTOM OF THE 10TH

The tournament continued the next day as we faced off against a team called the Racers. When we got to the field, the reporters were like a swarm of wasps. My parents arrived a few moments later and took the sting away from me. The Senator held court, but he waved the reporters away a few minutes before the game started. I was surprised and impressed.

Coach started Freddie over me. I didn't know if it was because of my poor performance at the plate the day before or just because Coach wanted Freddie in the lineup. The crowd booed Freddie as he took his place at third. I cheered him on, getting a nervous thank-you nod in return.

Unfortunately for Freddie, it didn't take long for Coach to send me in. He blew an easy grounder in the third which cost us a run. Bottom of the fourth, I took my place. The first batter winked at me. I rolled my eyes and exaggerated it enough that he would see it. It irritated him, and I knew he'd be gunning for me. Boys are idiots.

He smashed a hard line drive down the third base line that went foul. I dove anyway with my hand outstretched. My face slammed into the dirt and sent my hat flying. But I raised my glove with the ball firmly in the webbing.

Taught him not to wink at me.

Of course, cockiness on my part didn't stop my knee from opening up or my elbow from getting scratched. It was getting to

184

the point that I couldn't play without bleeding. I bent over to wipe the sweat and dirt from my eyes and left a trail of blood on my jersey. Apparently, there was a gash on my cheek as well. Coach jogged out from the dugout.

"You alrigh', Hudson?" he quipped. He lifted my chin to assess the damage.

I shoved his hand away. "Yeah, I'm fine. Get off the field."

He started back to the dugout and shouted over his shoulder, "Stop gettin' hurt."

Walter waited for me to catch my breath before throwing the next pitch.

The other team had it in for me that inning. The next batter hit a hard grounder that took an odd bounce and I had to backhand it while running to my left. I made the throw, beating the guy out by half a step. Two outs.

The third batter shot a base hit up the middle. Walter walked the next guy. Now they had runners at first and second.

Walter's struggles continued. He threw two more balls. With two outs, I hung closer to the bag. The guy at second had taken a bigger lead with each pitch. Walter wasn't looking him back. He took his biggest lead on the third pitch, a called strike. Daniel glanced my way. We were thinking the same thing. On the fourth pitch, a ball on the inside corner, the runner took off.

Daniel threw the ball from his knees as he fell back behind the batter. I straddled the bag and caught the perfect throw at my ankles. The runner slid to the outside of the bag, into my glove. His foot caught my right ankle after I tagged him. I fell forward but held onto the ball.

Walter and T.C. helped me back onto my feet. My ankle throbbed, but I ignored it. The guys smacked my back and high fived me. Daniel sat by me on the bench and got out the first aid kit. Without a word, he cleaned the scratch on my cheek with antiseptic. I could feel the prying eyes on us.

"You realize that you're going to be in the paper tomorrow?" I asked as he smoothed ointment over the spot then put a bandage on it.

He didn't smile. "Now let me see the elbow."

I held it out to him. He cleaned my elbow and started to bandage it when I pulled away.

"Daniel…"

"Vic, you're on deck," Coach shouted. "Cho, you done doctorin' her?"

Daniel nodded. "Yep, all better."

I grabbed my bat and took my spot in the on-deck circle. It didn't make any sense. I shook off the thoughts clouding my brain and focused on the game. T.C. struck out swinging on a nasty curveball on the outside corner.

"Watch the outside," he said as he slumped back to the dugout.

"Go get 'em, Vic," Calvin shouted as I made my way to the plate.

A slew of other people cheered as well. I tuned them out. It was something I'd become very accustomed to lately.

First pitch was down and in. So far down it hit my foot before I could move out of the way. The pitcher looked pissed as I trotted to first.

"Wasn't intentional," the first baseman said.

I grinned. "Didn't think it was."

Calvin moved me to second with a long fly ball into left. I waited for Coach to give me the sign. The guy that knocked me on my ass in the last inning was also playing third. I wanted to take him out. Coach signaled for me to steal. On the third pitch, I took off.

There wasn't even a throw. I doubt they expected me to run. I was glad to get third, but I really wanted that guy to eat dirt.

Reggie stood in the batter's box with a nasty sneer on his face. If I'd been facing him, I would've thought he would swing for the fence. He surprised them with a soft single over the first baseman. I trotted home, tying the game one to one.

We stayed tied until the eighth inning. Their pitcher made two mistakes during the game. First, he hit me. Second, he left a ball in the middle of the plate and Jayden smashed it over the fence, breaking the tie.

We won by that lone run.

Daniel touched my elbow in the dugout. "You okay?"

"Yeah, great. Why?"

"Just checking." He backed away without breaking eye contact.

I wanted to reach out to him, but he dumped me. He made that decision. He couldn't handle the spotlight. I didn't blame him in a way, but he was the reason we weren't together. Was he changing his mind?

"WooHoo," Adam shouted in my ear, throwing his arms over our shoulders. "Boys and girl, we are in the finals." Adam squeezed me hard enough that I couldn't breathe. My security detail moved in to separate us. "Party time tonight."

An hour later, we took over Hansen's. We moved to the second floor to get us out of the way of the regular crowd. They were packed and I wondered how many reporters were in the mix. Robert came in before we were forced upstairs. I brought him with me and let Wilson guard the stairs. He talked with Reggie's mom and Calvin's dad. Daniel's parents stood in a corner alone, watching their son. I felt his mother's eyes on me the entire time.

"Vic, may I have a word?" Mrs. Cho asked me as I stuffed a piece of cheese in my mouth.

"Um, yeah. I mean sure." I wasn't sure.

We moved into an unoccupied corner. Daniel's eyes widened when he saw me alone with his mother, but he didn't make any effort to stop this conversation from happening.

"My husband and I were very upset about the article regarding your relationship with our son," she said. I started to defend myself, but she waved her hand to stop me. "Personally, I don't want to know how involved you are with him. Some things are not for a parent to know. But I thought you might want to understand why we've asked Daniel to stop seeing you."

What? They told Daniel to... it wasn't his idea! Still, he didn't have to go along with it. I waited for an explanation, afraid of what might fly out of my mouth. Shaking my head, I finally said, "I don't understand. Not at all."

She smiled at me like I should know. "Your life is so much different than ours –"

"So?" I interrupted as my irritation rose.

"Please, let me finish." She paused. When I didn't say anything, she continued, "Your parents hold onto different values than we do. Your family is in the news –"

I opened my mouth, but she cut me off before I could say anything.

"Yes, I know you didn't ask for this. But, in many ways, you did whether you realize it or not." She grasped both of my hands

187

and shook them. "I know that you and Daniel care about each other deeply, but you have to see that he could be hurt by all of this. He's my only son. We just want to protect him."

Hope swelled in my chest. Things could go back to normal. Back to the way they were before the media, before the Senator. "What about after this is over? After the election?"

She smiled as if it hurt to do so. "Will it ever really be over, Vic?"

I couldn't answer that.

TOP OF THE 11TH

I knew I was in trouble the minute I found out what team we'd be playing for the championship game. The Cyclones was made up of boys from Hillside. I went to school with half of them and knew them all.

Grandma let me sleep in on Sunday morning. The game started at three and Coach wanted us at his house by one for a team meeting. Daniel was waiting outside when I pulled up to Coach's house ten minutes early. I'd hoped he would be early too. He looked as miserable as I felt. I smiled as he rushed over to me, but that didn't change the look on his face.

"What did she say to you?" he demanded.

"It's okay –"

"No, it's not." He ran his hands through his hair and spun in a circle. "God, I can't believe ..."

"Stop, Daniel. Just please stop." Once this game was over, then things could go back to normal. We could get back together. "Your mom's just being overprotective. After today, it's not going to matter much. The media will be after the Senator and I'll only be a pawn in the game. Besides, we aren't ..." I couldn't say it. "It won't affect you anymore."

He turned on his heel and stormed into Coach's house. I followed, leaving my bodyguards waiting in the SUV. Coach had few words to say to us before we left for the field. He wanted to get there early to show dominance. He wanted us there as a team. He didn't talk about the Cyclones at all and we weren't given a chance to say anything either.

Grandma and Charles arrived at the field at the same time as the rest of us. Wilson stopped and let her get in the middle of my security circle. Grandma reached out and squeezed my shoulder. When I glanced back, she was holding Charles' hand.

Dad held center court of the media circus, talking about the state of our country's economic crisis. Once the team was within eyesight, Robert came over to me and led me to the Senator's side.

"Vicky, some of the reporters would like you to make a statement," he said, beaming at me out of reach of the microphones.

"Are you kidding me? We're so not having this conversation." I couldn't believe him. After everything that was said, after finally understanding what was wrong, he asked me to make a statement to the press?

His face fell. Only for a second. "One last time, Vicky. That's all I'm asking."

"No." I tossed my bag into the dugout and turned to face him. "I'm not doing this for you or for your campaign. If you want to talk to the reporters, fine. Leave me out of it. I'm tired of living in your world. I'm tired of doing everything you ask of me when you can't do the one thing I ask you to do.

"You put me in the beauty pageants. You entered me into academic bowls. You enrolled me in Xavier. You wanted me to be at the best, remember? You never once asked me if I wanted any of it. God, I thought you understood. I thought you finally got it. Mom may have been behind it, but you never stopped any of this from happening. You did it for you and for your campaigns. Not for me." I paused. "Never for me."

"Victoria –"

"Even my name was all about you. Just … leave me alone. All I wanted was to play baseball." I stared at my father. "All I wanted was to be normal."

I shook my head and turned away from him. Daniel stood in the dugout, pretending to put his gear on. I knew he'd been listening. I grabbed my bag and fought back the tears.

"Vic, what the hell is going on?" Daniel asked just loud enough for me to hear.

I shook my head. "Your parents aren't the only ones making life tough, Daniel. Just leave it at that."

Adam slapped my back and offered to warm me up.

When I trotted on the field, Reggie shouted, "That's right, Vic. Get angry and take it out on the Cyclones!"

"Right on," Calvin cheered.

The rest of the guys started in on me. I couldn't hold back the laughter. Their attitude was infectious. We were still on the field when the other team showed up.

"Hey, Vicky," Colby Bender shouted from their dugout. He ran out to greet me. "We're playing your team?"

"Haven't been talking to Erik, have you?" I fake laughed. Erik knew what team I was on.

He chuckled. "No. You know I hate Perday's guts. Oh hey, I heard about your dad though. Ready to be First Daughter?"

The thought made me shiver in a bad way. "No, not at all."

He looked back at his dugout. "Well, good luck, Vicky. I'll see you after the game."

I watched him jog back to his team.

"You know that guy?" T.C. asked.

"Yep, I know all of them."

"Are you kidding?" Ollie's face showed what I thought was disgust.

"No. Why?"

"Inside information," Reggie whispered and then he shouted, "Dugout, guys!"

They pushed me into the dugout and pointed to the bench for me to sit. Adam sat on one side, Daniel on the other.

"Tell us everything you know."

I smiled. I meant to tell them that I knew the guys on the Cyclones earlier, but Coach went on and on about team unity. It slipped my mind.

"Okay, give me their lineup."

I ran through everything I could remember about each one of the guys, not leaving out a single detail. The one thing that surprised me most was that Erik wasn't pitching. I wanted to ask Colby but didn't risk it. We were better off without Erik on the mound.

We were the away team so I led off the game. When I stepped into the batter's box, Dylan gave me a small smile. Last year he was in most of my classes and we shared notes. He was pretty cool. I wondered if Andrea would give him a second chance. He asked her out at the end of the year and she shot him down. Now I knew why.

If I thought Dylan had any qualms about pitching to me, the first strike on the outside corner proved me wrong. I ended up hitting a soft grounder to Jake at second for the easy put out.

Adam started pitching the bottom of the first like it was a continuation of his no hitter. He struck out the first two batters and got the third to hit a grounder to T.C. The second and third innings went by in much the same way. Neither team could manage so much as a single.

Top of the fourth and I was at the plate again. Dylan had no pattern that I could see or had spotted anyway. Instincts took over. I looked for everything and anything that he might throw. Dylan didn't disappoint. He threw me a ball in, a ball out, and then a strike up in the zone. With the count at two and one, I hoped he'd just try to get me to swing. I focused on his fastball.

And got it, right down the middle.

I turned on it, hitting a line drive between third and short.

Brendan stood at first. "Dylan's going to be pissed you hit that."

"He shouldn't have left it in the middle of the plate."

He laughed. "He won't do that again."

"Probably not."

I took a short lead off the bag. Dylan tried to pick me off. I figured he would. Boys get that revenge mentality. Ollie walked on four straight balls. Dylan's frustration was clear on his face and in his pitches. I took a huge lead at second.

But I didn't need it.

Dylan made another mistake to Jayden on the first pitch. Jayden crushed the ball over the wall in dead center. We were up three to nothing.

We scored another run making it four to nothing in the seventh. Unfortunately, Adam's one hitter turned into a mess in the bottom of the frame. They scored two runs off him. He remained calm enough to get us out of the inning without further damage. He threw his glove into the dirt when he entered the dugout and Coach told him that his day was over. Walter and Gil warmed up in the bullpen.

Gil melted in the bottom of the ninth, giving up two runs to tie the game. The tenth was scoreless.

I was set to lead off the top of the eleventh. The Cyclones had a new pitcher, Erik Perday. He'd arrived just before the first pitch and sat alone on the bench for the last ten innings. I took a deep breath to calm down. Erik's hatred of me was well known in both dugouts. I doubted he'd risk his team a championship for revenge.

I couldn't have been more wrong.

The first pitch flew inside at a neck breaking speed. There was nothing I could do but turn my back to it. The ball slammed into my ribs in the same spot I'd taken a pitch the very first game of the season. Only ten times harder. I went down. My bat hit my helmet as I fell. I couldn't get my arms up to brace myself before my head collided with the hard infield dirt. The helmet flew off and it felt like a million bees were stinging me on every inch of my body at once.

"Oh no, Vicky," Jason, their catcher, said. He said something else, but he sounded like he was fading away.

Then I blacked out.

"Vic." A thick hand slapped my left cheek. "Wake up, kid. C'mon. Vic, open 'em eyes."

I did as the gruff voice commanded. Coach Strauss knelt beside me. I laid on my right side.

"We'll get an ambulance on the way, kid," he growled.

"I don't need an ambulance." I tried to sit up on my own. My head spun, and the bees were back. "Crap."

"Yeah, I think you do. You got a broken rib or two this time."

"What the hell just happened?" my father bellowed as he rushed onto the field. "Vicky, are you okay?"

"Shut up, Senator," I moaned as I tried again to sit up. It was hard to breath.

"Yeah, Senator, keep your trap shut for a change," Coach snapped. He winked at me and added in a softer tone, "Now, if I help you to the bench, you think you can make it?"

I nodded and then winced. It felt like a dozen little guys were hammering the inside of my skull and jackhammering in my back. Coach helped me to my feet. The low rumble of pain increased to a full symphony. I wanted to scream, but my shallow breaths wouldn't allow it. I leaned more on Coach than my father who flanked my right and held me steady by the elbow. Only then I realized that the rest of the team surrounded us.

"Freddie, take first," Coach yelled. "We got a game to win. Ollie,

Jay ... make 'em pay."

The guys cheered, and I whispered my own "woohoo" as I sat on the bench.

"Your mom called an ambulance," Daniel said as he knelt in front of me. "She's waiting for the EMTs by the parking lot. Do you want an aspirin?"

I shook my head no, which flamed in agony. Maybe I did need one. "How long was I out for?"

"Not that long, maybe a minute. Enough to miss the fun stuff." He smiled, but the concern never left his eyes.

"Fun stuff?" I shifted to my left. Big mistake. Stars erupted in my vision.

"Don't move, Vic. Wait for the ambulance."

"Now you tell me." I heard the wail of sirens entering the park. "I don't need an ambulance."

"Victoria," my father began. I'd totally forgotten he was there. "You need to see a doctor. You can barely breathe."

"They're here," Daniel said and stood to look toward the lot.

"They can wait. I want to see how this ends," I motioned to the field with my right hand. That side hurt but considerably less so than my left.

"Vicky, you need –" the Senator started.

"Just listen to me for a change," I snapped. "Please."

Daniel sat beside me as we watched the game resume. I wanted to read more into this than there was. He wouldn't sit by me like this if he didn't care.

The EMTs were heading our way with a stretcher. I could already see tomorrow's paper with a black and white of me lying on that thing and a caption that read "Senator Hudson's Daughter Gravely Injured."

Ollie smacked a base hit off Mark Law. Erik was nowhere to be seen. Dad stood and clapped then left the dugout to greet the EMTs.

"Distract me, Daniel." I touched his leg and felt that familiar shock that I missed. "Tell me about this fun stuff I missed."

"After that douchebag hit you, Jayden and Adam took off toward the mound. Erik ran like a pussy." Daniel glanced around before adding, "He's lucky they didn't get to him."

"They shouldn't have done that. They could've gotten booted."

"He shouldn't have thrown at you. He did it on purpose, Vic.

When you went down, he smiled."

"But they didn't need to —"

"Yeah, they did. You take out a member of our team, we take you out." His hand hovered over mine, but he didn't touch me. "He did manage to take himself out of the game though. The ump tossed him before you ate dirt."

I nodded and returned my attention back to the field. Jayden was locked in. The look on his face was almost serene. No way Mark was going to pitch to him. That would be stupid.

"Vicky, the EMTs are here," my father said.

They left the stretcher at the end of the dugout. A young guy with brown spiked hair sat down beside me. "Let's have a look."

"Shhh. Wait a minute, okay? I'm fine as long as I don't move." I didn't want to miss the end of the game. We'd worked so hard to get here.

"Victoria ..." my father scolded.

"Back off, Senator. I'm staying until the end of this game." I didn't look at him to see his expression. It could've been shock or he could've been pissed. At that moment I didn't care what he or anyone else thought. I was going to finish this. Sort of.

"Fine," the EMT said, "Let me take your vitals first." He strapped the blood pressure thingy around my arm and started pumping the air. "You don't have to move for this." Under his breath, he added, "But you need to get on the gurney."

"In a minute," I snapped, looking back at him. "The game will be over on this pitch. Just watch."

He glanced toward the field. The stands were quiet. The dugouts were quiet. The game would be won or lost here, even with another half inning to play. We all knew it was up to Jayden now. He stood in the box, calm and relaxed.

Mark, however, was like a pig in an oven. He spun the ball in his right hand and ignored the runners. Freddie took off to third as Mark threw the pitch. It happened in slow motion, like these things always do. The ball floated toward the plate, hovering over the middle. Jayden's head was down, his eye on the prize. Then his bat connected with a loud thwack.

The cheers in the stands and in our dugout drowned out anything the EMT said. I tried to stand up, but my body collapsed from the pain into the arms of the EMT. My father grabbed my hand. I looked at him for the first time since I had gotten hit.

The Senator was scared.

Somehow this calmed me down.

"Okay, take me to your gurney," I said, gritting my teeth.

They led me to the stretcher at the end of the bench and lifted me. I crumbled face first into the tiny, antiseptic-smelling pillow. The scissors were cold as they cut up the back of my jersey. There wasn't a collective gasp like the first time I'd been hit. The guys were watching Jayden cross home plate. They screamed and jumped and celebrated.

The gurney was pretty comfortable. The EMTs poked and prodded around my back and the pain was too much to bear. I passed out again, listening to the roar of the crowd.

I woke up in the emergency room. And I was feeling no pain. My head was groggy. My vision blurred, but I felt lightweight and fluffy. The bright lights of the room blinded me. Blurry vision and bright lights do not make it easy for a girl to recover.

So I asked a stupid question that I already knew the answer to, "Where am I?"

"You're at the hospital, honey," Mom said. She leaned over me and ran her hand through my dirty hair.

"Did we win?" I smacked my mouth together. I don't remember ever being this thirsty.

"We don't know for sure," she said. "But I think so."

"Where's the Senator?"

"In the waiting room. A lot of reporters followed the ambulance."

"Great, just fu –"

"Watch your language, young lady," she barked without any bite to it.

"Sorry." My eyes finally focused, and I could see that she'd been crying. "How long have I been out?"

"A couple of hours."

"Really?" I tried to sit up but couldn't feel my arms or my legs. "Is anyone else here?"

She nodded. "Your grandmother and Charles are in the cafeteria."

"And anyone else?" I started to slip. My mind drifted. For a moment I'd forgotten what I'd asked. "Well?"

"No, honey," she said. "No one else."

A small part of me wanted to cry. The non-drugged up part to be more specific.

"Vicky, I am so sorry if I ..." she started crying and sniffling at the same time. She blew her nose and composed herself. "I never meant to hurt you. Your father's political aspirations were all for you. Did you know that?" She waited for me to reply, but I didn't. "He decided that he wanted to make the world a better place only after you were born. In college, he'd leaned toward politics, but once he started working with your grandfather, he was happy with being a lawyer. Then you came along. That's when he decided to run for office. He wanted the world to be better for you than the one he grew up in. And we named you 'Victoria' because you're our greatest achievement." Mom shook her head and wiped her eyes. "Neither one of us ever meant to bring you pain."

She squeezed my hand and kissed my forehead. I didn't know what to say to her. My head grew foggy after a few minutes. I lost consciousness again and dreamed of the game. Of being the one that hit that homerun.

When I woke for the second time, the room was dark.

"Mom?" My throat burned as it cracked.

"She went to the cafeteria for coffee, Vicky," Grandma said. She sat in a chair to my left, just within my peripheral vision.

"Tell me what's going on, please," I pleaded. I felt out of the loop with myself and everything around me. Probably because my brain was pretty loopy.

"You have three broken ribs. One of them was dangerously close to puncturing your lung. The doctor prescribed a powerful pain medication. That's what has kept you unconscious. Drink some water." She leaned forward, offering me a cup with a straw. I sipped as she continued, "Your parents insisted you be kept overnight. The doctors thought you might be able to go home, but your father didn't want to leave room for doubt."

I leaned back on my pillows. "Yeah, and I bet having his daughter in the hospital overnight will give him a boost. I can only imagine what he's telling the reporters," I grumbled.

Grandma put the cup down and sat on the bed next to me. "His statement was 'no comment.'"

"Really?" Somehow I didn't believe that as possible.

"Yes. He's told them your condition and that you'll be fine, but he's asked that they respect the family's privacy in this matter."

"No 'women's rights'? No 'bullies need to be punished'? No big grand speech?"

"None." She patted my arm. "Do you want me to get your parents?"

I thought of Daniel. That was who I wanted to see, but he wasn't here. "Do you know if we won the game?"

Grandma smiled and sat straighter. "Ian struck out the side in the bottom of the eleventh. You won."

"Are they … did anyone …" I fought back the tears that threatened. "Have you seen any of them?"

"Not since we left the field. Charles stayed back to watch the end. I knew you would ask what happened." She stood and stretched her arms over her head. "But I haven't seen them here. Your father insisted on tight security, so they may have come. And only family was allowed in the ER. I'm sure he wants to see you."

I looked away from her, aware for the first time that I was in a private room and not an ER bed. Still, it wasn't much to look at. "What time is it?"

"Around nine-thirty."

They would be celebrating at Hansen's now. Without me.

"The Perdays came by –"

"I hope Dad punched Erik."

She chuckled. "I'm sure the thought crossed his mind. Erik wasn't with them. Your mother screamed at them, but your father accepted their apologies. They didn't think Erik was capable of anything like that. And you two used to be such good friends."

Erik was the last person on my mind. "Should I call Daniel?"

She handed me my cell.

It rang.

And rang.

And rang.

I hung up.

"Would you like something to eat?" Grandma asked as she took the phone from me.

"Yeah, I guess. I am kind of hungry."

"I'll go downstairs for something. Will you be okay?"

I nodded and turned on the TV. There wasn't anything on, but it kept me distracted from the pain that crept into my back as the drugs wore off. From the lack of concern from my team. From the fact that I wasn't there to celebrate after we won. The 1950s sitcom I settled on kept my mind from thinking too much.

A soft knock at the door drew me out of my self-imposed TV coma. Just when Ricky was about to yell at Lucy for doing the same stuff she always does. I looked over as it opened, but couldn't tell who it was. Then he walked into the light of the TV.

"Mind if I come in?" Daniel asked. He had a small tan teddy bear in his hand.

Tears spilled as I nodded. I never thought I'd be this happy to see anyone as I was at that moment.

He hurried over and sat on the edge of my bed. "Hey, don't cry, Vic. There's no –"

"I didn't think you were coming," I sobbed, wiping my eyes with the sheet. "I didn't think –"

"I've been here since the game ended. They wouldn't let me see you. It didn't matter how much I screamed." He leaned in and kissed my forehead. "We've all been here."

"All of you?"

"All of us. We got tired of the waiting room. And some of the guys got hungry so we found the cafeteria. That's where we ran into your grandma." He glanced over his shoulder toward the closed door. "Adam's in the hall. Can he come in?"

One by one, my teammates came in to see me. They each told me they were glad I was okay. They told me how the game ended, which varied a little depending on who said it. They told me about the big party tomorrow night at Hansen's. Jayden was the last player to come in.

"Hey, Dan, split for a minute, alright?" Jayden said in his deep bass voice.

Daniel's face screwed up in confusion, but he left without arguing.

Jayden looked me in the eye. "I've given you a lot of guff for playing ball. I'm sure you've heard most of it. And I talked to that dick reporter even after you asked us not to." He jammed his hands in his pockets and shrugged his shoulders. "So, I'm sorry about that.

Okay?"

I knew it took a lot for Jayden to admit he was wrong. "Yeah, okay."

"And you play good. Even for a girl." He smiled and looked at the floor. I think he was blushing. "You going to be okay or what?"

"Yeah, I'll be fine." I tugged at the sheet. "Once I get my parents off my back."

He laughed. It was the first time I'd ever heard that from him. I didn't think he had a sense of humor.

"So, are you going to make it to Hansen's tomorrow?" he asked.

"I hope so."

There was no way I was going to miss that.

THE POST GAME

I left the hospital Monday morning with my ribs wrapped so tight it felt like I had on a Victorian corset. Mom and Dad wanted to hole me up at their house, but I begged to go to Grandma's. They didn't fight, which was the first sign that something was up.

Plus, we still needed to discuss my desire to change my address on a permanent basis. That was another argument that could wait for another time.

When we got to Grandma's house, Daniel was there with his mom and dad. My parents were polite, thankfully. Mom went so far as to tell Mrs. Cho that Daniel would make a great doctor someday. After they all left, I took over the couch.

Daniel stayed behind. After twenty minutes and the best foot massage I ever had, I broke the silence.

"Are we ... good?" I didn't know how else to put it.

He took a few minutes to answer. "If you want me, yeah. If you don't, I can't blame you." His hands covered mine. "I know what Mom told you. They did ask me to stop seeing you, but ... It was stupid. I shouldn't have ... Victoria, breaking up with you was the stupidest thing I've ever done." He kissed the palms of my hands. "Forgive me?"

I closed my eyes, hoping that when I opened them he would still be there. When I did, I fought back a grin. "This time."

Grandma insisted I eat chicken noodle soup even though it was ninety degrees outside. I slept off and on throughout the day. Around six, Daniel woke me up to get ready for the party.

Daniel helped me into the passenger side of my car, giddy about driving until I reminded him why he had to.

Everyone else was already there when we got to the second floor of Hansen's. Daniel held my waist as I navigated the stairs. The guys smiled and waved. I was winded by the time Daniel lowered me into a chair. Coach stood up and made his way behind a makeshift podium.

"Alrigh', settle down. Let's get this started," he growled. He yanked a sheet off the table behind him and uncovered the individual trophies we'd won. "Now, y'all are gettin' one of these, but we got some player awards to hand out. It comes as no surprise to any of you that two of the awards go to Jayden. He had the highest batting average for one. And, as y'all voted last week, he's team MVP."

Jayden walked up and took the two plaques Coach handed him. We clapped. He totally deserved it.

"This is cool," I whispered to Daniel. When I started the season, I'd never expected an awards banquet.

"Coach Strauss is the only guy in our district to do it," Adam whispered across the table.

"Now, this is the first time for this next one since it's the first year we've been in the championship game, and the first time we'd made the playoffs. But the league votes on a championship game MVP. The players from all the playoff teams vote I mean. Since we won, they had to choose one player from our team. And," he pulled a small trophy from underneath the podium, "the winner gets this. Now, I doubt this comes as a surprise either. Winner's Jayden."

Like there was any doubt.

"Damn, Jay, save some awards for the rest of us," Reggie shouted from the back.

Jayden flipped him off and we laughed. It hurt, but it felt good too.

"Let's eat," Calvin added, sticking his nose in the air to sniff the food.

"Not so fast." Coach stuck his chest out a little more. "We got something else. Daniel, help that girl up here."

Daniel put his hands under my elbow and pulled me from my seat. What in the world was happening? I didn't deserve anything. I put my hand on the podium to steady myself as Daniel abandoned me for his seat.

"Vic, I knew you was something special that first day you smacked the ball off Delvin at practice." He put his hand on my shoulder and grinned. "When you started showing up in the paper, my wife saved the articles. I know it ain't how you want to remember playing this year, but you might look back on all this with a smile when you end up as ancient as I am."

He handed me a leather-bound scrapbook filled with the newspaper clippings from the entire season, even the box scores when nobody knew who Hudson was. There were clippings from other papers and a couple of articles from the internet. I wiped away the tears.

"That's everything local up through yesterday's papers."

I hugged him. It hurt like hell, but I hugged him. Coach patted my shoulder and handed me my championship trophy. He smiled wider than I'd ever seen him smile before.

"We're glad you played with us this year, Vic," Coach Strauss said with a gleam in his eye.

"Yeah, me too."

ABOUT THE AUTHOR

Lynn Stevens flunked out of college writing her first novel. Yes, she still has it and no, you can't read it. Surprisingly, she graduated with honors at her third school. A former farm girl turned city slicker, Lynn lives in the Midwest where she drinks coffee she can't pronounce and sips tea when she's out of coffee. When she's out of both, just stay away.

www.lstevensbooks.com

ALSO BY LYNN STEVENS

WESTLAND UNIVERSITY SERIES

FULL COUNT

GAME ON

GIRLS OF SUMMER SERIES

EXTRA INNINGS

THE REBOUND

JUST ONE... SERIES

JUST ONE SUMMER

ROOMIES

SWIPE LEFT FOR LOVE

Made in the USA
Monee, IL
26 October 2021

80384608R00121